Something Wicked

Monsignor Jack Myslinski

Michael McKinley

FIRST EDITION, MARCH 2025
LIBRARY OF CONGRESS CONTROL NUMBER: 2023950669
ISBN 978-1-953136-88-6 HARDBACK
ISBN 978-1-953136-98-5 PAPERBACK
ISBN 978-1-965784-04-4 AUDIOBOOK

Cover Graphic Design & Book Typography by Kurt Lovelace.
Cover photo ROME, VATICAN CITY licensed TTstudio.
Cover title set in **Fang** by Matthijs Herzberg.
Author names, chapter numbers in **Jenson** by Robert Slimbach.
Chapter titles in **Baskerville**; Body text set in **Nimbus**.
Chapter dropcaps set in **Mrs Eaves XL**
by Emigre Foundry designer Zuzana Licko.
Flourishes set in Emigre Foundry **Dalliance** by Frank Heine.
Emigre Foundry **ZeitGuys** by Bob Aufuldish, Eric Donelan.
Typefaces licensed Adobe, Linotype, Emigre, & URW GmbH.

Pierian Springs Press

PSPRESS.PUB
PIERIAN SPRINGS PRESS, INC
30 N GOULD ST, STE 25398
SHERIDAN, WYOMING 82801-6317

*"By the pricking of my thumbs,
Something wicked this way comes."*

WILLIAM SHAKESPEARE
MACBETH ACT 4, SCENE 1, LINES 44–45

CONTENTS

 **About the Authors**   **294**

Something Wicked

1

Jerusalem

The sunlight slanted through the blinds of the window of the small bedroom in Jerusalem, and lit up the host, a piece of unleavened bread, which was being transformed into the body and blood of Christ for the women gathered to celebrate the Eucharist. The presider held the host above the heads of the five nuns as if the eyes of the divine were shining down through it, and landing upon each one of them.

"Behold the Lamb of God, behold him who takes away the sins of the world. Blessed are those called to receive the supper of the Lamb," the presider said.

"Lord, I am not worthy that you should enter under my roof, but only say the word and my soul shall be healed," the nuns replied.

The presider then broke the bread into six pieces.

Sister Marie Therese De Bruyne was the last nun to receive Holy Communion, and as she did, she looked into the eyes of the presider. Sister Maureen O'Connor returned the gaze, her own blue eyes stunningly clear in the belief that what she was doing was right.

"The Body of Christ," Sister Maureen said in a low, trembling voice.

"Amen," Sister Marie Therese replied firmly. Then she took the host from Sister Maureen and put it in her mouth.

Marie Therese then bowed to Sister Maureen and to the other nuns, and quickly left the bedroom. As the executive director of the *Donne del Vaticano,* or Women of the Vatican, Sister Marie Therese was keen to support her fellow nuns and faithful laywomen.

But she knew, at age twenty-nine, that she was going to be tested at every turn, and when Sister Maureen invited her to Mass on this special morning, Sister Marie Therese did not feel as if she could say no. Sister Maureen, an American, had thirty years on Marie Therese, and she was a guest in this house.

So was Sister Marie Therese a guest of the Jesuits who ran the Pontifical Biblical Institute here in Jerusalem. But there were no priests in sight on this morning, as they had left the nuns alone to hold their conference as they saw fit. Was what had just happened fit? A woman celebrating Mass? Sister Marie Therese thought yes, and no.

As soon as she stepped out of the bedroom, Sister Marie Therese felt a pang of guilt wash over her. She couldn't help but feel that what they had just done was wrong, but at the same time she couldn't deny the feeling of empowerment and liberation that came with it. For too long, women had been excluded from positions of power within the Church, and this small act of rebellion felt like a step towards change.

Jesus was helped in his ministry by women. They fed him and his apostles, and supported his travels, and did not desert him in life, nor in death. They were the first to witness his resurrection.

And women had been a crucial part of the early Church, with St. Paul's letters saluting Priscilla and Julia and Phoebe and Junia. These women were important to the early Church, and had no doubt participated fully in the rituals of it. Paul makes it clear in Chapter 11 of his first letter to the Corinthians that the faithful must reenact the Last Supper, and so eat the bread which is the body of Jesus, and drink the wine, which is his blood.

He also makes it very clear in that chapter that women are subservient to men. Sister Marie Therese does not think women handed out communion, no matter how central they were to the early Church. But she doesn't know. So she takes what she just did as part of a small act of rebellion that women had been denied. To her, an act whose time had come.

As she walked down the hallway, she heard footsteps behind her. Turning around, she saw Sister Maureen striding towards her, a look of concern on her round, kind face.

"Are you okay, my dear?" Sister Maureen asked, her voice trembling slightly.

Sister Marie Therese nodded, suddenly overcome with emotion, and trying to hold back tears. "I'm fine, Sister. Thank you for inviting me to your Mass," she said in her soft Belgian accent.

Sister Maureen smiled. "I'm glad you could join us. You're doing important work with the *Donne del Vatican*."

Sister Marie Therese reached out and embraced the older nun. "I will be back in time for your talk," she said.

Sister Maureen grinned. "I hope so. The beginning is the best part. The middle and the end are pretty good, too."

Sister Marie Therese knew that if she didn't hurry, she might not make it back in time to hear Sister Maureen's keynote address. She had to hear it and see how her fellow women reacted to it. But of course, Cardinal Wolfram Friedrich knew that reality as well, as that was probably his point in summoning her to a breakfast meeting at his hotel on the day of Sister Maureen's keynote speech.

Sister Marie Therese got out her phone and swiped her

Gett Taxi app. There was a car just one minute away. Sister Marie Therese smiled. She would be there early, and so, she prayed, early to return.

The American Colony Hotel, please," she told the driver, who checked her out in the rearview mirror as if planning what he would do with her in the sack. To him, she looked like she was supposed to look, a handsome young woman with shining brown hair in a modest skirt and jacket that fitted nicely over her curvy figure, as that was Sister Marie Therese's mission. To change the way the Catholic Church looked at its women.

Sister Marie Therese got this "hey babe!" look all the time when she was studying theology at the Leuven in Belgium, where she was from. And now she got it back at home base in Rome from the men who hung around St. Peter's Square, whistling at her, and calling out to see if she would submit to their charms. She responded to the searching eyes of the taxi driver as she always did, by looking away, and down at her phone, scrolling through the cardinal's latest offerings on Google.

The streets of Jerusalem were free of traffic, as it was a Saturday morning, and so the sabbath. Marie Therese suspected the driver, a tawny-skinned man, clean shaven, about her age was either an Arab or one of the secular Israelis who didn't live in Tel Aviv.

The cardinal, on the other hand, was a German who was prefect of the Vatican's Dicastery for the Doctrine of Faith. Marie Therese knew that this august body had formerly been known as the Inquisition, whose form of faith was infamously brutal in its early years, and she expected as much from the conservative German cardinal today. Why else would he want to see her at 8 a.m. on Saturday? If only to echo what she found him saying on Google. "The Church was to become smaller and more faithful to its origins if it hoped to reach the soul of the twenty-first century."

Sister Marie Therese smiled. She could read through the

coded language. A smaller Church was another way of saying let the boys run the show as they always have and keep the women at the back of the church. And she would not let that happen. Not anymore.

Sister Marie Therese alighted the taxi at the American Colony Hotel in East Jerusalem. She added a 10% tip for her driver on her app as she walked into the small boutique hotel, with its golden Jerusalem limestone walls and its red tiled roof. She knew she'd need to get back to the Institute fast, and the last thing she needed was Gett Taxi drivers marking her as a cheapskate.

She was ten minutes early, and so she had time to herself before she was to meet the cardinal in The Courtyard, an outside dining area surrounded by mulberry and palm trees with a cool fountain in the middle. Marie Therese liked this stylish hotel, with its vaulted ceilings and Ottoman vibe, having once been the palace of a pasha. She knew that it had begun as a home to devout American Christians in the late 19th century and had now turned into the definition of luxury and service. She also knew that only a cardinal could afford to stay here.

She also knew that because of its location, in East Jerusalem, and because it was owned by Americans and the British and the Swiss, it was a neutral oasis in this country of strife, more so now after the terrible war that had ravaged the land about 50 miles to the west.

As such, the hotel was popular as a meeting place for those Israelis and Palestinians trying to solve an ancient problem, and for journalists and UN staffers on fat expense accounts. Then there were the spies poking around the bars and picking up whatever on conversations fueled by Taybeh beer. There were a lot of ears in the place. So, she was going to let the cardinal do the talking.

"Sister!"

Marie Therese looked up and saw Cardinal Friedrich's massive frame looming towards her. He was wrapped in a black soutane, with the cardinal's scarlet sash encircling his substantial gut, and the scarlet zucchetto, the scarlet yarmulke that cardinals wore, capping his massive head. The cardinal had his hand outstretched. She was not going to kiss his gold sapphire ring, so she quickly grabbed his hand and shook it three times, then released it. "Good morning, your Eminence."

"My dear Sister Marie Therese!"

The cardinal, a six-foot German in his early seventies had not shrunk with age He loomed over the five-foot-seven nun, and seemed to raise himself even higher as he looked down upon her. Then he started to pray over her."It is a day the Lord has made. Let us be glad and rejoice as we bow our heads and ask for God's blessing. God our Father, help us to always look to your Church as a Mother and seek her guidance through the wisdom of the Magisterium, the successors of the Apostles. Bless this servant of yours as she serves the Church with the spirit of obedience which she has professed in your presence. Amen"

Sister Marie Therese smiled as kindly as she could and said "Amen". It was going to be one of those meetings.

And so it was, as she made her way through a cup of delicious Turkish coffee and an almond croissant baked in the hotel's kitchen as the cardinal talked.

He told her about the hotel's history, which she acted as if she didn't know, widening her eyes, and pausing the coffee to take a sip of sparkling grapefruit juice as she absorbed the lesson being delivered.

"Imagine, Sister," he said, abruptly sweeping an arm to his right to take in the palatial majesty of the place, then quickly adjusting the scarlet zucchetto on his head, that his gesture had nearly sent flying. "You lose your four daughters in a shipwreck, and then Horatio and Anna Spafford, leave their hometown of Chicago in 1881 to find peace in the holy city of Jerusalem and to offer aid to families in distress. Together with sixteen other members of their church, they call themselves The Overcomers, and they settle together in a small house in the Old City. They were never missionaries, but receptacles. Active ones, whose charity was so great that the house became too small, and so they bought this place, which was initially built as a palace for a pasha and his four wives. And so, it eventually became The American Colony Hotel. It has endured all this Holy Land has had to challenge it with, the wars both of armies and religions, and indeed, it was the venue from which the white flag—made from a bed sheet from one of the Colony's hospitals—was taken in 1917 to initiate the truce that ended Ottoman rule in Jerusalem. Lawrence of Arabia even stayed here. That was not in the movie!"

The cardinal paused to shovel in three mouthfuls of scrambled eggs and Sister Marie Therese looked at the time on her phone. If she didn't leave in twenty minutes, then she would miss Sister Maureen's keynote address.

The cardinal seemed to sense this, as he smiled at her, with the smile of an assassin. His big blue eyes were hard, and his full mouth was stretched thin as he said, "But then, I expect you didn't come here to have a history lesson."

"It's fascinating, your Eminence," Marie Therese replied. "It's such a beautiful place. So tranquil."

The cardinal swallowed his eggs and took a slurp of tea, then said "Indeed, Sister. And tranquility is what we want."

Sister Marie Therese leaned back. She had an idea of what was coming next.

"Your conference has been going well?"

"It has, your Eminence. It has been most fruitful."

He nodded, and bit off a chunk of toast. "Well, I am not certain why the Women of the Vatican needed to come to Jerusalem to speak to each other about your women's issues."

Sister Marie Therese smiled. "It's because we women and our issues walk in the footsteps of Jesus, here in Jerusalem," she said.

The cardinal stopped eating. He folded his hands together in front of him, and Marie Therese caught the flash of his gold and sapphire ring as a beam of sunlight landed on his hands.

"Exactly, Sister. You are following in the footsteps of Jesus."

Marie Therese knew, even though English was her third language after French and Flemish, that she had said "walked," not "followed." But at least the cardinal was getting to the point.

"And as Prefect for the Dicastery of the Doctrine of the Faith, it is following that I urge you and your fellow women to do. The Holy Mother Church is a woman, and she has given us all a place. It is not yours to change what God has ordained."

He chomped into another piece of toast and Sister Marie Therese counted to ten. She knew this man was someone who could shut down her organization with a few strokes of his pen. She had to be careful.

"What makes you think God does not want us to more fully participate in the Holy Mother Church, your Eminence?" Sister Marie Therese said, finishing her coffee.

The cardinal looked at her as if she had just told him a very funny joke, and then burst into laughter. It was a deep and rumbling laugh, and it lasted far too long. When he finally had recovered, dabbing his eyes with the linen napkin, he told her what he thought.

"Because I am a cardinal, and you are a nun. God speaks to me differently than He speaks to you. And He told me to tell you to stop trying to take over the Church." He paused, to tee up the "or else' that was coming. "Or I shall be compelled to find other work for you and your women to do. Missionary work. Far from Rome."

Sister Marie Therese knew what this meant. He'd find some leper colony for her somewhere on the far side of the world. So, she played the only hand she had, and thanked the cardinal for breakfast as she rose.

"I must depart, your Eminence. My women are waiting for me, and I cannot lead them, from behind or otherwise, if I am not with them. I wish you a safe trip."

And with that, her cheeks red, her heart beating as if she'd just done a few fast laps in the hotel pool, she walked out of the hotel and headed back to the Institute. She would just make it in time for Sister Maureen's address, if God was paying attention to this nun.

2

Jerusalem

The conference room at the Pontifical Biblical Institute was filled with at least fifty women, seated in rows of ten, facing the podium from where Sister Maureen O'Connor would give her keynote address about the state of women in the Roman Catholic Church.

Sister Maureen, tall, and lithe, like the basketball player she was in her younger days at Georgetown, surveyed the room as she sat waiting for Sister Marie Therese to return to introduce her. The women in front of her ranged in age from early twenties to their later seventies, but they were all here this week in the holy city of Jerusalem to find a way forward for their gender in the Church which claimed to share it, as a Holy Mother.

Sister Maureen knew, from the classes she taught in Political Science at Georgetown, that women of any persuasion were far from equality. Be they the Islamic sisters who were veiled by their men—at least veiled nuns had chosen the veil. Be they those Orthodox women wigged and dressed in black and wrangling a brood of children, the way Irish mothers used to do. Or be they the Catholic women around the world who could dress as they liked and think whatever they wanted and marry each other. And believe that this all added up to having a voice that was heard.

Sister Maureen knew that it did not. It was just noise, and the men who ran the Church, some of them as if it were a private business for their own ends, could let the noise swirl around them as if it was a summer wind in Rome, and nothing more. She needed to find a way to change that.

Sister Maureen looked at her watch. Clearly Sister Marie Therese had been detained by that odious German autocrat, as Sister Maureen thought of Cardinal Wolfram Friedrich. So, she rose, and walked to the dais, and smiled her electric blue eyes on the women before her, who broke into applause.

Sister Maureen held up her hands, and grinned. "If only all my audience applauded before I spoke, my work would be done, sisters!"

The room rippled with laughter, as the women were already in the palm of Sister Maureen's hand, the one that only a couple of hours earlier had been dispensing the body of Christ.

"Thank you, sisters," the American nun continued. "It would seem that our esteemed director Sister Marie Therese has been delayed, so let us not stand on ceremony. For those of you who do not know me, I am Sister Maureen O'Connor, a member of the Sisters of Mercy. I teach politics at Georgetown University, in Washington, D.C., and I am a counselor to your group, *le Donne del Vaticano*, or as we Americans know you, the Women in the Vatican. Thank you for inviting me to speak to you today. And so, let me get on with it.

"I promise you, that unlike those homilies we have all heard from too many male priests, ones that should have ended in a quarter of the time that they took to say not much, I shall be brief.

The sisters replied with a surprising burst of laughter.

"This is our time, sisters. It is our time to take our rightful place at the altar. No more being the handmaids. We want to be priests. If the church hopes to survive, that is what must happen. The men of today's Roman Catholic Church must do as Jesus did, whose ministry was made possible by women.

"These female disciples of Jesus both followed him and financially supported him and the other twelve men. Not only that, but they also stuck with him to the cross and remained when all the others fled. And they were the first to see him when he rose from the dead.

"The Gospel of Luke tells more stories about women than any of the other synoptic Gospels. In fact, Luke's first letter to Theophilus contains twenty-three stories that are never mentioned in any of the other Gospels. In Chapter 8, we meet a group of women who consider their high status less than important in contrast to the blessing of being able to serve alongside Jesus. This is what Luke tell us:

"Soon afterward he went on through cities and villages, proclaiming and bringing the good news of the kingdom of God. And the twelve were with him, and also some women who had been healed of evil spirits and infirmities: Mary, called Magdalene, from whom seven demons had gone out, and Joanna, the wife of Chuza, Herod's household manager, and Susanna, and many others, who provided for them out of their means.

"These patronesses of Jesus' ministry were not just following. They were actively involved in his ministry. In fact, the word used for their activity in Greek is *diakoneó*—where we get our modern word "deacon." They were not just supporting Jesus with their finances. They were following him as disciples and ministering alongside him."

Sister Maureen paused and looked at her audience, who were looking back at her with the adoring zeal of apostles themselves. She smiled with maternal warmth at them all.

She felt a kinship to these women, these sisters who wanted what she wanted. A voice that was heard. And then she delivered her knockout punch.

"So, we need to honor where we began, and to resume our ministry alongside our brothers. As fully ordained priests."

Outside the Pontifical Biblical Institute, Sister Marie Therese heard the sound of cheering and applause as she hustled from the taxi into the PBI's courtyard.

She shook her head in dismay at herself. She was not too late, but Sister Maureen was someone who got straight to the point. From the raucous cheers Sister Marie could hear Sister Maureen had made her point and her audience adored it. And so Sister Marie's only reprieve against the pressing guilt she felt was that she had asked one of her fellow nuns to film Sister's Maureen's speech on her phone, for posterity.

She would share some of the blame with the taxi driver, who had not only been slow, but he had been difficult. Maybe he had a thing about driving people to Christian buildings. Who knew? But he did not pull up to the door of the Institute, as suddenly he found some energy and had another fare and so he had to go. He dropped Sister Marie Therese on the street in front and sped away.

As she hurried through the parked cars toward the door of the Pontifical Biblical Institute, she swiped the Gett Taxi app on her phone and was debating whether to tip him at all when the air before her turned hot and powerful, and sent her sprawling to the ground just as the front of the Institute crumbled like it was made of sand.

The explosion sent Jerusalem limestone raining down, and Sister Marie Therese curled herself into a ball, her hands over her head, as the stones fell around her.

Then she turned to the front of the building and saw bloodied women staggering out through the rubble.

She rose and hobbled, her leg having twisted in the fall, to the front of the building. Dazed nuns and laywomen struggled past her, one of them cradling her severed hand in her arm, her face frozen in shock.

Sister Marie Therese coughed as the smoke and the dust in the foyer filled her lungs, but she was determined to get to the conference room and to save whomever she could save.

But when she reached the doorway, which looked like shredded oak, it was clear from the debris and blown out windows and the pools of fresh blood on the floor that the conference room was where the explosion happened. And that there was no one to save. Before her were twelve bodies, all of them nuns in various states of death: some intact, some in pieces. And the thirteenth body was not one at all. It was just the head of Sister Maureen, her blue eyes open in surprise, lying at the foot of the podium.

Looking at Sister Marie Therese.

As Sister Marie Therese stood there, looking at the gruesome scene before her, a fire ignited inside her. She had never felt such a fierce desire for vengeance coursing through her veins.

She knew that it was not becoming of a nun, but she couldn't help it. She needed to find the person responsible for this heinous act and make them pay.

She walked over to the podium where Sister Maureen's head lay and knelt down beside it. She whispered a prayer and closed the eyes of her fallen sister. Then, she reached out and picked up the head, cradling it in her arms like a baby.

Then she got up, holding Sister Maureen's head close to her chest, and walked towards the exit. She knew that had she been on time, she would have been one of the dead. So maybe God had been on the side of this nun this morning. She also knew that she was standing in the middle of a crime scene. And that she would use every breath that God had put within her being to find out who had done this, and to bring them to justice. Or, she thought darkly, tears streaming down her face streaked with the dust of murder, to get her revenge.

3

Rome

Whenever Dan Lanaham came to Rome, he had a date with a woman in the Gesù, the mother church of the Jesuits, which had sat in baroque splendor in the center of the city since it was consecrated in 1584.

Dan had kept this date for nearly fifty years now, and while he had changed, so had the woman. She was more radiant, her complexion glowing with adoration and maternal protection for the child she had held in her arms for seven hundred years. Dan smiled when he saw her, and she met his gaze, her eyes bright.

"Hail Mary, full of grace..." Dan began the prayer, kneeling before her. With his full head of curly gray hair, his strong jaw and aquiline nose, and a tall, lean physique that still offered proof of the All-American soccer goalie he had been in college, no one would have guessed that Dan was seventy-five years old. He looked, easily, fifteen years younger, and his fellow Jesuits would joke that there was a painting of him in some dingy attic that was getting stooped and gray for him, because Dan seemed to be dodging it with no signs of surrender.

Dan had been a Jesuit priest for forty-five years, but he had been visiting the *Madonna della Strada* since he began his studies for the priesthood in Rome a half century earlier. The painting, which had once been a fresco, then transferred to canvas, hung in a chapel in the church which his order called home.

The founder of his order, St. Ignatius Loyola, had seen the painting too, and had been devoted to it since he first saw this face of Mary. Dan felt a connection to the saint in that reality, and he thanked Ignatius as he prayed to the Madonna, and to the child Jesus in her arms, to help guide him through the days ahead.

Dan had come back to Rome to join his fellow Jesuits in electing a new superior for their order. He had come back from Jerusalem, a city he loved, and where he served as the director of the Pontifical Biblical Institute. He prayed to the Madonna to help him to return to Jerusalem to continue his scholarly work. He was really asking her to keep him from being elected the new superior of his order.

He had heard the chatter about him being the new man, and he had tried to tune it out. He had made a vow when he took holy orders never to strive for ambition, and he made that vow again now, as Madonna looked down upon him.

"Holy Mary, mother of God, guide me to do the life that will serve you and our lord, your son Jesus with humility, and devotion, to the best of the blessings I have been given, for as long as I can. Amen."

The Madonna and Jesus looked at Dan with compassion, but also with a touch of wariness. That maybe, just maybe, there was more in his path than he had yet imagined. He smiled. He knew that there always was. He had long learned not to fear the future, because one day, his future would be in heaven, with the woman and her son whom he prayed to now. He just had to get there, and to get there, he had to do the Lord's will.

He rose and took a breath. Even though it was early on a Saturday morning, there was a tour group in the Chapel of St. Ignatius, looking at the tomb of the saint, decorated as it is with silver, gold, bronze, and marble. Dan glanced at his phone. He had to get back to the Jesuit headquarters near the Vatican to begin the proceedings to elect their new superior for the order, and he had about forty minutes to get there on foot. He smiled. Google maps told him the walk took thirty-seven minutes, so he would be early. He bowed to the altar and promised that he would come back to see St. Ignatius before he left for Jerusalem.

As Father Dan walked out of the church, he noticed a man sitting at the rear, not looking up at the magnificent fresco on the ceiling, but looking at him. He was African, his dark skin in stunning contrast to his blue eyes. He smiled at Dan, who returned the smile. He felt for Africans in Italy, who were more often than not treated as if they were from a different, hostile planet. Dan said a silent prayer for the man as he passed, wishing him the blessing of the Madonna and her son Jesus. He could not know that the man did not want his prayer, or her blessing. But soon, Dan would know it well.

The morning sun beamed down on the travertine stone building which housed the global headquarters of the Jesuit order on *Borgo Santo Spirito*, just a short walk away from the Vatican. The proximity between the pope, the earthly head of the Roman Catholic Church, and the Black Pope, as the head of the Jesuits was known, was something that had always amused Father Dan, as a Jesuit himself.

And it was especially amusing to him until this Saturday morning. For today, the two hundred Jesuit fathers from around the world had gathered in their convocation hall at the global HQ to elect a new superior for their order, one founded by St. Ignatius Loyola nearly

500 years ago, in 1540. The priests had spent the previous four days in *murmaratio*, or holy murmurings to discern who should guide them into the next decade. And from their conversations and their prayerful reflection, one name kept coming up: Dan Lanaham.

Father Dan looked at his own reflection in the glass covered painting of St. Ignatius, looking at the heavens that hung above the hall, as he walked with his fellow priests into the room where the voting would take place. He was taller than most of them, easily six-two in his socks, and still lean and with good muscle tone. If he could avoid dementia, everything else on his body was working as if he were twenty. So, he reckoned he could lead the Jesuits for a decade, at least, if he got elected.

But did he want to lead them?

There were more than 16,000 Jesuit priests spread across 112 countries, and that diversity was abundantly visible as Dan watched his fellow priests proceed toward the hall. Every color of the human rainbow was on the march to vote, and every human body type imaginable. "The world is our house," said an early Jesuit, and it was true. The reach of the order, through its presence on the ground, and its reach through history with its schools and universities and colleges and its legions of martyrs, who died for proclaiming their faith, had created a world within the Church known for its intellectual rigor, and its progressive demeanor, meeting people where they were, and taking it all from there.

Dan loved being a Jesuit, and he loved the brotherhood, but he also loved his life in Jerusalem, where he was the director of the Pontifical Biblical Institute. He had been as surprised as the rest of his Jesuit brothers when their Father General Alonzo Rivera had dropped dead on his way to meet Pope Leo. Just collapsed of a massive heart attack in St. Peters' Square at age 85. Ten years older than Dan was now.

So now, Dan knew, the Jesuits wanted to elect someone who had experience in administration, as Dan had in running the Institute in Jerusalem, and someone who was in good shape. To be sure, there were younger candidates, but the fact that Dan was also an American, from Boston, figured strongly in the equation. The Jesuits felt they needed American muscle to keep their mission happy and healthy when the next pope came to pass. For it was no secret that Pope Leo XIV was not long for the world.

That troubled Dan as well. Leo was his friend, and the two Irish Catholics spent years together in Boston studying, tending to their faith, and watching soccer. He did not want to think of his own future as being a reaction to Leo's impending death. It was not that death was something that troubled Dan, for his faith considered the end of earthly life the beginning of a new life of the spirit, but it was the naked politics of it all. And that was the thing that bothered him most about coming back to Rome.

The politics of the Church was something that Dan could largely avoid in Jerusalem, dealing with biblical scholars from around the planet who just wanted to know more about the treasures of this city that was holy to Jews, Christians, and Muslims, and not to employ the best means to accomplish their mutual destruction, as the last war had done.

But here in Rome, the politics were at the heart of the Church's daily life, and those politics were also fraught with danger and deception.

Dan had already seen the politics in play during the four days of murmurings, when one of his fellow Jesuits had shown that most un-Jesuitical quality called ambition and had invited Dan to consider his majesty in a ten-minute audition for a place close to the power that he thought Dan would become.

Dan saw him now, hanging near the door to the hall as he approached. He was in his early forties, and spoke

English like it was his first language, but he was as Italian as the city in which they were. Fortunately, he was standing next to Father Martin Gerrard, an Irish Jesuit in his mid-thirties whom Dan thought was exactly the kind of man he needed around him. Capable, smart. A man who had a light touch.

"Good morning, Fathers," Dan said.

"Top of the morning to you, Father Lanaham," the Irish priest replied.

The Italian priest looked like he was about to make another pitch for a place at the power table when Dan's phone pinged with a text.

"Excuse me," Dan said, and looked at the text.

The color drained from his cheeks and shock popped from his eyes.

"Is everything OK, Father?" Father Gerrard asked, concern in his voice.

Dan shook his head. "No, it is not. Please tell the fathers to continue without me. I have to see the Pope."

And then he turned and walked as fast as he could go. As if he were already too late.

4

Rome

Pope Leo had missed his weekly meeting with his Curial cardinals, those priests who ran the Vatican's bureaucracy, because his physician had told him he had walking pneumonia, and to stay put in his apartment on the third floor of the building to the right of St. Peter's Basilica, at least until he gave the Angelus on Sunday.

The apartment was more like a messy Southie study than a Vatican palace. Leo had brought in his own chairs, overstuffed floral beasts, and a green divan that had been given to him by his first parish, so one that had seen better days. There was a laptop on his desk, and there were books everywhere: on shelves, on the floor, under the desk, books mostly of theology and philosophy and history. Leo was a linguist, and he could greet his luscious brown teenage Lab, Chocolate, in six languages.

It was, in modern times, unusual for a pope to have a pet, and it was actually forbidden for a pope to have a pet inside the walls of the Vatican, until Pope Benedict more or less broke it by having a cat. Which was nothing compared to Pope Leo X's elephant in the early sixteenth century, or Pope Leo XIII's ostriches, deer, goats, and African gazelles in the late 19th century.

Pope Leo XIV had his beloved dog, and that dog Chocolate was a test: Chocolate loved the world, pretty much, but if he didn't like you, then you might well be in partnership with Satan.

Leo was sipping a mug of tea with Chocolate snoozing at his feet and listening to the BBC World Service when Dan was ushered into the papal apartment by Monsignor Van Ardt, a blonde and friendly Dutchman whom Leo had chosen as his secretary for his ability not to panic. Van Ardt had made himself scarce after letting Dan inside the papal chamber, knowing the two old friends needed time alone.

Leo had heard the news of the bombing in Jerusalem from the BBC, and he saw the sorrow now on his friend's face.

"Thank you for seeing me, Your Holiness," Dan said.

"I am so sorry, Dan," the pope replied, and held out a hand to his friend, which Dan took in both of his. He would need all the help he could get, Leo knew.

Dan sat opposite the Pope in a red leather armchair, while Leo reclined on the green divan.

"Who would do such a thing?" Leo asked. "Who would want to blow up a room full of nuns and religious women? Who would blow up Sister Maureen?"

Dan knew that Sister Maureen and Leo were friends. He did not know her well, but he knew how admired she was in academic circles for her scholarship. And for her faith. She was motivated by the mission and the message of Jesus.

"She was supposed to see me next week," the pope said. "She had news of a great crime."

But then she had been silenced by one.

The two men had known each other for more than a half century, going back to their days together at Boston College, and then onward into the Jesuit order. Leo had been Patrick Malone back in those days, an archbishop of Boston eventually, then a cardinal, and now the pope. Dan had been a biblical scholar and a teacher, and now, a man whose world had just exploded.

It was Pope Leo, however, who looked as if the news could be the last of him. They were the same age, but Leo looked a decade older than Dan, and it had been a hard decade. He had been pope for seven years, but from the look of the thin, frail, pale man who sat opposite Dan now, his hands trembling as he held the mug of tea, he did not look like he would see an eighth year as the Supreme Pontiff of the Catholic Church.

"Your Holiness," Dan said. "I need your permission to go back to Jerusalem. I need to find out what happened to Sister Maureen and those women. And the "why" what happened."

The pope put down his mug of tea and struggled to sit up. "I know you do, Dan," he said. "And you have my permission." Then a little smile, one not of mirth, but of irony, played at the corners of Leo's full mouth. "Just remember, you can still be elected Black Pope even if you're not in the room."

Dan grimaced. He knew. How odd it would be if these two Boston guys would be the popes, in their very different ways, at the same time? Not as odd as blowing up a roomful of religious women in Jerusalem. Because Dan knew that wasn't odd at all. That was evil. And he would do everything he could to find out why that evil had targeted these women of his Church.

5

Jerusalem

Father Dan Lanaham had seen what bombs could do when he had taught in Beirut in the 1980s. Car bombs, mainly, built by professionals and aimed at targets. Human targets. He remembered the burned-out hulks of the bombed cars and the shattered windows of shops and apartments, and the human blood that stained the streets after someone had decided that blowing up the world was the best way to solve whatever issue you wanted to solve.

What he saw now in the conference room at the Pontifical Biblical Institute, what he saw now in his own home, was no different than what he had seen back in the 1980s when it came to the attackers. This was no gas explosion, or grenade tossed through the stained-glass window by some anti-Christian zealot. Someone had wanted to kill the women in this room, and they had planned it.

Dan was standing in the doorway, watching the Israeli crime scene technicians and the Bomb Disposal Unit still studying the wreckage as if it were the Talmud, with no fragment too small to be examined. It was impressive, in a perverse kind of way. Dan did not want to be impressed by this.

Sister Marie Therese stood next to him, her brown eyes heavy with grief. "I don't understand, Father," she said, softly. "I just don't understand."

Dan did not understand it either, and he put his hand on her shoulder, as a fellow traveler in their shared sorrow. He hoped that the Lahav 433, the Israeli National Police who were Israel's equivalent of the FBI, could shed some light on the darkness. Lahav 433 Chief Inspector Hillel Bennett was striding toward them now, carefully avoiding the forensically tagged debris on the floor.

"Father Lanaham," the Chief Inspector said, extending a hand. "I am very sorry."

Hillel Bennett looked to be in his mid-thirties, with the burly build of the former military man he had been, who was now the INP's top investigator. His black hair was cropped tight to his head, and his eyes, almost as black as his hair, conveyed both compassion and purpose as he shook Dan's hand.

"Shall we speak in my study, Chief Inspector, Sister?" Dan said. He could not bear to watch the science of studying murder anymore.

Bennett swept his arm forward in a "lead the way" motion, and so Dan did, down past the main entrance, with its blown off door, then up the stairs to the library, and then to the right and into a small, orderly room that had a desk, three chairs, and a potted palm. Its wall-to-wall shelves were lined with books on theology, history, archaeology, and philosophy, along with American and British literature. A silver laptop was in sleep mode on the desk. Behind the desk, on the wall, hung a simple crucifix made entirely of wood.

"Please, sit down," Dan said. "Would you like something to drink?"

Both Sister Marie Therese and Chief Inspector Bennett

declined, so Dan popped open a bottle of Neviot mineral water and took a deep swig. He had come straight to the Institute from the airport, and still had the gritty throat from his flight from Rome. It is a short flight, just three and half hours, but when you are bearing grief in your heart, airplane air is particularly harsh.

And Dan was grieving, for Sister Maureen, and the dead women, and the destroyed room. He was especially sad for Sister Marie Therese, who had started her mission to reform the role of women in the Church with such zest. Now, sitting across from him, she seemed to have folded into herself, her eyes wounded and angry. Would she ever recover from this?

"So," Dan said, putting the water bottle on his desk. "What do we know, Chief Inspector?"

Hillel Bennett bit his lip slightly, then said "It was definitely a professional job."

"How can you tell?" Sister Marie Therese asked, her voice much stronger than her body seemed.

Bennett folded his hands as if he were praying. Then he said, "It was planted to detonate inside the... Amud..." and he said the word in Hebrew, searching, even though his English, like so many Israelis, was excellent.

"Lectern," Dan said.

"Yes, lectern," Bennett smiled in thanks. "We are not positive what the explosive was yet, but the fragments of shrapnel that we found in the room, and in the bodies, but the apparent elements such as an initiator, switch, a main charge and a container definitely indicate an improvised explosive device or IED. Because the package or container was small enough to fit in the lectern, and the destruction so vast, the Bomb Disposal Unit is surmising that it was Semtex, more commonly referred to as C4."

Dan leaned back in his chair. He was trying to digest the fact that he was in his office, not discussing biblical scholarship, or theology, but terrorism which had attacked his own house.

Chief Inspector Bennett leaned forward in his chair, as if to give himself support for the question he was about to ask. "I must ask you both a difficult thing," he said. "Do you know who would want to do this to these women?"

Dan looked to Marie Therese, whose eyes were still hot with pain. Then there was a quick rapping on Dan's closed office door, and before he could say "Come in," or "piss off, we're trying to deal with a crime," the door swung open on Archbishop Marco Sanseverino, the sleek and aristocratic Papal Nuncio, the official representative to Israel.

"I am so sorry I am late," the archbishop said, and Dan could read from the flash in Sister Marie Therese's eyes that she had not invited him. Neither had Dan.

"Please, take my chair," said Chief Inspector Bennett, quickly standing and offering the archbishop his seat, which he slid into as if it was a throne.

"*Grazie*," the archbishop said. He did not offer the cop his ring to kiss, for which Dan was greatly relieved, as Sanseverino was the kind of priest who liked his power, and all the ways he could display it. He smiled thinly at Dan, as if to say, "you're out of your depth."

He was sixty-six years old, and still wore his dyed black hair slicked back, like the Sicilian playboy he had once been, before, the story went, he got in too far with the daughter of a Mafia boss who liked the cut of his jib. But he knew enough not to touch, and so he went quickly into the priesthood. His reputation today was of a man who could deal effectively with muscle, which is why the Vatican sent him to Israel, preferring to have someone in the fractious Holy Land who could deal with trouble should trouble come. As it had just done.

"Chief Inspector Hillel Bennett, this is the Papal Nuncio, Archbishop Sanseverino," Dan said, breaking a silence that had grown uncomfortable. "Archbishop Sanseverino, Sister Marie Therese."

Before she had to kiss the archbishop's ring, the Inspector shook the archbishop's hand. "I think we met once before.

When you first arrived."

The archbishop smiled at that, and nodded, but Dan knew that he probably had no memory of the meeting. He was the kind of guy who only remembered people who could do him a service, and at the time they met, how could that be an Israeli cop?

"So, what is the conclusion?" the archbishop said to Bennett, then turned his gaze on Dan. If he had been already introduced to the nun sitting next to him, he showed no sign of it.

"There isn't one," Bennett replied. "Yet."

The archbishop folded his hands in his lap, his large gold ring with its amethyst stone set in the center on the top hand, so everyone could see it. Then he turned to Sister Marie Therese.

"You are part of the group who was bombed?" The archbishop directed the remark at Dan, but he was speaking to the woman next to him.

Dan nodded at the nun, and then said, "Sister Marie Therese is the executive director of the *Donne del Vaticano*, your Excellency. It was her conference that was attacked."

"Yes, it was my friends—" Marie Therese began but the archbishop cut her off, glancing his head in her direction, and giving her a paternal smile.

"Ah, that women's group. You do good work, I know, but you have many enemies, I think."

Sister Marie Therese smiled, as if this was the finest thing she had ever heard said about her organization. Then she said, "Your Excellency, we have dialogue with many different people and organizations in our work. None of them would do this."

"No, no, sister, I am sure that they did not," the archbishop said, now placing his hand for a brief second on her arm. She flinched.

The archbishop then looked at Dan. "Father Lanaham?"

Dan knew that he was asking him a question about his past, without saying it, so Dan said it for him.

"Your Excellency, I was in Beirut forty years ago. And I did not get my Hezbollah membership card." If he knew others at that time who joined Hezbollah, and he did know one, Dan did not know him now. On that, Chief Inspector Bennett cocked an eyebrow. "You lived in Beirut?"

"I taught there at the university for a couple of years."

"During the civil war."

Dan nodded. "Yes, during the civil war."

Bennett thought about that. "Lebanon is a beautiful country," he said.

"Yes, it is." Dan guessed that Bennett had served in Lebanon in one of Israel's wars there.

Then Chief Inspector Bennett walked to the window and looked out on the date palms below. "But here, in Israel, which is also a beautiful country, there are many who want to do us harm, as we have so recently seen. And attacking a group of Catholic nuns and holy women in Jerusalem like this will do us a lot more harm."

"In addition to the harm it did to them," Sister Marie Therese said, with a flare of annoyance in her voice. She was not concerned about geopolitical imagery; she was still seeing the severed head of Sister Maureen staring at her from the bombed-out floor and at night, as she tried to sleep looming above her in the middle of the night looming above her.

"Of course, of course, Sister, that is the most important thing, to get justice for those murdered women," Chief Inspector Bennett replied with what sounded like real sympathy. Or maybe it was his accent.

Sister Marie Therese suddenly flashed back to a memory that lit up her brown eyes. "When I arrived here, Chief Inspector, just seconds before the explosion, my taxi driver did not want to drive up to the door. He let me out on the street, and then sped away."

Bennett looked at her with interest. "Was he... could you tell his nationality?"

She shook her head. "I got him on the Gett app. It would

be easy to find out, I think."

Hillel Bennett nodded. "We will check him out, Sister. Thank you."

"So, who do you think did it?" the archbishop asked the cop, taking command of the story.

Hillel Bennett turned away from the window and looked at them like a math teacher about to deliver a quick lecture on calculus, his lips pursed, his arms crossed. "Well," he began," if someone wanted to hurt both the Church, and Israel, who would that be, in all likelihood?"

Dan knew where this was going, and he didn't like it, but knew it was something that could not be ruled out.

"The Islamic groups who hate us both," Chief Inspector Bennett was careful to say, and not blame all of Islam for the slaughter.

"And which one do you think it was?" Dan asked.

Bennett shrugged. "We don't know yet." He looked out the window, then back at the group. "But in my experience, they are very fond of telling us. So, until they do, we will suspect them all." Then he gave a weary nod to Dan, like a man who was not constrained by history, his own or anyone else's. "Of course, we will try to suspect them along with everyone else. I have learned in my work you cannot afford to be surprised."

Dan knew that the same applied in his work, as he opened the text app on his phone after they had all departed. There were fifty seven texts in his in-box. All from fellow Jesuits congratulating him on the thing he did not want, and now had to do. He would be moving back to Rome as superior general of the Jesuits. As the text from the Irish Jesuit, Father Gerrard put it "Elected almost unanimously!" Almost unanimously, Dan thought. He was sure that he would soon find out who did not want him in the job that he did not want either.

6

Rome

Pope Leo sat behind a dark oak desk in the Papal Library. Across from him sat Cardinal Alfonso Sanchez, the Vatican's Secretary of State, and Dottore Vincenzo Pericoli, the commander of the *Corpo della Gendarmeria*, the Vatican's police and security force, both for the city state, and for all its properties beyond. The Swiss Guard, with their colorful uniforms designed by Michelangelo, are the army that protects the pope and the Vatican. But it is the *Gendarmeria* which is the brain of the operation, reaching into every aspect of Papal security with its deep intelligence.

Sanchez was short and plump, in his late 60s, whose relaxed Venezuelan manner belied a sharp mind and deft political skills. Pericoli, tall and thin in his dark navy suit, with intense brown eyes that never seemed to blink, and a lush handlebar mustache, leaned his shaved head into his hands as the three men listened to the other person in this room, Dr. Rachel Ben-Simon, the Israeli ambassador to the Holy See.

Dr. Ben-Simon, at 40 years old, was young to be holding such a politically important job given the history between the Church and the Jews. She was tall and energetic, her black suit matching her black hair, her face lightly made up but clearly out of respect for the job and the journey this morning, and not to impress. Ben-Simon was a psychiatrist by trade, who had made her name studying the impulses behind religious fundamentalism in the world's major religions and concluded that they all shared the same quality: a willingness to harm others in the name of their belief. Harm, as in kill, to preserve their idea of the divine.

Today, however, she was here to convey a simple message to Pope Leo and his colleagues. "The State of Israel condemns this violent attack on the Pontifical Biblical Institute, and by extension, on the Roman Catholic Church, and we are committed to find the perpetrators and bring them to justice." Her voice was low and strong, her Italian, without accent.

It was the message that Pope Leo had expected, and he thanked her for it, but really, he only had one question for this esteemed student of the human mind. "Madame Ambassador," Pope Leo said, his head throbbing from the omeprazole the doctors were giving him for his stomach ulcers, "who do you think would do this?"

Rachel Ben-Simon had been expecting the question, but even so, clasped her hands in front of her, and lowered her head in thought, before she looked the pope in the eye and spoke.

"One possibility was a fundamentalist religious group that opposed the idea of women's empowerment, of the kind happening at the Institute on that morning of the attack. Or it could be a group with a political agenda that sought to further destabilize the region after the progress we have made with our Arab neighbors since the Gaza war ended. This group might view them as a soft target that would attract international attention and sow fear and chaos. Which leaves a list of suspects not quite as long as the Bible, but long enough."

"Iran?" Cardinal Sanchez asked.

"They would be top of the list," Dr. Ben-Simon replied.

A silence filled the sunlit library as the men thought about this, then Cardinal Sanchez asked, "Which do you think, Dr. Ben-Simon? Fundamentalists, or some terror group backed by Iran?"

Rachel considered this for a moment, and then said "I think, given the target, we cannot rule out either. But it would seem to have the hallmark qualities of fundamentalist grievance, against women, and against women of a different faith than the attackers. Which, of course, has also been an issue in Iran."

Pope Leo thought of the Iranians protesting in the streets at their government's harsh treatment of women who disobeyed the rules of their theocracy. It hurt him to see such cruelty in the name of religion, just as it had hurt him to see such cruelty his own Church had inflicted on the Jews. He knew, in that simple fact, that anyone could have committed this crime.

"So, the radical Islamists did it is what you conclude, Ambassador?" Dottore Pericoli said, his voice as thin as his frame, but his eyes dark and unblinking with the pursuit of justice, or perhaps with the story that he wanted told. So much easier to blame the Muslims and start another Crusade.

"I do not know, *Dottore*," Dr. Ben-Simon replied. "And as a psychiatrist, I know not to jump to hasty conclusions about the human mind. So, until the group who has committed this atrocity identifies itself..." she opened her hands, as a question, but Pericoli took it as a surrender.

"Then we must leave no stone overturned. You agree?"

Rachel Ben-Simon nodded. "I do agree, *Dottore*, and I am working with my government to make sure that all the rocks in Israel are examined." She then rose and bowed to the pope.

"I must depart, your Holiness, Eminence, *Dottore*, as I have to consult with my Minister of Justice shortly to receive an update. What I learn, I shall share."

Pope Leo rose shakily, his hands planted on the desk to support his weight, and the other two men stood as well. "Thank you, Madame Ambassador, for coming to see us. We know you are busy, but your work is very much valued, and may it be blessed."

The Israeli ambassador smiled warmly at Leo, like she might at a favorite uncle, then said, "I will take all the blessings I can receive, Your Holiness."

Then she left the room.

The pope sat down, and so did Sanchez and Pericoli.

"They have no idea," Pericoli said, his voice edged with dismissal.

"Neither do we, *Dottore*," Pope Leo added.

Cardinal Sanchez squeezed his lips together with his right hand, as he always did when thinking. "I would suggest, Your Holiness, that we use all our resources to find the culprits."

"Yes," agreed Pericoli. "I can call on Interpol with your permission. Your Holiness."

Pope Leo leaned back on his chair. He had never imagined that he would be involved in trying to solve such a horrible crime. Yet he also knew that the best resources were already devoted to it. He had great admiration for the Israelis, and how they had built their country and kept it as safe as it could be, given all the bad actors who wanted to do them ill. Of course, they had their problems, but who didn't?

"Thank you, both," Pope Leo said. "I will consider your ideas, and in the meantime, let our friends in Israel proceed with their investigation. They know the world from which this wickedness comes. I am confident that they will have answers for us soon."

The pope gave them a grateful nod, then looked down at his papers to indicate the meeting was over. Pericoli rose, bowed, and walked stiffly out of the room. Sanchez lingered, watching Leo like a sympathetic brother.

Leo had his eyes shut, as if in holy contemplation, but what he was really trying to do was hide the pain that was radiating from his stomach, up his sternum and into his throat. It was as if a bolt of lightning had exploded in his gut.

Sanchez put his hand on Pope Leo's arm. "May I walk you back to your study, Your Holiness?"

Pope Leo gave the Secretary of State a slight nod, and

Sanchez helped Leo to his feet. The Secretary of State hid his alarm at how frail Leo was with a broad smile at his friend. Leo was at least half a foot taller than the Cardinal, but with his stoop they were almost the same height.

They walked slowly through the Apostolic Palace towards the Papal Apartment, as Leo's breathing was heavy with the strain of all that he was enduring.

Lately, he found his mind connecting with the pope whose name he had taken, Leo XIII. He had chosen to reach back further in time than the popes immediately before him to pick his name, because Leo was a pope who changed the Church.

Leo XIII was the pope who followed the insular, bigoted Pius IX, the pope who had kidnapped the Jewish lad, Edgardo Mortara from his family because the child, when an infant, had been secretly baptized by a Catholic maid. Mortara was raised here, in this very palace, and became a priest himself. Extraordinary, Pope Leo XIV thought that the Jews would give us the time of day.

It was his predecessor, Leo XIII, who sought to correct the Church, opening its Secret Archives to the world's scholars, and even helping rabbis to get inside to transcribe tractates they needed to complete the historic Vilna Talmud. Leo XIII embraced the world, and took the Church forward in radical new ways, supporting the rights of workers to a fair wage, safer working conditions, and even the formation of trade unions.

He was known as the "Pope of the Workers", a man devoted to the Blessed Virgin Mary, and who revived the theological system of Thomas Aquinas, as the official heart and mind of the Catholic Church. He was the first pope to rule his faith without the benefit of the papal States, and he focused not on temporal power, but the power and dignity of humans, no matter who they were.

"Do you want to rest, Your Holiness?" The Secretary of State's voice filtered through Pope Leo's thoughts, and he turned to his colleague and smiled.

"I think my eternal rest shall come soon, Alfonso. So, while I am here, I want to get things done. One of them is to know who killed Sister Maureen and those holy women and why?"

Sanchez nodded and grabbed Leo's arm more tightly. "Do you really think the Israelis will find the criminals?"

Leo knew the unspoken part of the Secretary of State's question. He knew that the cardinal was thinking what Leo had just been thinking. That the Church's history with the Jews, of burning their holy books and their people, of herding them into ghettos and depriving them of rights, of the silence when the Nazis tried to kill them all, provided more than enough reason for the case to remain unsolved. But Pope Leo did not believe that it would.

"Yes, I think they will." The pope knew in his heart the goodness of other hearts, and he saw it in Dr. Rachel Ben-Simon. She would move heaven and earth to help solve the crime, because to do so was in her mind as a doctor, and in her spirit as human, and as a Jew. She would heal the world by helping them. Leo knew that the people who had founded his religion would once again help him to find the truth.

That truth, he also knew in his heart, might be closer to home than anyone thought. It was also why he wanted to keep the investigation away from Rome. The pope knew that Rome could destroy it. If it had a reason to do so. And until the pope knew what the Israelis had discovered, and their reasons, he did not want to give anyone in Rome a chance to tell a different story that became the official one.

Of course, he would let them tell that story, and then he would compare the two. If they matched, well, Leo knew from his own experience that this would be a kind of miracle. Because something wicked was out there in the Roman air. And Leo knew that it was coming for him, and for his Church.

Jerusalem

Agent Mimi Shapiro, 32 years old, lean and freckled with auburn curls and a ready smile, looked at Father Dan as if he was her own father, who might not be telling her the whole truth.

"So, no one from your time in Beirut would have a, how do you say, ax to grind with you, Father?"

"No one."

Father Dan knew that this was not strictly true, but this attractive Mossad agent didn't need to know the details.

Chief Inspector Hillel Bennett brought her along with him to see Dan on this warm morning in the middle of May, and when he introduced her, he did it in a way to convey to Dan that the less he said to Mossad, the better. By emphasizing the word Mossad in a way that made Israel's vaunted intelligence agency seem more like a nuisance, than a necessity.

Which of course, was an improvement from what they had been seen as after their catastrophic intelligence failure that led to the Hamas attack on Israel a couple of years earlier, and that terrible war that followed. Incompetent. Inept. And no longer invincible. Dan suspected that Agent Shapiro might have something to prove.

"How goes the investigation?" Dan had asked her, in an open-ended way. He had drawn no conclusions. He couldn't even find suspicions. He was sitting in his office when Bennett and Shapiro arrived, searching online for any news of what the Israelis had learned of the blast that had killed so many, but the internet after two days had gone silent.

"We know it was an IED, and we know they used Semtex. We don't yet have enough materials to determine where that IED came from."

Dan nodded. It was as much as they had told him the other day. And so maybe the fact that Chief Inspector Bennett wanted him to clam up for Mossad was a ruse, to get him to say something else.

"The nun who was with you the other day, is she still in Jerusalem?" Bennett asked.

Agent Shapiro quickly answered for Dan. "She flew out last night. To Rome."

Dan nodded, betraying nothing. It was clear that these two were playing some kind of inter-agency tennis match, and he was not going to be the referee. "Yes, she has to organize the funeral for Sister Maureen. And the memorial for the others."

Chief Inspector Bennett leaned back in his chair. "Yes, you have the luxury of time when it comes to funerals."

Dan gave the inspector a weary nod. The Jews followed their ancient custom of burying a body within twenty-four hours of death, at least, that's what the Orthodox did. In ancient times, leaving a body out too long attracted wild animals and, in the absence of refrigeration, an unseemly decomposition disrespectful to the dead.

In the time of Jesus, the body would be put in a tomb and sealed with a rock for a year, until the flesh had dried from the bones. The bones would then be put in an ossuary, a small bone box with the length of about two-and-a-half feet, to contain the longest bone in the adult body, the femur. And then stored away forever on a hillside, such as on the Mount of Olives. But as Dan believed, there was no ossuary bearing the bones of Jesus. He had risen from the dead, and gone to heaven, to return again in glory to judge the living, and the dead. And of the dead he had plenty to judge.

"Yes, we do have that luxury, Chief Inspector," Dan said. He was going to spare them his lecture on how Christian burial traditions had developed over the course of time to accommodate different pagan rituals and aristocratic necessities. "And while you need a body, you can also have funerals for the dead, no matter how they exist." He paused. "We have a body for Sister Maureen. Or most of one."

A silence lingered after Dan said that, as if the two Israelis were offering a moment of respect for the dead.

Then Agent Shapiro said, "Can you think of anyone who would want to kill Sister Maureen? She taught politics, did she not?"

Dan sighed. "Sister Maureen did teach politics, focusing on human rights in Africa."

"So she could have angered the Africans?"

Dan smiled. "Sister Maureen could not anger anyone, She was a gentle soul with a wonderful mind, and a wonderful mission, who only wanted to heal the world."

"You knew her well, Father?"

Dan shook his head. "Not as well as I hoped to. I knew of her work with the *Donne del Vaticano*, which was very important to her. You will want to speak with Sister Marie Therese."

"Oh, we shall," Agent Shapiro said, then she leaned forward in her chair. "The Islamic terrorists don't use Semtex. Pipe bombs, ball bearings, metal shavings, those kinds of things, but not C4. To use that suggests you have a connection to the military."

Chief Inspector Bennett looked at her and shrugged. "Or you can buy it on the dark corners of the internet."

Agent Shapiro smiled at him like he was in the special learners' class, and she was its substitute teacher. "But why would you do that? It takes time, you can get exposed, and you could get entrapped, and arrested by us. It would be very hard to get away with that in Israel. And in my experience, the terror groups who attack Israel want to do it the fastest, simplest way."

Chief Inspector Bennett paused, as if considering a response to what happened the last time the terror groups attacked Israel. Then he leaned forward to make his point: "Iran is supplying Hezbollah and Hamas and other proxy terror groups, so their weapons have become much more sophisticated. Maybe they supplied them."

Mimi Shapiro held her smile. "Well then, Chief Inspector, I guess we had better find out if that plastic explosive came from Iran."

Father Dan liked the ease with which she conducted her business, and the fact she used a "we" and not a "you" to Bennett, but then, that was the point. Mossad were now part of this process, and if anyone could find out who had killed these holy women, they thought that they could.

But first, Shapiro had another item of business, as she turned her smile on Father Dan. "Let me congratulate you on your election as the superior general to the Jesuits."

"Thank you," Dan said, surprised and a little impressed that she knew that fact, which clearly, from the look on his face, Chief Inspector Bennett had not.

"You're welcome," she said, and leaned forward. So, tell me Father General, about your time in Beirut. And please, begin at the beginning…"

Dan had hoped not to go into detail, but now he had to think back to his time in Beirut, four decades ago, now. What was the beginning of that story? His birth in Boston? Stepping off the airplane at the Amman Civil Airport, to make the five-hour drive to Beirut? Landing in Damascus would have been faster, but Syria was too dangerous, then, as now.

No, the Mossad agent didn't want that. She wanted to hear him name names so she could process the players and see if somehow Father Dan was connected to this crime. He knew that he was not, for Beirut was not about death for Dan, even though the terrible Civil War that so scarred the country was in its eighth year when he arrived in the country. No, Beirut was not about death. Beirut was about love.

8

Beirut, 1983

Father Dan Lanaham knew he should take a different route to the Institute of Oriental Studies from his room in St. Joseph's University, a two-minute walk away across the Damascus Road. He was in Christian East Beirut, and the Green Line, lush foliage that had grown in the destroyed streets and buildings, was what separated them from the Muslims of West Beirut.

Dan knew, as he inhaled the warm September air, perfumed with the smell of sweet lilac and bitter cordite, that he was unlikely to run into any groups of Muslim militiamen on his morning walk to class.

But then again, this was Beirut, and he was an American. The fact he was a priest of Rome made him doubly valuable, and the university had warned all of its priests and faculty to keep to their own side of the line at all times. In this civil war, anything had proven to be possible, with sudden death a constant reality. From a car bomb, from a sniper's bullet, from an Israeli jet dropping bombs, from someone who just didn't like the look of your religion.

Dan had grown up in Boston, which had its own forms of segregation and violence, but nothing like this. Dan was unlikely to get shot by Shia militias walking down College Road on his way to class at Boston College, though he would have received a thrashing if he'd been wearing a New York Yankees hat.

Or if he'd been Black. Dan was finishing his doctorate in theology in Rome in 1974, when Bostonians violently resisted desegregation, particularly in his old neighborhood of South Boston, which was the city's Irish-Catholic ground zero. These white protests led to school buses transporting Black children to desegregated schools getting bombarded with eggs and bricks and bottles. But not bombs and bullets, so a mercy, small, nonetheless.

No, it was in Rome that he had discovered his passion for the Middle East, at the Pontifical Oriental Institute, where he was mentored by the rector, Father Hans Kolvenbach. The Dutch Jesuit had also taught at University of St. Joseph, which had been founded by the Jesuits in 1875 as the first Jesuit university in the area. Father Kolvenbach saw Dan's keen desire to work and study in the Middle East, and so he helped him get the job in Lebanon.

Earlier this month of September, Father Kolvenbach had been elected superior general of the Jesuits, Dan's order. Dan felt sympathy for his mentor and friend, knowing that such a job came with almost as much responsibility as being the pope.

It was no accident that the superior general of the Jesuits was known as the Black Pope, referring both to the black robes that the Jesuits wore, but mainly to the power that they had as purveyors of education at its highest levels around the world. The pope in white, then Pope John Paul II, certainly had his powers, but Dan suspected that Father Kolvenbach would win a battle of the intellects. Kolvenbach's mind was so powerful and he used his intelligence with such ease that Dan felt that even as a longtime student he had never seen its power at full bore. Even so, Dan hoped it was enough to help his mentor rule this fractious order. And he prayed that he would never be in such a position of responsibility himself.

In Beirut, Dan was only responsible for himself, and his students. He had to prove himself as a scholar so that he could then teach and learn for the rest of his life. He was not really on his own, for his fellow scholars and priests all had similar missions, but Dan knew that he was the one responsible for his own success, or failure, in this beautiful, captivating, war ravaged city.

As Dan entered the Human Sciences compound, where the Institute of Oriental Studies lived, he admired the beauty of the building's sandstone façade, which, like the university itself, was free of any excessive ornamentation, save for the detailing which was typical of Renaissance architecture.

There were modillions along the top cornices, those projecting brackets beneath, which helped give them support, and added elegant texture; there were blind arcades surrounding arched windows. And Dan loved the vertical and horizontal flat stone buttresses which divided rhythmically the long façade, both on the main campus façade and here, to give the building a classical kind of order. In that order, there was beauty.

Dan walked into the Institute's cool lobby, and greeted the friendly young concierge, Amir, a student making some extra money, with a wave and a smile. Then Dan walked to the end of the corridor, and entered *La Salle des Etudes*, or the Room of Studies, which was the lecture hall where today he would speak to his class, which had grown by five students, and as such, needed a bigger room.

As Dan entered, he counted about fifty students in a room built to hold four times that number and smiled. What had been too small a room was now a room too large. No matter, he would fill it with words.

Dan's class was called "The Peoples of the Book", and the plural of people was deliberate. In this region so riddled with death because of religion, Dan hoped to find a way to bring together, through ideas, Judaism, Christianity, and Islam, as moving together, and not in opposition.

As Dan arranged his papers at the front of the class, he looked up at the clock on the rear wall to check the time and noticed a young woman entering the class who was, without exception, the most beautiful woman Dan had ever seen, with black hair and alabaster skin and bone structure as fine as roses. And she was looking out at the world with eyes the color of the Mediterranean when the sunlight struck it to make it seem a silvery blue.

Yes, he was a priest, but before that, he was a single man who had dated women. He had not come close to marrying one, but in the free love late 1960s, and early 1970s, when Dan was not yet a priest, he had shared a bed with a half dozen women and knew the power of carnal desire.

Watching this woman now take a seat near the front of the room did not fuel Dan's carnal desire. It fueled his general desire to know who she was and where she came from and how her eyes, the bluest he had ever seen, had come to be. What divinities had sired her?

Then he smiled at himself. He was the teacher, and he was a priest, and he had to maintain both roles in order to maintain his class, and his sense of his higher purpose. If he was to find out more about her, then the Lord would make it so.

Dan began his lecture today about the idea of the messiahs. He sketched out a messianic arc for the class, how the Jews, and Christians and Muslims all saw a way of deliverance through a messiah to a better world.

Then he focused on Simon Bar Kokhba, as today's example of how messiahs can rise up, and change the world in a way that they had not intended.

Dan told the class how this second century CE Jewish warrior was hailed as the long-awaited Messiah and proclaimed the King of the Jews who would rescue God's chosen people from the yoke of imperial persecution. His renown and popularity were once far greater than that of Jesus. Bar Kokhba was a messiah who nearly succeeded in doing what the man from Nazareth could not, or would not do: liberating the Jewish people from Rome and giving them their own kingdom.

Unlike Jesus, Dan tells the class, Bar Kokhba didn't turn the other cheek. He was a warrior messiah, and in his battle against Rome he risked and lost the entire Jewish nation.

His military failure haunted Judaism to the present day, and his messianic legacy was soon eclipsed by the religious triumph of Jesus and his followers—thus consigning Bar Kokhba's achievements to the black hole of history.

Dan paused and looked at the young woman in the front row as a sample reaction to his lecture so far. She stared at him as if he was telling her the greatest, or perhaps the most fantastic story she had ever heard. She smiled at him. He continued.

"It's 132 CE and the Jewish people are under siege. They've already lived through decades of Roman rule that reached a nadir with the destruction of their holiest site, the Temple in Jerusalem, in 70 CE. Now an extraordinary Jewish figure emerges, as if by Providence. His name is Simon bar Kokhba. And Bar Kokhba's messianic stage is set when the Roman Emperor Hadrian decrees that a blasphemous Temple to Jupiter will replace the destroyed Temple of Solomon. Hadrian also bans circumcision, and this prohibition combined with desecrating Judaism's holiest site foments the Jewish people to rebellion against Rome.

"Bar Kokhba the warrior is stunningly successful against the overmanned Roman garrisons, piling up victories– and Roman corpses –setting up a provisional government, building a network of fortresses, minting his own coins— thousands of which remain on the market –and inspiring the Jewish people with visions of biblical prophecy and political liberation."

Dan looked up again. He had the attention of the entire

class. They did not know this story, nor did they know where he was going with it.

"For more than three years, from 132-135 CE, Simon bar Kokhba leads Jewish forces in a remarkably successful revolt against the overwhelming power of the Roman Empire.

"But there's a twist to the story, one revealed recently in the ancient Jewish writings known as the Dead Sea Scrolls, discovered accidentally in the caves near Qumran.

"What emerges in the new translation of the Scrolls causes a sensation: the Jewish people of the first century CE were actually looking for two messiahs. One would be a priestly leader and prophet who would raise up the faithful and renew the faith of Abraham. The other, however, would be a monarch who would free the Land of Israel and rule over a restored biblical kingdom.

Did Jesus of Nazareth and Simon bar Kokhba fit the bill, each in their own way?"

Dan paused, and let the question hang over the class. Students rustled nervously, as if he was expecting an answer, and Dan smiled. "It's a rhetorical question, ladies and gentlemen. As is this one: why did the name of Jesus survive, and inspire a new religion, while Simon bar Kokhba pretty much disappeared from history?"

Dan the scholar then kicked in and delivered the set up. "The answer to this question lies in a dark forbidding cavern in the blistering desert east of Jerusalem in modern-day Israel. In the 1960s, an Israeli archeologist found a trove of letters—the largest cache of ancient correspondence ever uncovered in Israel—that included messages from Bar Kokhba. Bar Kokhba's letters show him warning his followers not to trust the "Galileans"—a common name for the followers of Jesus of Nazareth—because he says they are too eager to keep Rome happy and won't support the revolt."

"The Galileans, who already are being called Christians, are in the ascendancy. While the Romans are fighting the Jews of Judea, the Christians are gaining power and converts in the heart of the Roman Empire. This is not their war with the Romans, for the Christian messiah is the Prince of Peace. And without the support of the Galileans, Simon bar Kokhba's revolt is doomed."

Then Dan scanned the room and nodded, as if to say, you're not going to believe what happens next.

"But this massive insurgency launched against Rome by the warrior Prince of Israel terrifies the Emperor Hadrian. And he will make the Judean Jews pay for it. For the first time in their Middle Eastern occupation, the Romans bring in shock troops from Gaul to augment their local soldiers. Before then, the Roman troops were locals. Syrians. Egyptians. But now they are the blonde haired, blue-eyed forerunners of the SS. This ancient surge allows the Romans to finally crush the Bar Kokhba rebellion, but the Pax Romana is harsher than ever: nearly 600,000 Jews are killed, according to the Roman historian Cassius Dio, and more than 1,000 towns and villages are razed. The survivors are exiled or sold into slavery, and Bar Kokhba himself is killed."

Then Dan smiled, like an ace Red Sox pitcher who knew the exact pitch he needed to deliver to strike out the batter to win the inning, and the game, and the World bloody Series.

"The Romans not only destroy Bar Kokhba and his rebels, but they also declare the Holy Land to be "Jewish-free"— *Judenfrei*, as a later persecutor would term the policy—meaning that no Jewish person can remain in the land that God gave to Abraham, that Moses restored to the enslaved tribes of the Exodus, that Solomon built up after the Babylonian Captivity.

"And in a final, ominous effort to eradicate Judaism from the geography, the Emperor Hadrian renames Judea after the Philistines, a historic enemy of Israel whose Latinized name was "Palaestina," or Palestine. And so begin the Palestinians. From that point on, the separation of Judean Jews from their home becomes a sad reality for the next two thousand years— while Christianity begins its inexorable domination of the Roman Empire, and Western Civilization. And the

Palestinians harvest, quite literally, the spoils of a war in which they were bystanders."

Dan surveyed the class, who regarded him as if he had told them a story that could explain the world in which they live. And so he had.

"As you can see ladies, and gentlemen, that Jewish rebellion of nearly two thousand years ago echoes on the streets of this beautiful, battered city. Jews, Christians, and Palestinians all proclaim their identities through the harm they inflict upon each other."

A student at the back raised his hand. "You mean the Palestinians as Muslims, professor?"

Dan knew he had to be careful not to start a civil war in his classroom. "I mean, the Palestinians as an identity, one which sees them suffering in refugee camps here in Beirut and across the region."

"Because of the Jews!" the student said to Dan, as if completing his thought.

Dan shook his head. "Maybe we can say it's because of the Romans, and Emperor Hadrian, and his fear. But we shall deal with all of that going forward. Any questions?"

The students stared back at him with the young woman in the front row smiling like the Mona Lisa.

"That's all for today, ladies and gentlemen. My office hours will be on Thursday from two p.m. to five. Please drop by."

The students all rose slowly and quietly, having taken in this story which explained so much, and yet it was still going on in the world around them.

The young woman approached the lecture podium and stuck out her hand.

"Professor, my name is Layla Khoury."

Dan shook her hand. Her grip was firm, confident, yet soft. Her eyes, unblinking, stared into his very heart, it seemed.

"A pleasure to meet you."

She smiled. "My family are Palestinian Christians. Well, my mother is, I am, my father converted, and my brother is a

Muslim."

"Sounds like an interesting family."

She nodded. "Yes, and I think they would like to meet this American priest who can tell them about their origins on so many levels."

Dan waited, to see if she was going to start screaming at him, but her smile was as gentle as a summer breeze on the Corniche.

"So, I would invite you to tea with us, after Mass, on Sunday? Can you come to us, please?"

Dan knew that he should say he was not available, that he had to go to Amman for a conference. But he wanted to know everything he could know about this young woman. The Lord had provided. So, he said "Yes."

9

Rome

Jacqueline Brussard sat in the *Cappella Altemps* in the Basilica of *Santa Maria di Trastevere*. This chapel, dedicated to Mary, mother of Jesus, was a place that Jacqueline had always loved, ever since she first saw the *Madonna della Clemenza*, this ancient painting of Mary dating from the 7th century CE, with her own mother, 25 years ago when she was just 7 years old.

She remembered asking her mother on that day if the portrait of Mary, wearing a crown of pearls, and with Jesus in her lap, was really how the mother of Jesus looked. There were many answers, Jacqueline knew now, as an adult, about how badly the Church had treated people who were not white. Especially so in her own country, the United States. But her mother was much wiser than to deliver some lecture about race to her daughter in the face of such ancient art. Instead, her mother had smiled, and said, "Mary looks like whoever is looking at her."

Jacqueline had thought about that then, and now. Mary

did not look like the tall African American woman regarding her from a seat in the cool chapel, but her mother's wisdom washed over her as she knew that Mary was mother to us all, and you always looked like your mother.

Jacqueline smiled at the memory, and made a note to remind her mother of it when she next saw her back home in Washington, D.C. Then she checked her phone. It was nearly one o'clock in the afternoon.

She said a quick "Hail, Mary," and then rose. She walked down the aisle of the magnificent basilica, whose granite columns separating the nave from the aisles with their Ionic and Corinthian caps came from the Baths of Caracalla, the second largest public baths in Rome. Jacqueline knew that the columns were nearly 2000 years old, and felt a tingle run up the back of her neck. Time, in a place like this, puts your own time into a very clear perspective. It was short, and unless you became a saint, your existence on this planet would one day be completely forgotten. Jacqueline did not want to be forgotten. It was why she was in Rome.

She stepped out into the piazza in front of the Basilica, and squinted into the sun, making a note to pick up a pair of sunglasses. With her hand on her brow, she scanned the piazza, left to right, taking in the restaurants and the cafes, and the oldest working fountain in Rome at the center of the piazza. There she saw what she had come to see: Father Dan Lanaham, rising up behind one of the granite shells of the fountain, and walking down the steps to greet her.

"Jacqueline, how lovely to see you," Dan said, as he gave a hug to the woman who was an inch taller than his six-foot-two.

"Thank you for saying yes, Dan," Jacqueline replied, smiling at her former teacher, who she first met when she did a semester at the Pontifical Biblical Institute with Dan in Jerusalem, a dozen years ago. They had kept in touch when Jacqueline returned to Georgetown, and despite his best efforts, Dan could not turn her into a biblical scholar. Jacqueline was too interested in the present.

She thought Dan looked great, robust and still handsome in his mid-seventies. His eyes fired up with that intelligence she had found so captivating when first she met it. But now, there was a darkness, too, in those eyes, and Jacqueline knew a little about that. That was why Dan begged her to come, to use her faith and her journalist skills to expose the evil behind the bombing, and she said "Yes" because she also knew Dan could trust her.

"Sister Marie Therese is waiting for us at a nice little café just around the corner," Dan said, and led the way.

Sister Marie Therese was much younger than Jacqueline thought she would be, and she reckoned they were roughly the same age. "I am so sorry for what happened," Jacqueline said as they shook hands.

Sister Marie Therese nodded and gave Jacqueline a hopeful smile. "Thank you," she said. "Thank you for helping us find the truth. I have read about your journalistic exploits and I am sure we will not find the truth without you."

"I wish I did not have to," Jacqueline replied gently. "But Sister Maureen and I go back. I could not let this be."

"She was your teacher?" Sister Marie Therese asked.

"Yes, she was. I learned how to look at the world because of her. She showed me that you had to understand your own perspective before you could see anything. She was my teacher, and my friend."

"Jacqueline here is a fine scholar," Dan said. "But I could not convince her to follow my path backward. She is all about going forward."

Jacqueline gave a wry smile. "Sometimes you have to go backward to find the way forward."

They all laughed at that journey, knowing its truth. Then over a fine lunch of Roman salad, teeming with pitted black olives, tomatoes and anchovies, a bruschetta drizzled with olive oil so delicious you could drink it straight from the bottle, and a carafe of Pinot Grigio to wash it all down, Jacqueline listened as Sister Marie Therese told her about the *Donne del Vaticano.*

"We were established by Pope Francis to give women greater presence in the Vatican. It is open exclusively to lay and religious female employees and retirees of Vatican City State, the Holy See and related institutions. We want to provide greater visibility to the women in the Vatican, in the Church and in society. Another of our aims is to provide outreach and support to other women, especially those who are suffering, or in difficult situations, and there is no shortage of them. And we organize meetings and conferences on a variety of issues concerning women, social events, cultural tours, training courses, and so on. Like the one we were having in Jerusalem."

"And you are the director, Sister?" Jacqueline asked.

"I am the executive director, but I am responsible to all the women. Are you a Catholic?"

"I am," Jacqueline replied. "It was Sister Maureen who strengthened my faith through her example. She believed that justice was divine."

Sister Marie Therese smiled to hear the words of dear Maureen. "She did. And she worked to make it so."

"Who was Sister Maureen to you?" Jacqueline asked.

Sister Marie Therese took a sip of water, and closed her eyes briefly, as if saying a prayer. "She was, in many ways, our spiritual center. She had very progressive ideas about how the Church must change to meet the needs of today, and the future."

"And that meant creating female priests?" Jacqueline asked, silently cursing herself for getting so fast to the question she thought might be at the heart of the attack.

Sister Marie Therese's brown eyes softened at the question. "It did."

Jacqueline took a bite of salad and bought some time. "And what do you think about that, Sister?"

Sister Marie Therese glanced at Dan, who swirled his glass of Pinot Grigio and gave her a reassuring smile. He was the host of this meeting, but that was all. He wanted these two women to speak as freely as they could, and then smiled again to himself as he amended the thought: as freely as they could speak with a priest for company.

"I think that there is no reason not to keep women from being able to celebrate the holy Eucharist, and do all the things that priests do," Sister Marie Therese replied, her voice low, but firm. She knew that Dan had chosen this location far from the constantly listening ears inside the Vatican, but even so, what she was saying now was considered heresy by so many of her faith that she needed to be careful. She quickly glanced up and down the shaded street, and did not see any microwave vans painted in the Vatican colors listening in. "But I do not think that time is now."

"Why not?"

"Because the Church must sort out its other problems first, such as the criminal abuse of children. If women became priests, then we would have to sort all that out. We would be busy for a century, or longer, such was the depth of the crime. We need to begin with a tabula rasa."

"But if the pope made the offer now?"

Sister Marie Therese angled her head to the side, as if the question had its own gravitational pull. "We would say yes," she said slowly. "After all, it was women who funded the ministry of Jesus. Mary Magdalene, and Joanna, who was the wife of Herod's administrator, and Susanna, and, as the Gospel of Luke tells us, 'many other women'. We also did not abandon Jesus at the cross, and we were the first to discover his empty tomb. St. Paul's letters contain many references to women in positions of power in the early Church. We were there at the beginning, we were pushed out, and diminished, and it is time to be more fully here now. And if the pope asked, it would be foolish not to say yes. Because it could be another two thousand years before we were asked again."

Jacqueline leaned back in her chair and looked at Dan. "What do you think?"

"I agree with Sister Marie Therese. Women need to be full partners in the Church going forward."

Sister Marie Therese smiled at Dan as if he were her own father and raised her glass of wine to him.

"Do you think that's why you were attacked? Because someone didn't like your progressive stand on women in the Church?"

Sister Marie Therese shook her head. "I really do not know. But I am hoping that your skills as a journalist, which Father Dan has told me are formidable, will help us to perhaps find another way to the truth."

Jacqueline smiled. "You mean cut through the cop bull —" she caught herself, and quickly adjusted, "the copspeak that can be more foggy than clear."

Dan laughed. "Exactly that, my dear Jacqueline. You are an award-winning investigative reporter with the *Washington Post*, and we are so grateful for your offer to help us."

Jacqueline's smile faded into a look of resolve. "I have already begun."

"Begun your investigation?" Dan asked.

"Yes. Sister Maureen's death hit me hard. I had to begin."

Dan and Sister Marie Therese looked at Jacqueline expectantly.

"Did you know Sister Maureen was going to meet the pope this week?"

"Yes," Sister Marie Therese replied. "She was meeting Pope Leo and Cardinal Timothy Omahu."

"He's Nigerian, right?" Jacqueline asked.

"He is," Dan replied. "He's president of the Council for Justice and Peace."

Jacqueline thought about that. "Do you know what Maureen planned to discuss with them?"

Sister Marie Therese shook her head. "I don't. But Justice and Peace cover a lot of territory in our world."

Jacqueline nodded. "It does. I know how committed she was to helping Africa find its perspective. We need to find out what Sister Maureen was planning to talk to them about, and how it connected to Africa. If only to rule it out. As a reason for her murder."

Dan's eyes widened in surprise. "Are you saying that Sister Maureen was the target?"

"Maybe. And maybe the other women were cover up collaterals."

Sister Marie Therese frowned. "What does this mean?"

"It's a term organized crime uses. They kill their target along with a few others to throw the investigators off the scent."

"And you think that is what happened here?

"I don't know. But we're going to find out."

Dan admired the fact that Jacqueline had already dug down deep into the bombing and into Sister Maureen's life, as well. "If you find the truth, Jacqueline, we need the power of your voice as an outsider to tell it."

Jacqueline put on a stage whisper as she said, "So, you mean, I'm not officially here?"

Sister Therese handed Jacqueline a business card. "I took the liberty. It will open doors that might otherwise stay shut."

The journalist took the card, and her eyes lit up in amusement. "Aha, so I even got a doctorate out of this trip. Mama will be so proud." She spun the card so Dan could see what it said. Dr. Jacqueline Brussard, spiritual advisor, *Donne del Vaticano*.

"Very nice," Dan said. "But maybe we want to use your

mother's maiden name on the card, in case we have any sharp-eyed *Washington Post* readers in Rome. Which we do."

"That is my mother's name. My father bolted when I was a baby."

"What's your middle name?" Dan asked.

Jacqueline grinned. "Robinson. My mother was a baseball fan, and she thought if I were a boy, I'd be Jackie Robinson Brussard."

"But you can be Jackie Robinson on your card," Dan joked.

"I think Jacqueline Robinson will do the trick," she said, handing the card back to Sister Marie Therese. "To help us get that truth."

"Who do you think did it?" Sister Marie Therese asked the journalist.

"I don't know," Jacqueline replied. "But in my line of work you begin with one simple question: who stood to gain from this? Which is another way of saying, follow the money. And then let us find out if that was what Sister Maureen was doing."

10

Rome

"It's so beautiful, Renzo," Cardinal Antonio Matteo said as he and Renzo Bellocco looked out onto Rome from the rooftop terrace of Renzo's home, the *Palazzo dei Fiori*, a magnificent five-story townhouse just off the *Campo di Fiori* piazza in the ancient heart of Rome. "I can see the Basilica from here!"

The two men had met precisely twice before, at a Vatican reception for the new cardinal from Nigeria, Timothy Omahu, and at the funeral of Pope Benedict. This was the first time Cardinal Matteo had been invited to the palazzo, and even he who had inhaled the treasures of the Vatican had been impressed with the palazzo's elegant pink marble hallways, and crystal chandeliers, and walls filled with Modiglianis and Picassos and even a Michelangelo cartoon, of the Madonna and child. It was fit for the king that Renzo Bellocco was, of a sort.

The cardinal, his gray hair cut short, his face deceptively thinner than the portly body beneath it, looked older than his sixty-five years. But then, churchmen, in his experience, went from young to old with hardly any middle age to speak of.

His host, Renzo Bellocco, the same age as the cardinal, looked a decade younger, his body toned from regular exercise, his black hair thick and slicked back with gel, and his face smooth and free of the furrows of age. Perhaps that's what a life of sin does to you, the cardinal thought as he took a sip of champagne. All that looking over your shoulder keeps you fit.

"Yes, Antonio," Renzo replied. "This place where we are now is my basilica. Best of all, it comes with its own bar."

On that, a white-coated waiter slid over and topped up Renzo's glass, from a bottle of *Franciacorta*, the classic Italian sparkling wine made in the same method of the champagne from France. The cardinal chuckled and caught the eye of one of the two men in black suits who flanked the stairway down to the palazzo. He did not return the smile to the cardinal, but looked like he might do so if he had to shoot him in the head. He had the face of an assassin, and Cardinal Matteo, as a Sicilian, had seen that face too many times. He knew these men were Rocco's bodyguards, and he knew that Rocco needed bodyguards because, well, he lived in a dangerous world.

"The other Basilica looks so lovely," the cardinal said. The dome of St. Peter's Basilica was lit by a full moon tonight, just a mile away across the Tiber.

"And how are things going in that Basilica?" Renzo asked, his voice soft, his brown eyes thoughtful.

Cardinal Matteo was the Camerlengo of the Holy Roman Church, which is an office of the papal household that administers the property and revenues of the Holy See. He knew that was why he had been invited here tonight, for this solo drink on the roof with Renzo Bellocco, who was rumored to be the Mafia boss of Italy.

But that was just a rumor, Cardinal Matteo thought,

and he knew how rumor worked inside the Vatican. It had destroyed many, and he did his best not to deal in it. Unless, of course, he needed to do so. He knew that Renzo's success as an exporter of Italian food and drink, which the world could never get enough of, had paid for this grand palace overlooking the river and the city. And maybe some other things had helped, too.

Cardinal Matteo had grown up with the Mafiosi in Sicily, and they were roughhewn and savage. There was nothing savage about Renzo Bellocco. At least, nothing that the cardinal could see.

"Things are, shall we say, in a point of transition, Renzo, in the church."

"Mmm. I hear that my favorite order of priests, the Jesuits, have a new leader,"

Cardinal Matteo was curious as to why the Jesuits would be Renzo's favorite order of priests, but, since he was a Dominican, did not press the point. They were not his favorite order, that was for certain. "Yes, Father Lanaham was chosen to be their superior general."

Renzo looked thoughtfully out onto Rome, shimmering beneath them. "What do you make of him? Besides the fact he is American, and they always seem to find a way to mess things up."

Cardinal Matteo shrugged. He liked Americans, but it would seem Renzo Bellocco had some outstanding issue with them. "They say he has been so long in the Middle East that he has become less American and more... Levantine."

"You mean Jewish?"

Cardinal Matteo had meant "Jewish sympathizer" but again, he shrugged. "It's very sad what happened at his Pontifical Biblical Institute."

Renzo Bellocco took a sip of champagne. "You think someone was trying to send him a message?"

Cardinal Matteo had not thought that. He thought

someone was trying to kill progressive women and that was the message. But to whom? "I do not know, Renzo. Why would someone want to send him a message?"

Renzo Bellocco took a sip of wine and gave the cardinal the kind of tight smile he had seen before on the faces of so many Sicilians who knew something dark but weren't going to say what it was.

"I don't know," Bellocco replied. "I would imagine that he has made some enemies in the part of the world he lives in."

"But wouldn't his enemies go after him, and not those women?" The cardinal was curious now, as to Renzo Bellocco's calculus of revenge. If that's what it was.

Bellocco looked up and shrugged, as if this were above him. "I do not know about these things, Eminence. But I would think that if you wanted Fr. Lanaham's attention, to maybe get him to do something for you, that's one way of going about it."

Cardinal Matteo felt like draining his glass of wine on that opinion, as the way Bellocco said it, his voice warm and thoughtful, made it sound like he thought it was a good way of doing business.

So, Cardinal Matteo made a joke, of sorts. "All I know is that the Lord moves in mysterious ways." As if the Lord in which he believed would do such a thing, but maybe the one that Renzo did, would do. And that would be Satan.

"*Sic transit gloria mundi,* Antonio," Renzo replied with a reassuring smile. He liked to remind people, every now and again, that he had gone to university and had studied the classics.

The cardinal wondered, with all of his wealth and this life in a palazzo Renzo really thought of the passing glories of the world. But he was also making a point.

"I hear the Holy Father is not long for the world, Eminence."

Cardinal Mateo felt a chill run up his neck. He knew the

pope was ill, and old, but this statement, coming so hard after the message theory to Father Dan had suddenly changed the temperature of things.

"Well, Renzo, we know not the hour of our passing to eternity. All we know is that we must be ready."

Renzo put an arm on the brass, surely not gold, railing that ringed the rooftop terrace, and leaned into it. "But the Holy Father is not well. His hour looks to be soon."

"It is true that he is very ill."

"With stomach problems, so I hear."

"Yes, with some mysterious stomach issue that defeats the doctors."

Renzo nodded. "Perhaps I should send him to my doctor. To put him out of his misery."

Cardinal Matteo flinched at another surge of the chill, but he forced himself to acknowledge the idea. "I think, while the Holy Father is a most progressive soul, he would draw the line at euthanasia."

"Eminence!" Renzo laughed. "I wasn't talking about killing him. I was talking about my doctor giving him medicine to help him."

Cardinal Matteo now laughed, and the waiter topped up his glass, since to anyone watching, the evening was going so well.

"I think the Holy Father is more than prepared for his time, when it comes."

Renzo Bellocco nodded, and looked at the cardinal, his brown eyes heavy, and unblinking. "And when it does, Antonio, it is you, is it not, who closes down his life?"

Cardinal Matteo winced, but then covered it with a sip of wine. "I would say once upon a time, that was true. These days, my responsibility will be to cut the papal ring in two, in the presence of other cardinals, to be sure, to symbolically signal the end of this papacy. And to safekeep the Holy Father's will until it can be delivered to the College of Cardinals."

"Who will soon meet to elect the new pope," Renzo said.

"Yes, the conclave will happen as soon as possible after Pope Leo goes to his reward."

Renzo thought about this, and then turned his head back toward the Basilica. In profile, with his aquiline nose, and his strong jaw, he looked like the male partner to the she-wolf that represents Rome.

"You will not be the new pope, Antonio?"

"I will do everything in my power not to be the new pope, Renzo."

Renzo smiled. "So, when the pope dies, and there is not yet a new pope, who is in charge of the Vatican?"

Cardinal Matteo paused, and looked back at the Basilica, now softly lit as a haze had developed in the night sky. "That would be me, Renzo."

Renz Bellocco now smiled as if he meant it. "That is very good news, Antonio."

"I won't have much power, I mean, I can't appoint cardinals or anything."

Renzo kept the smile burning, now right into Cardinal Matteo's heart. "But you can make things safe."

"Safe?"

"I am sure there are things in the Vatican that need to be made safe." He paused. "As you know, I have helped the Church, and I want my help to be safe."

"Ah, yes, safe. I understand." Cardinal Matteo understood that Renzo Bellocco spoke of the money he had loaned the Vatican. It was a lot of money, which Bellocco had topped up when the pandemic diminished Church coffers to an alarming degree, which made the money he had already poured in when Benedict was still the pope cresting fifty million Euros.

"You want your money returned, Renzo?"

Renzo Bellocco shook his head. "No, I want it to be safe. To do its work for the Church."

Cardinal Matteo nodded thoughtfully. He did not know

exactly when Bellocco meant, but he would find out. "Of course, Renzo," he said.

"I am glad that you do understand, Antonio. It will make my life so much simpler. I won't need to send messages to get the Church's attention. I will just tell you."

"Messages?"

"Oh, you know, doing something big to make sure the Church understands me."

Cardinal Matteo blinked. The only big thing lately was all those women who had been blown up in Jerusalem. Would that be the kind of message a man like Renzo Bellocco would send? Surely, he was not telling him that.

Renzo watched the cardinal think it through, then he said. "What I want even more than my money to help the Church is a vote in the conclave to elect the next pope. In fact, I want my cardinal elected. And I want you to make that happen, Antonio."

Cardinal Matteo now felt as if he had been punched in the stomach, so he drew back his shoulders and took a deep breath. "Who might that be, Renzo?"

Renzo put a hand on the cardinal's shoulder, and Antonio Matteo could feel his strength as Renzo pushed down on him, flexing his hand like the lever of power that it was. "I will tell you when you need to know, Antonio. Can't have the news get out and spoil my betting odds now, can we?"

A bell chimed from below, and the white-coated waiter announced that dinner would now be served. Cardinal Matteo wondered how he could eat without throwing up. He would have to find a way to rig a papal election, not just for the good of his Church, but now, clearly, to save his own life. Once Pope Leo was dead.

11

Rome

It had barely gone 10 o'clock in the morning when Father Jared Rossi poked his head into the office of Gianluca Schmitt and said, "I have to postpone our 10:30. I have been summoned by the cardinal."

"The boss?" Schmitt asked in English, their office language.

Father Rossi shook his head no. He had not been summoned by the boss, Cardinal Konrad Pawlevski, who was President of the five cardinals who supervised the *Istituto per le Opere di Religione*, or Institute for Works of Religion, known as the Vatican Bank. He had been summoned by another one of the five cardinals who supervised them. Cardinal Antonio Matteo.

Father Rossi's intense blue eyes twinkled as he delivered the news to his colleague, with whom he played a delicate game. Rossi, with his doctorate from the LSE in economics, was the man tagged by Pope Leo to work with Schmitt, a forensic accountant, to make sure the Vatican's finances were as clean as the breath of angels.

Rossi knew that they were not, but he also knew that his predecessor, a Canadian monsignor who had been a banker before he became a priest had put guardrails in place to hamper people like Schmitt from discovering the truth with any degree of ease. As the Canadian had said to Rossi about the ability someone would need to undo his work: "He'll have to be a fucken genius."

And if Schmitt was that genius, and if the truth got out, then the sins that the Vatican Bank had committed in the past would look like a child's First Confession compared to the list of "burn in hell forever" sins that would play out in the media today.

Schmitt, at age 33, had already conceded to his baldness by shaving his head, so that his glistening dome and his round black horn-rimmed glasses combined with his lush black mustache whose ends he twirled upwards and waxed to make him seem out of time. With his hearty manner, he seemed like a Roman boulevardier from a century ago, who made up for his tall bald self with an exuberant Mediterranean personality, one not at all Swiss.

Father Rossi, just four years older, could have been a Vogue model, if Vogue had wanted a Mediterranean man with a sculpted jaw and a celestial nose, slightly turned up, and cheekbones you could set emeralds on. He had a full head of curly black hair and those impossibly blue eyes. Rossi was a head turner, to be sure, and here in the Vatican, that meant that the vast majority of the heads that turned his way were male.

The pink Mafia, as the gay priests and bishops and cardinals were known, were a potent force inside the city state, and far beyond it. Gianluca Schmitt was gay, and even he, with all his world experience, would marvel to Jared at the complexity of some of the transactions on offer, which, as a civilian, he could partake in if he wished. As he was dating one of the Swiss Guards, he was a wry observer, and a good source for Jared, who was, when it came to the pink Mafia, on the other side of the planet.

Father Jared Rossi knew in his heart that he loved women. He knew it in his flesh as well, for he had dated widely before he became a priest. Jared had taken up the priestly life of chastity and celibacy because of a broken heart. Renata, a woman he had loved more with each rising of the sun had risen herself one day when he was finishing up his thesis, loaded her pockets with rocks and walked into the Thames.

Jared Rossi was stunned into chastity. He could not understand how his love for Renata could not have seen this tragedy coming. If he had, could he have saved her? He blamed himself, and he vowed never to love anyone else like that again. In case it killed them, too. And then he sealed the promise by becoming a priest, joining the Dominican order because of their Four Pillars of holy preaching: community, study, prayer and service. Of course, he knew that his sealed promise sealed nothing if God had other plans for him.

This morning, he rushed from the Vatican Bank's office, on the *Via Sant' Anna*, just to the right of St. Peter's Square, and dodged tour groups as he cut across the Square and headed to *La Bella Donna*, a café just on the other side of it, on the *Via Porta di Cavalleggeri*. It was close enough to the Vatican to be a short walk, so that two priests meeting there for coffee wouldn't arouse suspicion about clandestine activity, nor would they be overheard by Vatican spies. If that's what the cardinal wanted.

Cardinal Antonio Matteo was at a table on the sidewalk as Jared hustled up the Via, and he raised his hand in a princely wave.

"Nice to see you again, Father Rossi," the cardinal said, extending his sleek hand. The cardinal's eyes were intense, and searching, as if Jared was about to spill a secret, one way or another.

Jared shook his hand, and replied, "The same, your Eminence."

The cardinal sat, and so did Jared, and just as a waiter appeared to take Jared's order, the cardinal abruptly plunked ten Euros on the table and suggested that a walk along the Tiber would be a much better thing to do on such a fine June day.

Jared smiled as if this was the best idea he'd ever heard. Then he stood, and turned toward the direction the cardinal was looking in when he decided to change venues. No Vatican spies there. So, he looked the other way, and saw Father Dan Lanaham, the new Superior General of the Jesuits, walking slowly with a tall African woman whose beauty raised the hairs on Jared's neck.

Why would Cardinal Matteo want to avoid Father Lanaham and this woman?

The cardinal was almost at the fountain on the Via when Jared caught up to him. They chatted about the weather as they walked toward the Tiber, a short ten minutes away, and then once they were on the walkway along the Tiber, the cardinal stopped, and leaned against the stone wall that flanked the river.

"Ah, the air is getting worse," the cardinal said as he took out an Albuterol asthma inhaler and gave himself a spritz of relief.

"Yes," Jared agreed. He looked at the air quality report on Accuweather every morning, mainly because of his job to forecast the economic future of the Vatican, and climate change could not be ignored. Today the air was dreadful. Just the walk from the café to here made Jared feel as if he'd smoked a cigar.

"Are you alright, Eminence?" he asked, thinking maybe the cardinal would call off whatever inquisition he had planned.

The cardinal held up his hand, then pocketed his inhaler. "I am much better now, thank you. I have to stay healthy so I will be ready when the time comes."

Jared knew that Matteo, as the papal camerlengo, was referring to the expected death of Pope Leo. He thought it an odd thing to say, and Cardinal Matteo read the look on his face.

"Yes, Father Rossi, change is coming, and we must all be prepared."

Jared nodded. He was still thinking about why Father Lanaham and the beautiful woman with him had made the asthmatic run for the river. Cardinal Matteo interrupted the thought.

"How are things at the IOR? How is that Swiss fellow working out?"

Jared took a breath of the bad air. The cardinal was asking him if the forensic accountant was a good colleague, or good at his job. "He's a very nice guy, Eminence. Easy to work with."

The cardinal turned to gaze at the great river, its water murky and sluggish today. "You know, I would expect that with this bombing in Israel, you will be affected at the IOR, no?"

Jared pretended to consider this, but now he was wondering why the cardinal would connect the Vatican Bank to a terrorist outage in Israel. "Our work in Israel will continue," Jared replied calmly. "We have a fine relationship with the state of Israel, and many properties of great spiritual, and I might also add, financial value there."

The cardinal smiled at him, appreciating the distinction. "Did you know, Father Rossi, that the Jewish banking Rothschild family loaned Pope Urban XVI the sum of $400,000 in 1832, to help with the Vatican finances after revolutionary zeal had stretched the Church? It would be the equivalent to—"

"Four billion dollars today," Jared said.

"Ah, so you knew?"

Jared knew, and he also knew how startled the Rothschilds had been to discover the chaos in the Vatican bank. There were no budgets or balance sheets, no independent reviews or audits, and the people in charge had no financial training. It had pretty much stayed that way up until the 1980s, Jared also knew. But he smiled reassuringly at the cardinal and said, "Yes, and they made a few subsequent loans. Saved the Church, so they say."

The cardinal nodded. "They also said the Jews ran the popes, but eventually, we turned that around. With Catholic bankers, and our Italian friends."

The cardinal stood up straight. He was a good half foot shorter than Jared, who was six-foot three, but he had the presence of power. "So, tell me, Father Rossi, when the changes come, as they will, how will things look inside the Vatican bank? For our Italian friends."

"I'm not sure I understand, Eminence," Jared replied.

"We have had good Italian friends help the Church by sharing their money with us, and when the time comes, we want to know that their money is safe."

Jared swallowed. The cardinal was referring to all that dark cash that had flooded in before Pope Francis had installed his reforms. Money that had no records, save for what was owed to whom when the debt was called. Mafia money. Washed by the Vatican.

"I think that we're working for the good of the Church," Jared said. "Me and my Swiss colleague."

The cardinal smiled at that. Then he put a strong hand on Jared's arm. "And you will tell me if anything becomes unsafe, won't you Father Rossi? Before it is too late?"

Jared nodded as an acknowledgement of the request. But in his heart, and in his formidable mind, he knew that if the question had to be asked, then it was already too late.

"That's good," Cardinal Matteo said. "Because the more I know, the more I can help you to stay safe, too."

12

Rome

Pope Leo looked as if he had somehow regained a little of his strength as he raised himself from the papal throne in St. Peter's Basilica and walked to the lectern to deliver the homily for Sister Maureen O'Connor, on this, the day of her funeral.

The Basilica, which could hold 60,000 souls, was filled to its capacity today. The Roman sunlight beamed through the stained-glass windows of the great Basilica and onto heads of state, and royalty; legions of nuns from every order from around the world; powerful women and business leaders; humble citizens paying their respects; and a delegation from Israel, led by Dr. Rachel Ben-Simon, the ambassador to the Holy See, who sat in a position of honor along with Chief Inspector Hillel Bennett, and Agent Mimi Shapiro. They watched this Catholic ritual in a choice spot to the right of Bernini's grand *baldacchino,* a magnificent merger of architecture and art that is the bronze canopy of columns and corinths and angels rising above the high altar, and directly under the dome of the Basilica.

Father Dan Lanaham, who had been asked to concelebrate the funeral Mass for Sister Maureen with Pope Leo, looked at the Jewish delegation as the pope walked to the lectern, sitting there with respect and reverence inside a Church which had done them so much harm.

Indeed, when the Jewish ghetto existed in this city, Dan knew, the Jews had to listen to Catholic preaching on their Sabbath, as part of their punishment for killing Jesus, which, of course, they did not do. And here they were today, listening to Pope Leo speak to everyone as a humble priest in mourning for the life that had been lost, and in joy for the heavenly life to come.

"If I falter," Leo had told Dan before the Mass, "then read 'em this." He handed Dan a sheaf of papers that was his homily, and Dan wondered exactly how he would pull that off, as he tucked the papers beneath his cassock, should Leo falter. He prayed that he would not.

The prayer was heard. Leo was not faltering, and he was not speaking from a script. He spoke from his heart.

"At Catholic funerals, eulogies are considered inappropriate," Leo said in English, in respect for the language of Sister Maureen, and also, he needed his own mother tongue to express the deep emotion that he felt for Sister Maureen. He could easily manage in Italian, or Spanish, or German, or French, but he could express her full truth in English.

"The reason is that the Mass is a formal liturgical rite that needs to be uncorrupted, according to our faith. Anything said during Mass must be related to the teachings of the Catholic church, and so, a eulogy that focuses on the life and times of the person we have come to bury does not meet that requirement, which is why we don't do them."

Leo looked up at the coffin in front of the altar, draped with the Vatican flag, and then out at the crowd before him. He caught the eye of Sister Marie Therese, sitting with Jacqueline Brussard, next to the delegation from Israel. He smiled softly at Sister Marie Therese, and said, "And today, I will break that rule. I believe, as pope, that I am permitted to give myself that permission."

That was the first laugh Leo got at Sister Maureen's funeral, and it would not be his last.

He spoke about how this Irish-Catholic girl from Maryland had put herself through Georgetown by working as a waiter in an Italian restaurant in Little Italy. It was there, Leo said, "Sister Maureen had her first encounter with the inequities of our world. Not that the *linguine alle vongole* wasn't as good as the veal *scallopini*," he paused, as laughter rolled up the nave. Then he smiled, but there was anger in his eyes. "Sister Maureen had met up with the fact that the men working at the restaurant and doing the same jobs as the women got paid more. When she protested, she was fired."

A murmur now went through the crowd, but Leo stopped it with another smile. "Oh, she was just getting started. When I first met her, she was a newly minted professor at Georgetown, and hadn't been a nun all that long either. She came to see me because I was part of the president's commission on interreligious dialogue when I was a bishop, and she said, 'I want to be on that commission.'

"And I said, as she knew I would, 'but we don't have any female members.' This would have been the late 1970s, Jimmy Carter was the president, Saint John Paul II was the pope. But even so, I blush to recall that conversation today. And I knew at that moment that Sister Maureen was going to change the world by changing her Church, and so we invited her to join that commission."

"And so, she did. She helped to create and advise the

Women of the Vatican, *le Donne del Vaticano*, many of whom I see here today. And many of whom were killed with Sister Maureen, in Jerusalem, a holy city to us, to our Jewish forebears, and to our brothers and sisters in Islam. And I ask, 'Why?'"

Leo paused and took a sip of water from the crystal glass that Dan had filled and left on the shelf under the lectern. "I don't ask why in the sense that I know we all die, and some of us here count on joining the legions who have gone before us in a place that we call heaven. But I think Sister Maureen was working to create heaven on earth for all of us, but especially for women who have been often unheard in our Church. Or silenced by it. And that's why she was killed. So, who would want to do that, and why? That's what I am asking."

He took another sip of water and winced as a flash of pain raced up his gut and into his neck. "There are good and experienced people investigating that 'why', and they will find the truth, and the justice, for Sister Maureen. That's all she would want. Truth, and because of it, justice. And in order to have justice, you need to have someone who can do something about it to listen to the truth."

Leo looked around the Basilica, as if he might just see Sister Maureen in the crowd. "Well, *le Donne del Vaticano*, Women of the Church," Leo said, and angled his head toward the sky, "and Sister Maureen, I have some power. And I am listening to you and your truth. We shall find justice for Sister Maureen, that I promise you. And in the meantime, take solace, and take power, from this, which was her favorite poem, by another Irish person, W.B. Yeats.

> *Had I the heavens' embroidered cloths,*
> *Enwrought with golden and silver light,*
> *The blue and the dim and the dark cloths*
> *Of night and light and the half light,*

I would spread the cloths under your feet:
But I, being poor, have only my dreams;
I have spread my dreams under your feet;
Tread softly because you tread on my dreams.

The reception after the funeral Mass for Sister Maureen took place in the *Domus Casa Marta,* the modest hotel for visiting Church leaders and dignitaries just south of the Basilica in Vatican City. Pope Leo stood at a table near the front of the cafeteria, as people came by to pay their respects to him, which many of them suspected was for the last time.

Father Dan stood across the room, with Sister Marie Therese and Jacqueline Brussard, sipping a glass of Sister Maureen's favorite wine, *Montepulciano d'Abruzzo,* and munching on mini bruschetta canapes.

"The only person who I wish was here is the one we're mourning," Dan said, and Jacqueline raised her glass to him.

"Pretty impressive crowd that came out for her," Jacqueline said.

"She was a pretty impressive person," Sister Marie Therese replied. She was drinking water, and her eyes were scanning the crowd.

"I know," Jacqueline said. "She was a force of good."

"And she still is," Dan added.

"Ah," Sister Marie Therese exclaimed, her eyes finding what she sought. "There he is."

Dan and Jacqueline followed Sister Marie Therese's gaze, which landed on a tall, powerful African man in his early sixties, who was greeting Pope Leo.

"That's Cardinal Timothy Omahu," Sister Marie Therese said. "He's from Nigeria. He was the one that Sister Maureen was going to meet. Along with the pope. And after what the Holy Father just said, I suspect she had some truth to tell him to get justice for someone."

Jacqueline considered this. "Do you think he knows what she wanted?"

Dan nodded. "Likely in a general sense. He and the Pope would have to know in order to take the meeting. But we can't just go up and ask them. We need some kind of evidence, the kind that Maureen was going to bring to them."

"Evidence of what?" Jacqueline asked. "Do you know, Sister?"

Sister Marie Therese shook her head and closed her eyes. As if no amount of prayer could reveal the mystery. When she opened them, she smiled.

"I think she might know."

Dan and Jacqueline followed her gaze, toward an African woman who was now speaking to Cardinal Omahu and the pope.

"Who's that?" Jacqueline asked.

"She's a woman I saw with Sister Maureen in Rome once, in a Chinese restaurant."

"And you think she knows because....?"

"Because she's also Nigerian. And if Sister Maureen was coming to Rome to speak with Cardinal Omahu and the pope, she would know."

"Do you know who she is?" Dan asked.

Sister Marie Therese squeezed her eyes shut, then opened them and shook her head. "No, but she'll remember meeting me, I hope. Time to reintroduce myself. You stay here. This has to seem like an accident, not an investigation."

Dan smiled at the nun, and Jacqueline gave her a thumbs up. They watched as Sister Marie Therese made her way through the crowd, toward the African woman. They watched as Sister Marie Therese spoke to her, and as the two women shook hands. Then they watched as Sister Marie Therese exchanged business cards with the woman. Then she turned to Dan and Jacqueline and smiled. It was the first true smile Dan had seen from the nun since they met. She was onto something.

"Father Lanaham, we offer the deepest condolences of our government and ourselves," Dr. Rachel Ben-Simon said to Dan, arriving at his side with Chief Inspector Bennett and Agent Shapiro flanking her.

"May her memory be a blessing," Agent Shapiro said.

"Amen," Dan replied. "May I offer you a glass of her favorite wine?"

Chief Inspector Bennett's eyes flickered a yes, but Dr. Ben-Simon smiled a no. "We are working, Father, to solve this crime, so best to keep our heads clear."

Dan smiled. "Me too. I find wine sometimes helps."

Jacqueline Brussard laughed at that, and Dan apologized. "I'm sorry, the wine has dulled my manners. Dr. Rachel Ben-Simon is the ambassador to the Holy See for the State of Israel, and Chief Inspector Hillel Bennett and Agent Mimi Shapiro are the lead investigators looking to solve the crime that killed Sister Maureen, and so many others."

Jacqueline shook hands and introduced herself. "I'm Dr. Jacqueline Robinson, though not a medical doctor like you, Ambassador. I can save you if you choke on moral theology, but that's about it. I advise the *Donne del Vaticano*."

Dan hid his smile as he took a sip of wine. Jacqueline was impressively smooth in her fiction, selling it with the detail about moral theology.

"Are you based here in Rome?" Dr. Ben-Simon asked.

"No, I wish. I came for the funeral and to help the *Donne* to get themselves into some kind of order," Jacqueline said. "I'm based in Washington, D.C."

"You are a professor?" Agent Shapiro asked.

Jacqueline smiled. Saying yes would be too easy a lie to expose. So, she said, "No, I work with the Archdiocese of Washington as a consultant."

"You must be a good one," Chief Inspector Bennett said, glancing longingly at the table filled with wine. "You are helping many organizations."

Jacqueline gracefully accepted the question as a compliment. "I do my best. There is much to do to make our world better for us all."

The three Israelis all agreed with that sentiment and in the pause that followed, Dan stepped in. "Any developments in the investigation?"

Chief Inspector Bennett looked to Mimi Shapiro who looked to Dr. Ben-Simon. "We are putting together the evidence so far. We should have a briefing for you and the Holy Father this week."

Dan noticed Sister Marie Therese watching in the distance. As if she did not want to reveal in front of Israeli cops and their ambassador what had made her smile.

So, Dan took action. "I look forward to that, Dr. Ben-Simon. Will you be staying in Rome long?" he said to Chief Inspector Bennett and Agent Shapiro.

"Just until tomorrow," Agent Shapiro replied.

"Then back at it."

Dan nodded, and waved to his assistant, Father Martin Gerrard, who was waiting on the sidelines for such a summoning.

"Yes, Father, and hello Madam Ambassador, Dr. Robinson," Martin Gerrard said as he ambled up to the gathering and smiled particularly warmly at Chief Inspector Bennett. Who smiled back with equal warmth. Dan took note. Maybe there was the fire of attraction there, forbidden as it was for them both.

Fr. Dan made introduction all around, and then added, " Chief Inspector Bennet and Agent Shapiro have only one night in Rome, so please show them our hospitality at our favorite restaurant in Trastevere, Father Gerrard. You can't solve crime on an empty stomach, and the food in Rome is quite... unmissable."

Father Gerrard smiled. "It would be my great pleasure. Now, come with me and let's make our plan," Gerrard said with Irish mirth. "I hope you won't mind having a drink, first?"

The two cops looked at Dr. Ben-Simon who smiled at them. "Go. Enjoy your evening."

Then she nodded to Dan and Jacqueline and said, "Thank you for that escape. I will use the time to catch up with my family. Who have begun to wonder if I am their mother, or a hologram."

Dan and Jacqueline laughed, and Dr. Ben-Simon bowed. "We will be in touch soon, Father, Dr. Robinson." Then she followed her cop colleagues out into the square.

Sister Marie Therese then stepped out of the shadows as if she was in a play and had just heard her cue. "Her name is Chinara Bukar, and we have a meeting," she said.

"That woman knew Sister Maureen?"

"Yes, she does. She did. She's based in Washington. But as I said, she's from Nigeria."

Dan and Jacqueline smiled at Sister Marie Therese. "It would seem you have two vocations, Sister Marie Therese. Nun, and detective," Dan said.

The nun blushed, and the rush of blood in her pale cheeks made her seem younger and even prettier. "I have one vocation only, and that is to the truth as we know it through Jesus Christ. And if he has led me here, then it is him we must thank. And pray that he keeps the path open."

"When do we meet with her?" Jacqueline said.

"I am to call her tomorrow morning. She leaves for Washington tomorrow night."

Dan poured two glasses of wine and handed them to Sister Marie Therese and Jacqueline, and then topped up his own. "To Sister Maureen," he said. "And the justice that we shall find."

As they clinked glasses, Dan saw Cardinal Alfonso

Sanchez, the Vatican Secretary of State, as well as Vincenzo Pericoli, head of the Vatican's *Gendarmeria* escorting Pope Leo out of the Domus cafeteria. Leo looked as if this day had finally caught up with him and had taken his breath away. Dan knew that Leo did not have many more breaths in him. He would do everything he could do to get justice for Sister Maureen and the dead women and the *Donne del Vaticano* while this good and just pope was still the head of his Church. Because once Leo was gone from this world, so too was his justice.

13

Rome

Chinara Bukar insisted that she meet with Sister Marie Therese and Father Dan and Jacqueline Brussard "somewhere that we cannot be seen."

Which is why they were meeting with the slender Nigerian woman with the intense brown eyes in the Chapel of the Madonna of Bocciata, the oldest chapel in the grottoes of St. Peter's Basilica and the closest one to the tomb of Peter, the rock upon whom Jesus said he would build his church.

Father Dan was vested in his green robes of Ordinary Time and standing on the altar. Behind him was the 14th century fresco by Pietro Cavallini of *"Madonna della Bocciata"*, which gets its name because Mary has a swollen face due to a drunken soldier having thrown a bowl into the holy image after he lost a game of bocce, or bowls, and making her face bleed. Today, the majestic and solemn Madonna holds Jesus on her lap, and intensely looks out on those before her.

Kneeling in the pews and looking back at the Madonna were Sister Marie Therese, Jacqueline Brussard, and Chinara Bukar. To anyone passing by, it looked completely normal, a priest saying Mass in this chapel beneath the great Basilica. It was how to be unseen in Rome, by being very public in church, and engaged in something that did not seem like what it was. Dan had already said a quick Mass, but before his blessing and dismissal, they had one matter to deal with. What was Sister Maureen going to tell Pope Leo and Cardinal Omahu?

"She was going to speak of a crime and criminals," Chinara said in her Nigerian lilt of alto, "that takes place in my country, that is, in Nigeria, and one that takes place in Rome."

"Where in Rome?" Dan asked.

Chinara extended her hands and turned both her palms upward. She was thin and delicate, with the face of an empress who looked younger than her five decades, dignified and certain and now, her brown eyes hot, angry.

"You mean right here?" Jacqueline asked. Chinara nodded once.

"What type of crime was Sister Maureen speaking of?" Sister Marie Therese asked in a low voice.

"Do you know of the Black Axe?" Chinara asked.

Jacqueline and Sister Marie Therese nodded. Dan cocked his head. "I'm sorry, I do not."

Chinara Bukar looked around, to see if anyone was listening, then said "The Black Axe gang began as a student movement in Benin City in the 1970s. Then it became a gang, attacking professors, and other students. Violent. Cruel. They kill people as if taking a breath, and they enjoy it."

She paused, her eyes closed, and Jacqueline picked up the story. "Today the Black Axe is a global criminal network that engages in drug and human trafficking and money laundering. And they are responsible for most of the world's cyber-crime. They have gone global. Sister Maureen was investigating them."

Chinara Bukar nodded, impressed by Jacqueline's research. "She was. And what Sister Maureen was going to tell the pope was that the Black Axe are now in Rome. She told me that she would tell the Holy Father and the cardinal from Nigeria first. If they agreed, then she would need my help."

Jacqueline quickly asked, "What kind of help would that be?"

"I work at the Nigerian embassy in Washington, Dr. Robinson. I would expect my help to be one of information, and its dissemination. After Sister Maureen reported back."

"Do you have any guesses what they are doing in Rome?" Dan asked.

Chinara smiled. "In my line of work, it is always about money, one way or another. So, I would ask myself, how do the Vatican and Nigeria connect through money?"

The question hung in the air as they all considered its angles. Their thoughts were interrupted by a loud male voice speaking German, thundering along as if it was the only language in the world and its speaker and his audience were the only people in the church.

Dan saw the source, Cardinal Wolfram Friedrich, turning the corner ahead of three men in suits. The cardinal saw Dan on the altar, and the women in the pews, and stopped talking and walking.

So, Dan finished the Mass. "Let us pray," he said, and the women all stood. "May you go forth with all God's blessing, in the name of the Father, the Son, and the Holy Spirit."

The women all made the Sign of the Cross, and then Dan said, "The Mass is ended, go in peace to love and serve the Lord."

The women all exited the chapel, and Cardinal

Friedrich watched them go, giving a nod to Sister Marie Therese as she passed, who was clearly obeying his dictum to listen to the men. Then he gave Dan a knowing smile. "Good day, Father. Nice to see you saying Mass for these women. It is good for them to see a priest of your stature in action."

He said it as if Dan was performing in a play, or in an arena, and not in a church.

"Thank you, Eminence," Dan replied, stepping down from the altar, and walking to the iron gate that enclosed the chapel. "I am honored to be able to say Mass for them, and to say it so close to the tomb of the first pope."

Cardinal Friedrich mulled this as he tilted his head to the side. He was about two inches shorter than Dan, and about seventy-five pounds heavier, the scarlet sash tied around his black cassock accommodating a substantial gut which bulged above it. The cardinal liked German food and beer, Dan knew, and seemed proud to show his appetite by how tightly he wrapped the sash. "Yes indeed, the first pope, the one after whom this basilica is named," the cardinal replied. "I wonder if he imagined he would have such power when the heathen crucified him upside down?"

The men with the cardinal clearly understood some English, as one of them nodded and grinned.

Dan smiled, too, and said "I think he was probably imagining heaven, Eminence."

Cardinal Friedrich chuckled. "Something in common with our current pope then, as well."

On that, he marched off, and the men with him followed. Though they wore business suits, they wore them in a way that suggested this was a special occasion, and not a daily ritual. The cardinal resumed his lecture in German, and Dan made his way up to the staircase to the sacristy, to divest.

As he changed into his black priest's suit, and fixed his Roman collar, Dan inhaled the elegance of the octagonal sacristy where priests put on their robes and took them off in the great Basilica, a sacristy built in the 18th century and supported by eight columns repurposed from the Emperor Hadrian's villa.

Despite the room's marbled glory, its silver crucifixes on antique altars, its Old Master paintings of Jesus and Peter and the disciples on the walls, Dan often thought the Basilica's sacristy was a bit like a very exclusive locker room, where men from around the world gathered in the early morning to don uniform to do battle. And if Cardinal Friedrich had his way, that battle would be against anything progressive.

"He was speaking to architects," Sister Marie Therese said when Dan joined her and Chinara and Jacqueline in St. Peter's Square. "I speak German."

"How do you know they were architects?" Jacqueline asked.

"Because he was telling them that this was the kind of chapel that would suit Castel Gandolfo. And one of them said their firm had done one in a similar style for some rich person in France."

Dan blinked in surprise. "Cardinal Friedrich was talking to architects about renovating Castel Gandolfo? That's the pope's summer residence."

The thought hung in the Roman sunshine for a moment, and then Jacqueline said, "Castel Gandolfo was turned into a museum by Pope Francis. So why can this cardinal renovate it? Could he be working with Pope Leo?"

Sister Marie Therese shook her head. "I met him in Jerusalem the morning of the attack, and he was about as patronizing as he could be. The kind of guy who thinks women are the maid service of the Church. He is not Pope Leo's kind of person."

"You met him the morning of the attack?" Jacqueline asked.

"Yes, he made me meet him at his hotel. He wanted to

give me a warning about my women's group getting too pushy."

"And then the bomb went off," Dan said.

The women looked at him.

"You don't think he had anything to do with the bombing, do you?" Sister Marie Therese asked.

Dan shuddered. "He's a pretty slick character, that cardinal. I'll check in with the pope about Castel Gandolfo. That's a question we can answer."

"But what about the attack?" Jacqueline asked.

Dan looked at Chinara. "When you said the money could connect Nigeria to Rome, what were you thinking, exactly?"

Chinara looked around, to see if anyone close by was paying them too much attention. "Nigeria has Boko Haram. Nigeria's Taliban. They kidnap girls from school and make them marry their soldiers, and rape them to make children, who they bring up in their same awful belief system. They hate women, except for breeding purposes. If you wanted to send a message, you would get them to do something like what happened in Jerusalem. And they could do it."

Dan looked at Sister Marie Therese. "Who would want to send you a message like that?"

Sister Marie Therese shook her head, but Jacqueline Brussard smiled grimly. "Someone who was threatened by the *Donne del Vaticano*. And my money would be on someone in the Vatican."

They all looked at her, with St. Peter's Basilica rising in majesty behind them, the center of the Catholic Church.

"But killing them?" Sister Marie Therese said. "Usually, the group that does such a thing wants the world to know why it has killed. But no one has claimed to be responsible."

Jacqueline smiled again. "My point exactly. The message was more important than the sender. For now, anyway. The message said, 'we can kill you wherever you are' and that's enough."

A silence hung over the group for a moment, and then Chinara said, "I will follow up on this when I get back to Washington. I will check into Boko Haram's contacts with..." Her voice trailed off. She didn't have to say the rest.

They had come to the point where it made sense to see if an African jihadi group had contacts in the very Church where they all worshiped. Dan had a feeling in his gut that the answer could be yes. And something much worse.

14

Rome

Cardinal Timothy Omahu was not surprised to see Father Dan Lanaham ushered into his office. He rose, gave Dan a broad smile, and extended his hand. "I want to congratulate you on your new position as boss of the Jesuits!" He let out a little chuckle, and Dan smiled and shook the cardinal's powerful hand.

"I think of myself more as a steward, than a boss, Eminence. It's safer that way."

Cardinal Omahu laughed at that remark. Thinking yourself boss of the Jesuits was like believing you could herd cats. Both being far too independent of mind to allow for that kind of perceived control.

"I thought I would be seeing you, Father Lanaham."

Cardinal Omahu was the Prefect for the Causes of Saints, and his office was just outside St. Peter's Square, in Piazza Pio XII. He was a decade younger than Dan, and about six inches shorter. He was built like the rugby prop he had been as a young man on Nigeria's national team. As if cut in a solid block from African granite.

"Yes, Eminence, but I bring you no miracles," Dan said. "I may need one, though."

The cardinal laughed at Dan's joke as if this was the first time anyone had said such a thing to him. His body heaved with mirth as his basso profundo voice choked out the ha-ha's. The job of his dicastery was to find those figures worthy of sainthood and begin the process. The would-be saint needed to have two miracles to their credit. Martyrs needed none. Then the cardinal stopped laughing and gestured to Dan to sit. His brown eyes were now lit with an idea.

"You have come to see if Sister Maureen could become a saint, Father Lanaham?"

Dan was surprised by the question. In his view, Sister Maureen was a saint already. She was also a martyr, it would seem. So, her sainthood was possible, but he also knew that five years had to pass after the death of a candidate for sainthood. Unless there was special permission from the pope. But Sister Maureen's sainthood was not why he had come to see Cardinal Omahu. He had come because of who had killed her.

"I would leave that exploration up to you and your fine staff, Eminence," Dan said. "But you are right, I am here to see you about Sister Maureen. She was coming to Rome to see you and the Holy Father, and I wonder if you can tell me why."

Cardinal Omahu leaned forward, his arms crossed on his desk, and his face as serious as if he was hearing Dan's confession. "I only knew a little bit of it, Father," he said.

Dan nodded and said nothing. He knew that silence was a powerful motivator for people to fill in their own conversational blanks, and so the cardinal did.

"She was coming here to talk to us about the Black Axe, who you know about."

Dan nodded again.

"They are here in Rome, now. They have gone global in exporting their heinous crimes. But Sister Maureen had a theory that they would try to get inside the Vatican. And do their damage from within."

Now Dan spoke. "Do you know exactly what her theory was, Eminence?"

The cardinal shook his head. "No, she was coming here to spell it out." Then he sighed and leaned back in his chair. "Corruption is so bad in Nigeria that she would have had a deep source from which to extract it." He smiled and shook his head. "A couple of years ago, $100,000 disappeared from a government account. When this was discovered, a government official said, 'A snake ate it.' That is how the government treats the people."

Dan leaned back, taking in the force of that reality. "Is the government Black Axe? Could this be them?"

"The Black Axe is a cult, a state within a state," he said. "They are just like the Mafia was in this country, and maybe still are: they bribe the police, so people are not willing to come out and give evidence or testify against them. And if you are so bold as to speak out, they will hack you to bits with machetes, and then shoot you in the face." He folded his hands, as if in prayer.

"The Black Axe offers a powerful attraction to young men without hope. Unemployment is more than twenty percent in Nigeria. Radio advertisements beg women not to have more children because right now, at current birth rates, Nigeria will move from being the world's sixth most populous country to its third by 2050. Young people often find that no opportunities await them upon graduation. Meanwhile, out of Nigeria's 225 million citizens, 112 million of them live below the poverty line. That's what we're up against. And it is why, to be brutally honest, many young men join the priesthood. It is a job for life."

Dan had been thinking about the various ways the Black Axe could get inside the Vatican. Had Cardinal

Omahu just given him a major clue?

The cardinal read his mind and smiled. "No, I do not think Black Axe has sent us a priest. They are their own priesthood; they don't need us. They will try to attack in a different way."

If not a priest, not an insider, then how would they get inside? They could try to bribe or threaten a priest or cardinal. To get them where they wanted to be. "They want to get inside the Vatican Bank," Dan said.

Cardinal Omahu slowly nodded. "Yes, that would make sense. But how would they get in?" He smiled at his own question. "They are world class experts in cybercrime, so they could come through that door, perhaps."

Dan thought about that. He knew that Pope Francis had installed all kinds of guardrails on the Vatican Bank, and that getting inside electronically these days was not impossible, but very difficult. They might pick an easier way.

"What do you think that easier way might be, Father?"

"Not sure. Do you happen to know who they have sent to Rome to establish their cell?"

The cardinal shrugged. "We have more than one hundred thousand Nigerians living in Italy. Most of them in Rome. So, who knows? It would be difficult to interrogate them all."

Dan sighed. He had not realized the Nigerian diaspora in Italy was so large.

"I would think, however, that the *Gendarmeria* might have a better idea of them," the cardinal said. "Maybe we should speak with them. Their boss has the reputation of being a serious man."

Dan nodded. Speaking to the *Gendarmeria* was a good idea. But he also knew that Pope Leo wanted the Israelis to take the lead on solving the murder of Sister Maureen and the other women. Maybe the Israelis would be able to help with the Black Axe. No, they needed to be left to do their work. They were solving a murder in their country. The Black Axe was now here, in his spiritual country. It was his problem to solve.

Dan rose. "Thank you, Eminence. Would you like to ask the Holy Father about the meeting with the *Gendarmeria*?"

The cardinal stood too, reaching up to clap a hand on Dan's shoulder. "Do not worry Father Lanaham. We have a saying here in the dicastery for the Causation of Saints. 'If the miracle exists, God will shine a light upon it for us to see'. We will find our light, and we will find you your miracle."

15

Rome

Every morning, Pope Leo would have a hard-boiled egg and a piece of whole wheat toast, washed down with orange juice and coffee as he sat reading the morning newspapers in his study, with his dog Chocolate curled up at his feet. He liked to read newspapers in his hand, and not on screen, so each morning, his secretary, Monsignor Van Ardt, would bring him his stack: *Osservatore Romano*, the Vatican daily, and the Italian stalwarts *La Reppublica* and *Il Corriere della Sera*, plus *The Guardian, The New York Times*, and *the Boston Globe*.

Leo would go first to the *Globe*, and after checking the obits in the "Irish Sports pages" to see who had died that he had once known, and to learn the stories of those he had not, he would check out the fortunes of the team of the season.In summer and he hoped, in autumn, the Red Sox. In autumn, winter and spring, the Bruins and the Celtics. And in summer, autumn, and winter, the Patriots, who had seen some bad weather ever since Tom Brady had left them.

Leo had admired Brady the athlete but thought the coach and the team which he had built made the quarterback look even better than he was. And yet, once that quarterback was gone, it all kind of fell apart.

Leo wondered what the Church would look like after he was gone, not that he thought himself a Superbowl kind of quarterback. He was more like a trusted tight end. A safe pair of hands to go to when it was third and long.

Leo knew that it was third and very long for the Church now, and for him, it was late in the fourth quarter.

This morning, he could barely swallow the egg, and the toast was dry in his throat, and his stomach hurt. The only thing that calmed him was the touch of Chocolate on his leg, and the orange juice, which seemed pulpier than usual, and sweeter, too. He rang a bell and asked the monsignor for another glass.

"Ah, you like Cardinal Matteo's gift, I see, Holy Father," the Dutch priest said with a jaunty grin. "He said he hoped that you would."

Leo blinked at this news. "Cardinal Matteo gave me orange juice?"

Monsignor Van Ardt nodded enthusiastically. "Six whole cases. It's from Sicily, where he said the best orange juice comes from. He said it will heal what hurts."

"It's very sweet," Leo said. "The orange juice."

The monsignor smiled. "He said that, too. But he said the sweetness is not added sugar. It was lovely what he said, in Italian..."

"Then say it in Italian, monsignor. I can still speak it..."

The monsignor blushed and said, "...*nasce dalla dolcezza celestiale del sole siciliano.*"

"It comes from the heavenly sweetness of the Sicilian sun."

Leo thought about that as he downed his second glass of the blood orange juice. Cardinal Matteo, the camerlengo, and so responsible for the pope's household, was keeping the pope healthy. Unless, of course, he had poisoned the orange juice.

Leo smiled ruefully at the thought. Maybe he should bring back the papal food tester, from the Renaissance, when popes feared being poisoned. No, Matteo was one of the good guys. He had always been straight with Leo, even if he was Italian. Unlike the others who believed the papacy was an Italian birthright, Matteo had made a point of telling the American Leo that he was with him, *contra mundum.* Against the world

Leo was not against the world. He was very much for it. But he knew that not everyone in the Vatican felt as he did, that the Church was for everyone who wanted it. That the choice had to come from them and could not be imposed.

But there were others who wanted to impose their will upon everything. Leo worried that when he was gone, one of them would be elected, as a totem of the time in which we lived, which had grown so mean and vengeful. He took a sip of orange juice, and it calmed the pain in his stomach. Still, he knew that he would have to impose his own will on the Church if he wanted to save her from the darkness ahead. For he knew with each labored breath, that very soon, his own clock would run out.

He reached down and petted Chocolate on his handsome head. "But not yet, right Choco? Not yet. We still have a few things to do." The dog wagged its tail. Leo smiled. He would have to make a note in his will to leave Chocolate to someone who could be trusted. He smiled again. There was only one candidate.

16

Beirut, Lebanon, 1983

It had become a ritual that Dan and Layla enjoyed. The civil war churned its bloody path around them, but every Sunday morning, Layla would come to Dan's room in St. Joseph's University, and they would tumble into bed and spend the next few hours creating the kind of deeds you might want to confess. That is, if you weren't sleeping with your confessor.

And then, when finished, Layla, her blue eyes ablaze with pleasure and purpose, would take demure leave of her professor, as if this Sunday morning consult on her senior thesis about the Bar Kokhba revolt was the most innocent thing on earth.

It had happened three months earlier, to Dan's surprise, and also, to his desire. Layla had been in his office, going over a paper she had written on early messianic figures in Judaism, and Dan had been so impressed that he told her she was going to be a great scholar, greater than he could ever be. "Your work is miraculous."

In response, she kissed him. It was a simple kiss on the mouth, but one that tasted to Dan like love. For that is what he felt for Layla. And now, he knew, that she felt the same thing for him. All they had to do was cross a line, in a place and time where the lines had been bombed and bloodied into the earth.

"You can make miracles, Layla," Dan had said, his arms holding Layla in front of him, as a barrier, and as a possibility.

"If you believe in them," Layla responded. "Do you?"

Dan pulled her close, and it began.

To Dan, it was innocent. He was not committing a crime against humanity. Yes, to many in the Church, he was "betraying a vow" he had taken to remain chaste, but he knew in his heart that this promise was more of an obstacle than a blessing for him, and for most priests. Dan knew, in the very depths of his being, that, to be totally alive, and fully human, was the glory of God.

The Church's insistence on chastity and celibacy would have to one day change to admit the very thing that fueled the world. Dan knew in his heart that if God was love, then God would not consider the love he felt for Layla ever to be a crime against the divine.

"Do you want to remain a priest?" Layla asked him, before she left, as she always did.

"I will always be a priest," Dan answered, and kissed her on the top of her black curls.

But Layla smiled at that. She knew he was getting closer to leaving the priesthood for her. Did she want that? Yes, she wanted that. She wanted to be with him as a partner. It was why she had invited Dan to dine with her family this evening, at their home. Until today, it had always been tea in the afternoon. Tonight, it was dinner. To see how he fit in front of the family in the truth of the night.

Dan bought a bottle of burgundy from the St. Joseph's kitchen, and dressed in civilian clothes, then waited on

Rashid, the family's driver, to take him in the family's Mercedes sedan to Layla's home in the southern part of Beirut.

Unlike the central city, where buildings dating from the twelfth century butted heads with buildings from other centuries, Layla's neighborhood was new. Their high-rise apartment building overlooked spacious undeveloped lots, with a view of the Mediterranean. Dan thought that it was the perfect place to live, except for the fact there was a Palestinian refugee camp just down the street.

The camp was called *Mar Elias*, and it was one of the largest and oldest Palestinian Refugee camps in existence. *Mar Elias* camp was founded in 1952 by the Congregation of St. Elias to host Palestine refugees from the Galilee region of Palestine. It was inhabited by mainly Christian Palestinians, as well as a large non-Palestinian population. It was two city blocks long by one block wide and bisected in the middle by Dr. Philippe Hitti Street.

Layla's apartment building was a half a block to the south on the other side of Gabriel El Murr Boulevard. The entire camp had walls, at least twelve feet high, surrounding it, with the entrances to each of the two halves of the camp in the center of its bisecting street. Buildings were wedged in tight beside each other, with multiple stories and shaky staircases letting not much light down onto the pathways. In places, they were barely wide enough for a bicycle or scooter to pass through.

Layla's father, Mahmoud, was an executive for a British bank, and the family had bought the apartment before the civil war. The fact that Mahmoud was a Palestinian gave the family a pass in the neighborhood, and the fact that her mother, Mirai, was a Maronite Christian meant that Layla could feel at home at St. Joseph's University, where she now lived, as it was safer than meeting the wrong gunman at the wrong checkpoint in the middle of the night.

The apartment was big, with three bedrooms and three

baths, as well as a spacious living room, dining room and kitchen. There was a maid's quarters and maid's bath, and Anna, a beautiful young maid from the Seychelles who catered to the family's domestic needs.

"*As salam alaykum,*" Mahmoud said to Dan as he entered, giving him a kiss on both cheeks.

"*Wa alaykum salam,*" Dan replied, and handed him the bottle of wine. Mahmoud, a handsome man with a smooth olive complexion and thick black hair graying at the temples, was a few years older than Dan, in his mid-forties, and he grinned at the burgundy. "That will go very nicely with the lamb, Father," he said, and ushered Dan into the living room, where Layla sat with Mirai.

Even at age forty-four Mirai looked like the stunning magazine model she had been in Paris when Mahmoud won her heart, her thick black curls falling over her pale sculpted cheeks, and with full red lips just like her daughter, but with even bluer eyes.

"Welcome, Dan," Mirai said, and rose to extend a hand, which Dan shook.

"Thank you for this generous invitation to Sunday dinner," Dan said.

"We wanted to save you from the French cooking of the St. Joseph's cafeteria," Layla said, and Dan laughed. "I am in your debt just for the thought."

Her blue eyes flickered with mischief to signal how she would make him pay off that debt.

"I thought the food was good at the university," Layla's thirteen-year-old brother Ahmad Hussain Khalil said, his voice just starting to break. The males of the family were Muslims, and the females were Catholic, and they managed to do what the country could not. Live in peace.

"It is good, but it's always the same," Dan said. "It's as if the cooks have not realized that they are no longer in France."

Mahmoud laughed. "They must be deaf then, as well."

As if on cue, an explosion rumbled close enough to rattle the glass in the windows.

"Let's eat before they blow us up," Mirai said, and so they all moved to the dining room, where the feast had been laid out by Anna, the maid.

There were crunchy pickles, and hummus with *zhug*, a Yemeni green hot sauce, topped with roasted chickpeas and chopped parsley. There was tomato salad with pine nuts and pomegranate molasses, and crispy pitta, and shish taouk, chicken marinated in garlic and grilled and skewered, and there was muhammara, a dip made from walnuts and red bell peppers pairs. The lamb chops had been grilled in coriander and cumin and paprika and cardamom and cinnamon and nutmeg, all of which paired perfectly with the burgundy that Dan had brought.

For dessert, there was baklava, and thick Turkish coffee, serenaded by the sound of occasional gunfire out on the street. And then Mahmoud got to the point of this invitation.

"Father, we have something to ask you," he said, his brown eyes serious, and tinged with fear that perhaps the request would be met with hostility.

"Of course," Dan replied, leaning back, smiling, open.

"We would like your help to get Ahmad Hussain Khalil out of Lebanon."

He let his request settle in the night air, and as Dan had not said "No," he continued.

"We cannot see this terrible war ending anytime soon. And we want to keep our son as far from it as we can."

Dan nodded at Ahmad, who looked like this was the worst idea he'd ever heard. Dan glanced at Layla, who did not meet his gaze. Did she know this when she invited me? he wondered. Even if she did, she was just being a good daughter, and sister.

"Have you been able to get any help from your employer?" Dan asked, knowing the question was a formality.

Mahmoud knew it, too. "I have tried, Father, but they said they would have to bring us all, and they do not wish to, how did they put it, 'lose a man of my abilities in this part of the world.'"

It was at this moment that Dan finally understood. How could a British bank be operating in a country engaged in a long and bloody civil war unless it was part of that war? Financing one side, or the other, hedging their bets, supplying arms, whatever they needed to do. Mahmoud was in the thick of it. And he was afraid that his son would pay the price.

"I can see what I can do, Mahmoud," Dan said. "Maybe we could get Ahmad into Georgetown Prep."

"What is that?" Ahmad asked.

"It's a Jesuit boarding school in Washington, D.C."

"It is *kafir!*" Ahmad said, using the Muslim term for infidel.

"Ahmad!" His father gave him a look that was as good as a slap. "Apologize for this insult!"

Ahmad lowered his head and muttered something.

"I did not hear that," Mahmoud said, "nor see you look at Father Dan."

"Sorry," Ahmad said. "But I don't want to go to a Christian school. I am a Muslim. I belong here, fighting with my people."

Dan then knew that the reason the family wanted Ahmad Hussain Khalil out of Beirut was not because of the war being a danger to him, but because Ahmad Hussain Khalil was a danger to them.

"I will see what I can do," Dan said, smiling at them all. "And if I succeed, then you can decide."

Dan knew that he had to succeed, if only for the sake of protecting Layla. He could not do anything to jeopardize his love for her, or his stature as a priest. Her brother needed to get out to save him and the fortunes of the family of the woman he loved. And as he rode back to St. Joseph's that night, he realized that he now had a wrenching choice to make. In order to save Layla, he would have to give her up.

17

Rome

Dr. Rachel Ben-Simon and Agent Mimi Shapiro exited the Great Synagogue of Rome into a balmy Roman Friday night in mid-May. They had met at the Synagogue, built in 1904 as a proud testament to the liberation of the Jews of Rome from their ghetto, to visit the Hebrew Museum within, where they would be among family, and could speak freely.

And so, they did. They talked about the bombing at the Pontifical Biblical Institute in Jerusalem, and the urgent need to solve it to prove that Israel, after its own tragic failures of both intelligence and hubris, would let no one again escape justice. Solving the murder of these religious women would be a triumph that would resonate from Jerusalem to Rome.Of course, Agent Shapiro could not compromise the investigation with speculation, and while the ambassador had the highest security clearance, it was habit that made Agent Shapiro speak in a kind of code.

It was something in that code when they were looking at

the instructions the Nazis had given to Rome's Jews in 1943, that the ambassador connected to now.

The two women walked across the *Lungoteveri di Cenci* to stroll along the sidewalk that follows the Tiber. Agent Shapiro had said, "For two thousand years the Catholic Church has been at kind of war with itself about us Jews. And even though today, with these most recent popes, things are much better, officially, the rise in anti-Semitism around the world is much worse, no matter what the pope says. Not quite as bad as the Nazis, but we would do well to recall that millions of Jews died because we didn't think the Nazis would ever be as bad as they were."

Now, Rachel Ben-Simon considered this as more than a message about anti-Semitism, and hinted at where the investigation was leading. "Do you think this war within the Church, as you see it, plays a part in what happened in Jerusalem?"

Agent Shapiro stopped and turned to look at the river. "I do not see how it cannot. I mean, why attack a group of progressive women, trying to get more power in their Church unless their attempt to get more power threatens you?"

"But the Church is not a terrorist organization."

Agent Shapiro offered an ironic smile. "Well, if they were burning you at the stake in the 15th century in an auto da fé, maybe you would feel differently. But no, they proclaim the message of peace that the rabbi from Nazareth delivered. However, if you wanted to send a message to the Church through violence, there is one man who has the means to do that."

Rachel Ben-Simon turned to Agent Shapiro, as if she didn't want her to say anything more. As if to deliver a name would forever taint the person who might well be innocent. But she also had to know, if only to protect the innocent. Or to bring the guilty to justice.

"Who?" she asked.

Agent Shapiro started to walk again. "Abu Hamza."

Now Rachel Ben-Simon stopped. "Why would he kill Catholic women?"

"Because," Agent Shapiro began, "because when he was a kid in Lebanon, Father Dan—"

Suddenly, out of the dark, a Vespa motor scooter blasted into the two women. The passenger behind the driver took out a pistol and Agent Shapiro yelled "Beretta seventy—" before he shot her in the head, the click click of the suppressed 22 caliber handgun dropping her where she stood. Rachel Ben-Simon had started to run, and the two men on the Vespa sped up behind her, with the passenger reaching out and pushing the ambassador hard to the ground. Her head smashed into the wall that ran along the Tiber walkway as she fell, and she was out cold.

The two men paused, looking at the ambassador lying on the ground.

"Her too?" the passenger asked the driver in Italian, his pistol ready.

The driver shook his head. "Just the one. That was the order. Now we get the hell out of Rome before they kill us, too."

18

London

Renzo Bellocco was jealous. He lived in a palazzo in Rome, but this massive Georgian townhouse in London, with its cool marble foyer, and gold and diamond chandelier hanging above it, and a George Stubbs painting of an eighteenth-century foxhunt at the end of foyer, perched above the largest rose filled porcelain vase Renzo had ever seen, was the kind of place that Anglo loving Italians like him dreamed of living.

The fact that its owner was a flower-crazed Swiss money machine was an insult to both this home in Belgravia, and to Renzo's idea of who should live here. If not a duke or an earl, then an Italian self-made prince like him, who could not just pony up the $50 million to live in Eton Square but have the style and breeding to pull it off.

An attractive young woman with blonde hair pulled back into a ponytail, and blue owl shaped glasses greeted Renzo, in English. He couldn't tell if she was really English or if like him, it was her second language.

"Do you need a towel?" she asked Renzo, looking at the water dripping off him onto the floor. He had been caught in a downpour walking from the Tube. He had taken the Tube because this meeting was off the books, and any kind of car service would keep a record, and he had come alone, giving his guards the morning off to go to the British Museum. As far as he was concerned, he was never here.

He wouldn't mind having this young woman dry him off with a towel, but she wasn't offering that. "No thank you. It will dry quickly."

She gave him a once over that suggested even if he was wet, she approved of this handsome, fit Italian, maybe late forties, early fifties, with his slick backed black hair, rainwater bonding with the hair gel to make it shine.

"Frau Oberfeldt is in the Conservatory," she said, gesturing for him to follow.

So, he did, checking out the alluring curve of her swaying buttocks under her orange Hermes skirt, while also marveling at the eighteenth-century décor in the drawing room to his right, and the gilded mirrors in dining room to his left, as they walked down through a book studded, wainscoted library to the Conservatory, which was really a carefully manicured outdoor garden under a wrought-iron and glass roof.

Alina Oberfeldt stood upon Renzo's arrival and gave him a courtly bow. She was renowned for her aversion to physical contact, which, Renzo thought, probably came from having a Nazi war criminal for a father.

Oberfeldt's father had been a Nazi doctor who performed experiments of such cruelty on Jewish inmates at Mauthausen in World War II that he was known as Doctor Death. Renzo also knew that the Vatican and the Americans had helped Oberfeldt's father escape to Argentina after the war because he wasn't as bad as the Communists.

He was a scientist, a chemist, and his knowledge could

help them kill Reds. Renzo smiled. It was information that the world did not know, as Oberfeldt's father had changed their name and had plastic surgery and had dodged the information machine and had died anonymously in his own bed at age 90. He had escaped justice.

So had his daughter, whom the Nazi father had dispatched to a Swiss boarding school when the girl was twelve and left her there. Alina Oberfeldt was not Swiss, despite her passport. She was the daughter of a war criminal who was never caught. Renzo's contacts in the Vatican ran as deep and wide as the church and its secrets. So Alina's secret would be kept quiet as long as Renzo wanted it that way.

Renzo bowed back now to his Swiss host, and sat in the chair opposite Frau Oberfeldt, who did not sit, but who instead walked over to a rose bush, with glorious pink and white flowers, open more like a tulip than a traditional tightly petal packed rose.

"Come, Renzo," Alina Oberfeldt commanded, her Schweizer Deutsch accented English betraying nothing of her Argentinian girlhood, so Renzo approached the bush.

"Ferdinand Pichard," Oberfeldt said, her voice a rich alto, accented with Swiss discipline. "That is the type of rose. It is my favorite. So colorful, so aromatic!"

She produced a pair of gardening shears and abruptly cut off a stem and held it for Renzo to take.

Renzo didn't have a chance to scan the stem for thorns, as Frau Oberfeldt thrust it at him so quickly that he had to grab it, and of course, it pricked his thumb. He didn't wince or look at the drop of blood that had appeared in response.

"What do you think it smells like, Renzo?" Alina Oberfeldt said, clenching the shears as if to stab Renzo through the heart if he gave the wrong answer.

"I think it smells like an English garden party in summer," Renzo said, having prepared for this moment by reading up on roses, which he knew were Alina Oberfeldt's obsession. "Fruity, with the fizziness of champagne."

Alina smiled at that description. "That is very good. Do you grow roses?"

Renzo shook his head. "I only buy them to give them to women I want to fuck. I have given a lot of roses."

Alina Oberfeldt looked as if Renzo's use of profanity had offended the gods of her garden, and then she burst into laughter. It was a loud, heaving laugh that surprised Renzo, as he wasn't sure if Oberfeldt was laughing at him, or with him.

"Yes, yes," Alina Oberfeldt said, calming down. "I would imagine a man of your stature, though, would only have to buy one rose, and not a dozen, to woo the lady in question."

Renzo angled his head, as if remembering. "Yes," he said. "One is usually enough."

Alina Oberfeldt smiled, revealing that for all her wealth, she did not like dentists, as her teeth were snaggled and yellow, like the fangs of a wolf. Maybe, Renzo thought, that was a legacy of her father. Doctors could not be trusted.

Alina Oberfeldt's Zug Gruppe, named after the canton where she claimed to have been born sixty-seven years ago, was one of the world's most successful private equity funds. And one of the most discreet. To anyone who didn't know, this house on Eton Square in London was just a rich person's house. To Renzo, it was the headquarters of a global empire of money, one that had brought him from warm Rome to rainy London today.

Oberfeldt was taller than Renzo, with her close-cropped hair more salt than pepper, and a gardening apron that she had belted tight, showing off her fit frame. She reminded Renzo of some jungle cat, ready to unleash fatal force when least expected.

"You are here today, Renzo, not to talk roses, I think," Alina Oberfeldt said.

"That's right, Alina. I am here to tell you that I think we will have our man in Rome where we want him to be soon."

Oberfeldt sat, and folded her hands, staring with her blue eyes at Renzo like some Nazi interrogator.

"Where you want him, Renzo. I am merely an interested investor."

Renzo felt like swearing at Oberfeldt's obvious fiction. He knew how much Alina Oberfeldt hated the Catholic Church, and the Jesuits in particular. He knew that she thought they tried to expose her father's service to the Fatherland as a crime and would not stop. She knew that the Jew loving Jesuit Dan Lanaham was first among them to try to ruin her father, but her clever father had escaped them all. Though Oberfeldt had abandoned his child, Alina told herself Papa had done that to ensure her safety, and the Church had forced him to do that. She wanted revenge.

Renzo pursed his lips and considered his reply. "Of course, Alina, your investment will be even more profitable when our man is in position."

Oberfeldt didn't blink. "What about the *schwarze?* Do you have them under control?"

Renzo didn't blink at Alina Oberfeldt's casual reduction of a nation to a color. "The Nigerians are under their own control, Alina, and like all independent entities, they, too, respond to profit."

Oberfeldt blinked now. "The Nigerians? I mean the Black Axe. They are a problem."

It was a statement, with a hint of a question mark.

"They are not a problem once we have our man in place."

"They also kill people," Alina Oberfeldt continued. "More so than your tribe, I think. Though I hear you had a big one in Rome."

Renzo felt the color rise in his cheeks. This woman, whose father killed Jews as easily as he would take a breath, had invoked some moral superiority card. One that suggested the killings, when they happened, didn't help her, ever.

"A big one in Rome?"

Oberfeldt smiled. "Don't be modest, Renzo. The killing of that Israeli agent was a very professional job, I am told. Not like the Black Axe, who would have hacked her to death with machetes. Just a..." She mimed a gun, and aimed it at Renzo's head, and made a *zip-zip* sound through her full lips. "... and the job is done. My question is, why her? Will this not bring trouble on your house?"

Now Renzo smiled so he would not look as outraged as he felt. "You mean on our house, Alina. She was already bringing trouble, and killing one Mossad agent doesn't kill them all. In fact, they will want revenge."

"And this is a good thing?"

Renzo looked at Alina Oberfeldt the way you might regard a simple child, though he knew the billionaire's brain was not at all simple, and indeed, more lethal than his.

"It is a good thing because the people who assassinated this poor woman were in fact Nigerian. I have it on good authority."

"Why would they want to get into a war with Mossad?"

"They don't," Renzo replied. "They didn't know who they killed. Just that we wanted it done."

"We?"

Renzo stood. "Unless you wanted her to find the culprits who killed those women in Jerusalem, and then to start looking harder at us, yes, we. Because our money is married, Alina, and the Catholic Church does not permit divorce. Until death do us part."

Alina Oberfeldt looked at Renzo with a mixture of admiration and disgust. Renzo bowed and said "I will see you soon. In Rome."

Then he walked back out the way he had entered and encountered the young woman who had let him into the house. He handed her the rose. "Come and see me in Rome. I will make it worth your while."

She smiled and took the rose. *"Grazie, Signor Bellocco."*

"Prego Signorina..." He realized he didn't know her name. "I will tell you in Rome," she said, her green eyes hot.

Renzo walked out the door into a now cloudless London sky, not knowing if she had made a promise, or a threat.

19

Jerusalem

The funeral for Agent Mimi Shapiro took place in the holiest burial site in Judaism, on the Mount of Olives, overlooking the city. Dan knew the Mount well, as the Jewish cemetery is located on the western slope of the mount, along with the Tomb of the Prophets, the Roman Catholic Church of Dominus Flevit, and the Russian Orthodox Church of Mary Magdalene. And at the foot of the Mount lies the Garden of Gethsemane, the place where Judas Iscariot betrayed Jesus, an event which, in its way, led to Dan standing here today. Wondering who had betrayed the woman being buried far before her time.

Today, the ancient tomb that would receive Mimi Shapiro was surrounded by a couple of hundred people, from Mossad agents to government ministers, to Mimi's parents, younger than Dan, with the black ribbon of mourning for the non-Orthodox over their hearts, sobbing as Psalm 91 was recited for the seventh and final time.

"He that dwelleth in the secret place of the most High

shall abide under the shadow of the Almighty."

Then her oak coffin was lowered into the earth.

The May sun was warm as the mourners took the spade and shoveled earth onto Mimi's coffin. Dan was one of the last, following the Papal Nuncio, the sleek and smooth Archbishop Sanseverino, who gave him a grim smile as he handed him the spade.

"It was good of you to come all this way," the archbishop said, as if Dan had no stake at all in the holy city.

"I would rather have not returned for another death, Your Grace," Dan replied, reminding Sanseverino of the murder or Sister Maureen and those other women in his house. Then he tossed a mound of rich earth onto the coffin bearing the assassinated agent, and said a silent "Hail Mary".

"You are the superior of the Jesuits now," the Archbishop continued. "I would imagine you are very busy in Rome." He said it as if Dan's presence was somehow a vacation.

Dan did not respond. He did not think this Jewish funeral was the place to admonish an uppity Catholic cleric, even if he was the Papal Nuncio.

"Father Lanaham, thank you for coming." Chief Inspector Hillel Bennett had suddenly appeared next to the archbishop, as if he had sensed an intervention was needed. "And you, Archbishop Sanseverino." He shook their hands.

"I will pray for the deceased," the archbishop said, as if Mimi was an object. And that this was something that Bennett and his fellow Jews would want most, the prayers from the Papal Nuncio.

Hillel Bennett nodded, then looked back at Mimi's grave, now rounded and full, as the last shovelful of earth had been placed on top.

"How are you, Chief Inspector?" Dan asked, knowing how hard this day must be for the Israeli cop.

"I am not unused to death, Father, and it is a reality here every day, but this one hit me hard. She was a very fine person."

"May her memory be a blessing," Dan said, using the Jewish expression to commemorate the dead and putting his hand on Hillel Bennett's shoulder. The cop smiled and grabbed Dan's arm and squeezed it.

"Thank you. It will be."

"Do you know anything about who targeted her, Chief Inspector?" Sanseverino asked with bluntness, his black eyes cold.

Hillel Bennett blinked, and in an instant moved from mourner to cop. He looked around, and then nodded for them to walk with him away from the mourners who were standing over the graveside, reciting their own prayers for Mimi.

When they had moved far enough from earshot, Bennett said "We think it was a hit job, for sure. This was no robbery."

"Why do you think they let the Ambassador live?" Sanseverino asked, as if he was now conducting his own inquiry.

"That's why we think it was an assassination, Your Grace. They could have easily killed Ambassador Ben-Simon, but did not." He paused and looked around to make sure no one was listening. "They also used a suppressor, a silencer. Who does that but assassins?"

"How do you know this?" Sanseverino asked, now with the tone of an inquisitor testing some heretic.

Hillel Bennett exhaled. "Because Ambassador Ben-Simon did not hear a gunshot, which she would have done, standing as she was next to Mimi."

"Do you think it is connected to the murder of Sister Maureen?" Dan asked.

Bennett shrugged. "Mossad has many enemies."

Bennett's tone indicated that he was saying no more

about this case. Dan wondered why the mention of Sister Maureen had shut it down.

"Well, do keep us posted," Archbishop Sanseverino said. "I think that, since no one has claimed responsibility for it, or for the murder of your agent, we can assume that we might never know."

Hillel Bennett's eyes flashed with anger, but he smiled and calmly said "Just because no one has said anything, doesn't mean we can't find them."

Archbishop Sanseverino smiled, too warmly Dan thought, and tilted his head to one side, as if deep on the hunt for the cop's logic. "I see," he said. "I will pray for your efforts as well. In our Church, we have a special saint for that prayer."

Dan hoped that Bennett would not ask who, but the cop's politeness did not consider Dan's hopes. "Which saint is that Your Grace?"

"Saint Jude. He was one of the twelve apostles who followed our Lord, Jesus."

"I hope he's not the Jude who betrayed Jesus, very close to where we now stand?" Bennett asked. Dan was impressed by the cop's willingness to take on the Archbishop's arrogance.

"No, he is not the same as Judas Iscariot. This Jude was a relative of Jesus, known as Thaddaeus, and a brother of St. James the Less. His mother Mary was the Virgin Mary's cousin."

"He sounds like a powerful saint, then," Bennett replied.

"He's known," Sanseverino said, with a smug smile, "as the patron saint of hopeless causes."

"You think my cause is hopeless, Your Grace?" Bennett asked, smiling now himself.

"We pray to Saint Jude when we need a miracle," Sanseverino replied. "That is what I am praying for you both."

Dan realized it was the second time that week that a

miracle had been invoked for him. Once by Cardinal Omahu, and now by the Papal Nuncio. The difference being that Omahu wanted one, and Sanseverino spoke about it as being the province of the hopeless cause. Why would he see it that way?

As Dan flew back to Rome that night, the answer came to him somewhere over Greece. Archbishop Marco Sanseverino wanted to see the cause of solving Sister Maureen's murder as hopeless because seeing it that way expressed the belief that it would never be solved. Why, Dan wondered, would he believe that? Unless he wanted that outcome. For the case just to vanish into the cold and dark.

Dan felt a chill run through his body, the kind you get when a fever hits and you can't stop shivering. Dan wrapped his arms around himself and turned in his seat to face the window. He looked at his reflection. And saw in his eyes the look of a man who now believed that evil was within his own house.

20

Rome

Pope Leo had asked Dan to be in the room when Vincenzo Pericoli delivered the unofficial report about the killing of Agent Mimi Shapiro, so Dan arrived early at the Apostolic Palace and went to the pope's apartment to get some time alone with Leo.

He assumed that Cardinal Omahu had asked for Dan to be there, so he wasn't surprised to see the cardinal already in the pope's sitting room with Leo, along with short, plump Cardinal Sanchez, the Secretary of State, and Chocolate, the pope's lab, who was lying in the middle of the floor. Cardinal Omahu looked happy to see Dan enter, his face broadening into a smile as he rose to shake Dan's hand.

"Father Lanaham, so good to see you," the cardinal said, his voice deep and mellow, with the lilt of Nigeria.

"It is good to see you, Dan," Pope Leo said. "How was your trip to Jerusalem?"

"It was, all things considered, good to be there, Your

Holiness." Dan wanted to say more, but until he knew how everything connected, if it connected, he had decided the best council was to keep Jerusalem to himself.

Pope Leo motioned to a tall wooden chair by the window. "Please, sit. Monsignor Van Ardt will get you some tea."

The Dutch priest, standing in the doorway, smiled at Dan. "Cream and sugar, Father?"

"No, I am fine as I am, thank you," Dan replied. He wanted a whiskey, but that seemed like a request that might send the wrong message. He gave Chocolate a pat on the head, and the dog wagged its tail at him, then he sat next to Cardinal Sanchez, and wondered why if he was early, the others were here before him. As if reading his mind, Pope Leo made it clear.

"Dottore Pericoli will be here shortly with his account of what happened near the Great Synagogue a couple of nights ago." Leo's voice was soft, but his words were strong. "He will want to bring Interpol into the investigation." He paused and looked into the eyes of each man in the room. "I do not want that..."

Leo then held up his hand as if to hold on to the thought. The pain in his stomach was like a military drum squad, beating out a particularly robust rhythm tonight, and he reached into his cassock for another omeprazole tablet. He had concluded that whatever was ailing him could not be tamed by these pills, but he washed it down with a sip of water from a glass on the coffee table.

Dan could see the pain in his friend's eyes, and Leo noticed Dan's distress. He smiled reassuringly at Dan, as if to convey that they both knew how it ended and believed in a better world in the afterlife. Leo conveyed a peace, however, that he did not feel. He still had things to do on earth. "I do not want Interpol involved," the pope said, "because I do not know what they will find."

His words washed over the room as if the truth had

suddenly fallen from the ceiling. Cardinal Sanchez then leaned forward and said, "That is wise, Holy Father. They could open a can of snakes."

Pope Leo nodded. "And I want us to open that can of snakes ourselves, right Cardinal Omahu?"

The cardinal nodded somberly; his long thin hands folded in front of him as if he were in prayer. "The snakes are most certainly in our house. They have been in mine for a long time."

"And now we hear that they are in Rome."

Pope Leo and Cardinal Sanchez looked at Dan. "Who do you speak of, Father?" Sanchez asked.

"The snakes who have troubled Cardinal Omahu's house. The Black Axe."

Leo frowned. "I do not know of them."

"I wish I did not either, Your Holiness," Cardinal Omahu said, giving Dan a nod of thanks for raising the issue. "They started as a criminal gang in Nigerian universities in the 1970s, and today have become an international criminal organization."

"What kind of crime are they known for?" Leo asked.

"They commit cybercrime and steal vast sums of money as easily as they will slit your throat with a machete and steal your wallet. They kidnap young girls and traffic them into prostitution. And now, they have established a cell in Rome. This is what Sister Maureen wanted to discuss."

Pope Leo nodded thoughtfully, but his face was white. With pain, with sorrow, with both, Dan thought, at the so deeply fallen state of humankind.

"We might want to ask Dottore Pericoli about them," Dan said.

Leo nodded. "I would think that is where Interpol could help them. Direct their attention to this Black Axe." Then he closed his eyes and smiled, as if he had just put a straitjacket on senility. "Goodness me, did I just not say we don't want Interpol in the Vatican? We'll see if he knows about them and leave it there."

Dan was about to suggest a framing for that very question when Dottore Pericoli entered the room with Monsignor Van Ardt hard on his heels, as if he had been overtaken by someone in a hurry. The Vatican cop looked even thinner and more haunted than when Dan had last seen him, his shaved head glistening in the soft lamplight of the papal apartment.

"Holy Father, Eminences, Father Lanaham, I am sorry for keeping you waiting."

Pope Leo waved the thought away. "We were all here early, *Dottore*. So keen are we to hear your news. Would you like some tea?"

Vincenzo Pericoli bowed. "No thank you, Your Holiness."

Leo flashed a smile at Monsignor Van Ardt, who nodded and disappeared. Vincenzo Pericoli then took a manila folder from his satchel and placed it on the coffee table. He sat next to Dan.

"Inside are pictures we got of the killers of Agent Shapiro from security cameras near the synagogue."

Pope Leo opened the folder and picked up the photo. He looked at it, and then passed it around. When Dan saw it, he could see two African men on a Vespa.

"Do we know who they might be?" Dan asked.

Pericoli shook his head. "They are not Italian."

Dan took a breath. It was always amazing to him how the Italians could be so provincial when it came to assessing who was Italian—white—and who was not—nonwhite, even though the guys on the Vespa could have grown up in the shadow of St. Peter's.

"Who do you think they are, *Dottore?*" Cardinal Omahu asked.

"I do not know. We have run their photos through our contacts in Interpol, but nothing has come up. All we know is that they are clearly African."

Leo shot a look at Dan. So, Interpol is already involved, and they don't know about the Black Axe?

"How is the ambassador, Dr. Ben-Simon?" Cardinal Sanchez asked.

Pericoli sighed. "The doctors think she will be okay, but at the moment, she can't seem to tell us anything."

Or doesn't want to, Dan thought. She had told Chief inspector Bennett that the killer had used a suppressor on his gun. Why would she not want to help the Vatican police?

"What do you know, then?" Pope Leo asked.

"That we need help, Holy Father. I do not think the *Gendarmeria* can solve this one on its own."

Pope Leo nodded. "I would think the Israelis would be very helpful. Now so many have died, including one of their agents."

Pericoli shifted in his chair and looked at the folder in the middle of the table, and turned over the other two photos, one showing Agent Shapiro dead on the ground, and then Dr. Ben-Simon lying unconscious against the stone wall. "We appreciate the Israeli help, Holy Father, to be sure, but they have their own interests."

"As do we, *Dottore*," Pope Leo said gently. "As do we."

Vincenzo Pericoli looked at each man with his unblinking brown eyes, then said softly, "But I think we need more help. From a neutral third party. Such as Interpol."

Pope Leo reached across the table and patted Pericoli's arm. "I appreciate your talents as an investigator, *Dottore*, and your thoughts. But I do not want to let Interpol inside the Vatican just yet. Until we know exactly what we're dealing with. And then, maybe not even then. Depending."

Pericoli looked as if he might want to argue but saw that the men in this room were aligned with Pope Leo, not one of them rising in protest of Leo's blocking of Interpol to help solve this crime. He could stay and try to finagle the point, or he could make his own point and leave. So, he rose. "I understand, Holy Father. I will do my best, as ever."

"Before you go, *Dottore,*" Cardinal Omahu said, holding up a hand. "Do you know anything about the Black Axe in Rome?"

"The Black Axe?" Pericoli said, looking blank.

"No matter," Cardinal Omahu said. He knew that if Pericoli did not know yet, he would know soon.

"Is there anything else, Holy Father?"

"Good night, *Dottore.* Godspeed," Leo said, and made the sign of the cross toward Pericoli.

Pericoli bowed, and left the room. He walked fast, as if he couldn't wait to get out of there, Dan noticed. Dan didn't blame him. The cop had asked for help and the pope had told him no. The cardinal had asked him about an international criminal gang, and he had been caught short. Unless, of course, Pericoli knew more than he was saying. That, too, was a Vatican bloodsport. Keeping silent on one matter to protect another.

Pope Leo sat back in his chair, and then picked up a little bell and rang it. Monsignor Van Ardt papal appeared and bowed.

"I think Irish whiskey could not do us any harm tonight, please monsignor," the pope said.

"The Red Breast, Holy Father?" Van Ardt asked, his voice as careful as the wine waiter at a convention of sommeliers.

"The Red Breast is just what I was thinking."

Van Ardt smiled and went to fetch the whiskey.

"I cannot stay long, Holy Father," Cardinal Sanchez said. "In fact, with your permission, I will take my leave now. I have an early meeting with some people at the IOR. I need to be sharp." He tapped his head and smiled.

"By all means, Alfonso," the pope said. "I won't make anyone drink the holy waters unless they want to!"

Cardinal Sanchez's brown eyes flickered, as if the pope had just suggested he might be some kind of heretic, but the lively twinkle of amusement in Leo's blue eyes made Sanchez smile. "I will look forward to the next taking of the holy waters," he said. "To your health!"

Then he left, passing Monsignor Van Ardt with a tray on which there were four crystal glasses, an ice bucket, and a bottle of Red Breast.

"Shall I do the honors?" Dan said, reaching for the bottle. He used the tongs to plunk a thick cube of ice in each glass, then poured three fat shots.

"Ah," said Cardinal Omahu after a sip. "The music of the Emerald Isle is upon my tongue."

Pope Leo chuckled, then took a sip. "Indeed, we need more music that is not funereal," he said. Dan saw the pope's face register pain, which Leo followed with another sip, and his face relaxed. "It's a better medicine, I think, than the one they are giving me."

Dan took a sip of whiskey, its smooth heat rippling through his mouth and down his gullet. Then he leaned forward. "I am glad the three of us are together," he said. "For many reasons, but one of them has to do with Sister Maureen O'Connor."

Cardinal Omahu put down his glass and folded his hands. "Yes, she was coming to see me and the Holy Father."

Dan admired the cardinal for getting to the point so quickly.

"She was afraid, Dan," Pope Leo said.

"Yes, I gather. But what was she afraid of?"

Cardinal Omahu looked to Pope Leo who nodded. "She was afraid of us."

Dan took another sip of whisky.

"She was afraid of what the Black Axe are doing in Rome," Cardinal Omahu said.

"Do we know anything more?" Dan asked.

Cardinal Omahu sighed and drained his glass. "Just that they are here."

Dan took another sip, then placed his glass on the table, and looked at both men.

"Did they kill Sister Maureen?"

Cardinal Omahu opened his hands. "We do not know if it was them directly, or an ally. They were putting pressure on Sister's group to stop them from interfering with their trafficking of women from Africa to Europe."

"Do you know what kind of pressure?"

Cardinal Omahu shook his head. "No, she was going to tell us the details when she came to see us. She said that her work with *Donne del Vaticano* was costing them money, and they do not like that."

Dan thought about this. If they wanted Sister Maureen to stop, killing her would be a way to do it. But why kill so many, so spectacularly, and not claim the victory?

"I know, Dan," Pope Leo said. "It might not have been them."

Dan thought about who else would want to stop a progressive women's group from doing work to make the Church more open and accessible, and to give women the power to do that, the power they deserved. He reached into his briefcase and pulled out a copy of the *Washington Post*. The front section was open to page 4, and Dan had highlighted a paragraph in yellow. He handed the paper to Pope Leo.

Pope Leo read the highlighted section aloud. "The attack on the *Donne del Vaticano* is thought by many experts on terror to be an attack on Israel. However, our investigation has learned that the Donne del Vaticano had enemies within the Roman Catholic church. The women themselves were the target."

Pope Leo handed the newspaper to Cardinal Omahu and turned to Dan. "Do you know this writer, Jacqueline Brussard?"

Dan was in one of those Jesuitical moments. To tell the truth could compromise Jacqueline's work in Rome if he said yes. "I do not," he lied. "I suspect that Sister Maureen did. She knew a few people on the Post."

Pope Leo nodded, choosing to believe this was true.

"Do you think someone inside the Vatican could have been the killer?" Cardinal Omahu asked.

Pope Leo gave Dan a look the way he had looked at him all those years ago back in Boston College. It was an "Is the pope Catholic?" kind of look, then turned with a grim smile to the cardinal.

"We think that because the crime took place in Jerusalem, our first suspects should come from that neighborhood," Pope Leo said. "But then, after that, we look in our neighborhood. And by 'our', I mean the Church, which is everywhere."

Dan thought about that as he walked along the outside of Saint Peter's Square just after midnight. The Church touched every corner of the world, and so, everyone was a suspect. The Square was empty of tourists. Two *poliziotti*, cops who patrolled the quarter at night, watched over the empty Square, which had closed to everyone half an hour earlier. One of them nodded to Dan as he passed.

Dan reached the Bernini colonnades that elliptically enclose the Square. The three aisles of eighty-eight pillars standing with four rows of two hundred and eighty-four columns made of travertine stone were Bernini's idea of the Church's arms embracing the world.

They provided a refuge as well, Dan always thought, when passing through them, a place of power and beauty, in between worlds. He stopped to take a breath, having drunk more whisky than he meant to, and that's when he saw the man in the shadows of a colonnade, from the glowing tip of his cigarette. The man crushed the cigarette underfoot, then stepped into the light, with his finger at his lips.

He was tall, and slender, built more like a scholar than a warrior. He had shaved off his beard, and now wore wire rim glasses, to complete the look of the academic on the wander, and to bring Dan back decades to Beirut when he first met him.

Dan had not seen him for more than twenty-five years, the last time in Jerusalem, after Khalil had graduated from Georgetown and had come to say thanks. But he had seen his face on news reports of international terror. And now he was motioning for Dan to come forward, to come closer. Dan took another deep breath, and then took a step toward the last person he expected to see again, and especially now, here. If he were here to kill him, it would be done already. No, he was here for another reason. And so, Dan took a step towards Layla's little brother, Ahmad Hussain Khalil. To find out why.

21

Beirut, 1985

The feast at Layla's apartment was even more lavish than the last time. Dan was glad he'd brought two bottles of Burgundy for this Saturday night dinner, because they were going to need them just to get through all the wonderful dishes Mirai had spent the afternoon preparing with Layla.

Dan was glad that Layla had arrived before he had. He had not told her what he was about to tell them all, and he hoped and prayed that the news would not cause him to be crucified, for it was, after all, a last supper.

The dinner that the women had prepared, with the help of Anna, the maid, was worthy of any restaurant that Dan had eaten in, anywhere.

For appetizers, there were slow-cooked lamb rolls, kohlrabi with lemon, maneesh flatbread made with Za'atar spice, which was perfect for dipping in the halloumi with tomato jam.

For the main course, there was sumac-and cardamom-spiced chicken and roasted potatoes alongside tabbouleh and Fattoush salads, with lamb-stuffed zucchini, which featured a cinnamon-spiced tomato sauce. If that wasn't enough, there was also a heaping plate of lamb shawarma, tangy and succulent thanks to the yogurt in which it was marinated.

"I would like to make a toast," Layla's father Mahmoud said, raising his glass and aiming it at Dan. "To Father Dan, for what he has done for us, and for my son, Ahmad Hussain Khalil."

Dan blushed and raised his glass in thanks. "And I would like to wish fair winds for Ahmad Hussain Khalil on his journey."

Mirai and Layla raised their glasses, and everyone sipped, though Dan noticed Layla was not drinking tonight.

As for Ahmad Hussain Khalil, he sulked at the table just like a barely teenage Muslim Lebanese kid about to be sent off to a Catholic boarding school in Washington, D.C.

"What do you say to Father Dan, Khalil?" Mahmoud said, his face smiling, but his eyes as hot as his son's attitude.

"Thanks, I guess," Ahmad Hussain Khalil said, and took a swig of cola.

His father reached out with astonishing speed and cuffed him once on the cheek, sending cola spewing onto Ahmad Hussain Khalil's shirt.

"Try again," Mahmoud said calmly, though fury burned in his brown eyes. Dan was alarmed by this sudden flash of violence. To be sure, the city was a violent place, and Mahmoud was under stress at the bank. Now that banking in a country at civil war was about one thing only: funding the side that would win.

"Thank you, Father Dan," Ahmad Hussain Khalil said, his head down.

"I think you will like the school very much," Dan replied, with muted cheer. He wanted to respect the boy's feelings, and glanced at Layla, who gave him a reassuring smile. "Washington is an interesting city, because the government of the United States is there," Dan said. "You will meet interesting people."

"Will I meet the President?"

"You are a schoolboy!" Mirai chided. "You will meet your teachers and obey them."

Dan leaned back in his chair. "I know a few of the teachers there. My good friend Paul, who is also a priest, teaches your favorite subject."

"They have chemistry there?" Ahmad Hussain Khalil asked, as if chemistry was a subject only taught in Lebanon.

"They do," Dan said. "They have a very fine lab, and you will like it."

Ahmad Hussain Khalil thought this over. "Do I have to go to church with the—" he caught the look from his father and bit back the word *kafir* which he was about to say, and changed it up— "Christian boys?"

Dan nodded. "Going to chapel is part of the life there. There are boys from more than eighty countries. Not all of them are going to be Christian."

"But they go to this chapel?" Ahmad Hussain Khalil asked.

"They do. Think of it as broadening your mind."

"What does that mean?"

"It means thanking Father Dan every time you see him for the rest of your life," Mahmoud said, then topped up Dan's and his wine glasses.

Ahmad Hussain Khalil looked resolved. "Will you be teaching there?"

Layla laughed. "Of course not! Father Dan teaches at USJ, where I study. Why would he leave?"

Dan took a sip of wine and figured that now was the moment to change the view.

"I have to leave," he began, looking at Mahmoud, but speaking to Layla, "because my..." he smiled at Ahmad

Hussain Khalil, "... church boss asked me to take up a very important job that connects to what I really want to do."

"I thought you loved to teach!" Mirai exclaimed.

"I will be teaching. Just not here."

"Where?" Layla asked.

Dan looked at her, and saw the pain electrify her blue eyes as if they were beacons of alarm.

"At the Pontifical Biblical Institute."

"Ah," Mahmoud said. "So, you are going back to Rome."

Dan smiled and took another sip of wine. "No, I am not going to the one in Rome. I am going to the one in Jerusalem."

A silence fell over the table. Not only was Dan leaving, but he was going to a country that the Lebanese saw as their enemy.

Ahmad Hussain Khalil, on the other hand, was intrigued. "You are going to Israel?"

Dan nodded, anticipating a torrent of vitriol. But it did not come.

"I would like to see it," the boy said. However, the way he said it was as if to take its measure, and then figure out how to knock it down a peg or two.

"Maybe you will, one day," Dan said.

Ahmad Hussain Khalil gave him a smile at once of childish glee, and fatal energy. "Oh, I am sure I will. Especially after my American school makes me safe to go there."

Dan realized that Ahmad Hussain Khalil was already on the path to doing something that could get the boy killed. Or others killed. He just didn't know yet how many dead would be on Khalil's tally, in the end.

Layla sat as far from Dan as she could on the ride back to the university. Dan made small talk with Rashid, but not enough to distract him from getting them safely home. Rashid knew where the checkpoints were, and managed to dodge them all, save the one on Damascus Road, to the university.

When the militiamen, Christians, saw Dan's Roman collar, they waved them through with salutes.

"I should get one of those collars," Rashid joked.

"It only works in one or two places," Dan replied.

"In this city, one is enough, depending..." Rashid said, then pulled the Mercedes into the driveway leading to Dan's dorm.

"Thank you, Rashid."

"*Allah maak*," he replied, shaking Dan's hand. God be with you.

He waved to Layla, then drove off into the night, his taillights fading into the west.

"Do you want to come up?" Dan asked Layla, hoping she would say yes so that he could explain why he had to take the job in Israel. To protect her from whatever her father was doing, and whatever her brother would one day, do.

"No," she replied evenly. "I have to do work."

"It's the end of term," Dan said.

She smiled at him like he was a dimwit. "If you are leaving Beirut, then I am leaving, too. I must go work on my application."

Dan's brain flashed with Layla, the Maronite Christian, coming to Jerusalem, but she read the look.

"No, I will be aiming for cooler places," she said. "Somewhere that people are not always trying to kill each other."

"Layla, look, there was no good way to tell you..."

Layla nodded. "I think there was. If you loved me, you could have told me that they had asked you to move to Israel."

"And what would you have said?"

"I would have said to follow your heart."

Dan wanted to tell her that his heart was here, with her, but he could not leave the priesthood to start a life with a woman in a country in a civil war. He would lose his job, and he would not be the man she said she loved. He was following his head.

"I do love you, Layla," Dan said.

She looked at him, her eyes lit by the light spilling from the building where Dan lived. "I think we love in different ways," she replied. "When do you leave for Israel?"

Dan looked at the ground. "Next Saturday."

Layla hid the surprise that jarred her body. One week. That was all they had together, before who knows what?

She reached out, as if to grab Dan's hand, then remembered where they were, and who they were. "I think I will come up," she said to Dan. "If one week is our long goodbye, then we should start tonight."

Dan felt love wash over him, and that he had made a terrible mistake in losing this woman who was sane and loving and so bloody gorgeous.

"It won't be goodbye," Dan said. "We will still love each other."

Layla smiled. Maybe they would, but she knew that time and distance could and would have its say in that. All she knew was that she was pregnant, and in the long goodbye of their week ahead, she could not become more pregnant. And that Dan could never know. Until maybe much later, when he could love their child like a father, and not like a priest.

22

Rome

It was a little after midnight when Dan ushered Ahmad Hussain Khalil into his office on the fourth floor at the Jesuit General House on *Borgo Spirito*, and saw, to his alarm, that his assistant, Father Martin Gerrard, was working late.

Father Gerrard looked up just as Dan and Ahmad Hussain Khalil entered. If he was surprised to see the superior general of his order smelling of booze, in the company of a handsome, slender, clean-shaven man with wire rim glasses, and the air of a scholar, his face did not show it. He smiled at his boss, and rose, walking toward them.

"Good evening, Father General," Gerrard said. "I didn't expect to see you here at such an hour."

"Likewise, Father Gerrard. What has you burning the midnight oil?" Dan could hear the whisky he'd drunk half an hour ago with the pope still swirling in his voice, making it deeper and more liquid.

Father Gerrard smiled. "Lots to do to set you up in style, Father General."

That was certainly true. Since Dan's election to lead the Jesuits, he had not been here much, and when he was, he was trying to solve a terrible crime.

Father Gerrard turned his green eyes toward Ahmad Hussain Khalil, and offered his hand.

"I am Martin Gerrard, the assistant to Father General," he said.

Ahmad Hussain Khalil took his hand and gave it a hearty shake. "Nice to meet you, Father. I am Pedro Garcia," he said. "I am an old friend of Dan's, from Jerusalem."

Father Gerrard nodded solemnly. The name was Spanish, but the accent was not. It had the twang of America, but not by birth. It was an accent from somewhere else. "Such a terrible thing, Jerusalem," Gerrard said, hoping to draw this man out and place that accent.

"Yes," Ahmad Hussain Khalil said, "it was."

Dan took Ahmad Hussain Khalil by the arm and ushered him toward Dan's office. "We have much to catch up on, Pedro. And don't worry, Father Gerrard. We'll turn out the lights when we leave."

Father Gerrard smiled. "Can I get you anything? Some coffee? Some wine?"

Dan shook his head, but Ahmad Hussain Khalil said, "I'd love some wine. Red if you have it."

Father Gerrard smiled again and hustled off to find the wine. He had the accent now. It was Arabic.

Dan took Ahmad Hussain Khalil into his office and shut the door.

"Pedro Garcia?" Dan said.

"It's the name on my Spanish passport," Ahmad Hussain Khalil said.

"Do you have a passport in the name Ahmad Hussain

Khalil Khoury?" Dan asked.

"Ah, you mean my international terrorist passport. The Italians wouldn't have let me in if I used it. And I am just Khalil now, to my friends. My time in America got Ahmad Hussain pretty much kicked out of me."

He smiled at Dan, just like he had done nearly forty years ago over those fabulous dinners in Beirut with his sister Layla and their parents. All dead, now, save Ahmad Hussain Khalil, or just Khalil. And the smile had the touch of death to it as well, for Khalil had caused many people to die. He was a killer. And he saw Dan as his friend.

"Why are you here?"

Father Gerrard knocked on the door, and then entered. He had an opened bottle of Spanish rioja in one hand, and two glasses in another.

"Here you go," he said, putting the wine and glasses down on the top of Dan's desk. "A little splash of the homeland."

"Gracias," Khalil said.

"Disfruta el vino," Father Gerrard replied. Fruit of the vine. Then he stifled a yawn.

"I think you should go get some much-deserved rest, Father," Dan said.

Father Gerrard looked relieved, and so did Khalil. "I think I will do that very thing. Raise a glass to my success!"

He grinned at Khalil, and then left. Dan listened as his footsteps retreated down the hallway. Then he heard the office door open and shut.

Dan poured a glass of wine for Khalil, who held up his hand.

"No, I do not drink alcohol, Father Dan. That was for the benefit of my Spanish persona."

Dan poured two glasses of wine and took sips from each.

"That's to help your Spanish persona. So, back to where

we were, why are you here?"

Khalil swiveled his eyes around the room, as if checking for anything that could overhear them.

"We're in my office, Khalil," Dan said. "No one is listening to you but me. And God."

Khalil nodded, then clasped his hands in front of him, as if in prayer. "When you got me that place at Georgetown Prep, I did not want to go," he said.

"I remember."

"But I am very glad that I did go. It gave me a perspective I would not have had on injustice. It gave me my life."

"And it took the lives of some others," Dan replied.

Khalil nodded. "People get killed in wars, Father."

"Even those who do not know they are at war?"

"Justice always has casualties, Father. Injustice has many more."

Dan was thinking of Khalil's last attack, on a train station in France. It killed a dozen people, and injured many more, but the reason for it seemed like anything but justice. It was to shock the French government into releasing one of Khalil's colleagues, his so-called bombmaker, whom the French had scooped up as he changed planes in Cameroon. The French did release him, and then the Israelis tracked him down in Senegal and shot him through the head. So, in the end, thirteen was the death total for a mission that Khalil had, at the time, called a success.

"And you came to see me because of the injustice of the attack in Jerusalem?"

Khalil smiled again. Without his beard, and with his wire rimmed glasses, he really did look like a scholar.

"Yes. It was worth the risk."

"Aren't you worried that all the facial recognition out there won't spot you?" Dan asked.

Khalil tapped his glasses. "These are very helpful. Not just any old glasses, but they create a distortion field for cameras that reads like glare, or a glitch. Who said AI was just for plagiarizing essays?"

He laughed, and Dan felt a chill run up his spine. It was a cold laugh.

"But even so," Khalil continued, "there are risks to everything we do. But I had to come here to tell you that it wasn't me. Out of respect for our long, shall we say, history together."

"I didn't think it was you, Khalil. It wasn't your style."

Khalil nodded. "The Jews will think it's me, or that I knew something. They always do."

"Are they wrong?"

Khalil shook his head. "Not always. Even a little bit right this time. I do know something."

Dan leaned forward in his chair, suddenly feeling like he'd been drinking nothing but coffee. "What do you know?"

Khalil leaned forward as well, and pulled out a notepad, and a pen. Then he scrawled something on the pad, ripped out the page and handed it to Dan. Khalil had written, *Archbishop Marco Sanseverino / Renzo Bellocco.*

Dan looked at Khalil with questions in his eyes. Then Khalil handed him the notepad.

Dan wrote, *The Papal Nuncio to Israel and an Italian billionaire?*

Khalil nodded. Then he wrote, *Mafia.*

Dan leaned back in his chair. He had heard talk that Sanseverino came from a difficult region of Sicily, one rife with Mafia activity and threat, but Bellocco was news. Dan didn't know much about him at all, except that he lived in a palazzo and was fond of beautiful women.

Dan then wrote, *You are saying the Mafia had something to do with Jerusalem?*

Khalil nodded again. *So I hear.*

Dan wrote *?*

Khalil shrugged.

Dan wrote, *Can you find out more?*

Khalil shrugged again and gave Dan a smile that was a punch to the heart. It was just like the one he had seen on the face of Khalil's sister Layla, so long ago. The one she gave Dan after he kissed her for the first time. One of delight. Poor dead Layla, news of whom was the last time he had heard from Khalil. A letter, saying Layla had died suddenly. That was it, and Dan carried the pain still. He did not want to open that wound tonight.

Now Khalil was delighted at being kissed with enlistment by the superior general to help solve a terrorist crime.

Dan had to shake his head at the mysterious ways the Lord moved. He also knew that Khalil was sitting here in his office in Rome and had been seen by his assistant. Then he realized that since Khalil had been seen, Dan had to continue the fiction that he was an old friend from Jerusalem.

He wrote, *If you're going to help me, can you stay in Rome?*

Khalil responded, *Three days only. Not a hotel.*

Dan knew just the place.

He led Khalil across St. Peter's Square again, past a different set of *poliziotti* now on patrol, and paying Dan and Khalil no attention. They walked through Bernini's majestic colonnades in silence, with Dan thinking about what Khalil had told him. The Mafia had a hand in the death of those women in Jerusalem. He would not have given it serious consideration but for the source. Khalil had no reason to risk his life by coming to Rome to lie to Dan. But maybe he had other reasons, as well.

They walked along the *Via Aurelia* to the *Villino Giovanni*, a starkly Gothic convent that also operated as a guest house, and which was run by the Sisters of Mercy.

Dan knew the nuns here, and that Khalil would be treated with discretion.

"This is a convent?" Khalil asked, his voice tense with

disbelief as he took in the crucifix above the entrance, and the Sisters of Mercy emblem of a lamb lit up by heavenly light on the glass door.

"It's the safest place I can think of," Dan said, not adding besides prison. "It's popular with Germans, so your Spanish won't be tested."

Dan rang the doorbell, and expected the stern night duty nun, used to dealing with beered up Germans, arriving late, to open the door.

But instead, the nun who came to the door was Sister Marie Therese, who gave Dan a look of surprise. He knew she was a member of the Sisters of Mercy, but he did not know that she lived here. Now he would have to lie to her, for the time being, and not let Khalil know that they knew each other.

So, before she could speak, Dan said, in Italian, "Good evening sister, we have to pretend we do not know each other, OK? Just smile."

Sister Marie Therese smiled. "Good evening, Father, sir, how can I help you?" she replied in Italian, and Dan switched to English.

"This is my friend Pedro Garcia, an old friend from Jerusalem. He needs a room for no more than three nights. Can you help, Sister?"

"I will pay up front in cash," Khalil added.

"You are most welcome, Senior Garcia," Sister Marie Therese said in Spanish.

"Gracias," Khalil replied. Dan was coming to the conclusion that his Spanish was not much more than that, when he said, *"Ha sido un largo viaje, hermana. ¿Puedes por favor mostrarme mi habitación?"* It has been a long trip, sister. Can you please show me my room?

Sister Marie Therese swung the door open wide, and Khalil entered. Sister Marie Therese widened her eyes at Dan, and he smiled.

"Buenas noches, Pedro. Dormir bien."

Khalil turned and nodded his thanks.

"I will be back in the morning, Sister," Dan said in Italian. "And I will tell you everything."

23

Rome

Father Jared Rossi stared at the screen that his colleague Gianluca Schmitt had swiveled around so they could both see it. There were two documents, one of them in Italian, and the other in code.

"What's that?" Jared asked.

"I think it's the smoking gun, so to speak," Gianluca grinned, happy at the result.

"What do you mean?"

Gianluca pointed to the coded section. "If you look here, you will see letters and numbers repeat themselves. We just have to figure out what the code is, and we'll know what is going on."

Jared could see part of what was going on. Next to each coded entry was a sum of money, not in code. The entries were for ten and twenty million Euros, adding up to nine hundred and fifty million Euros. Or more than a billion U.S. dollars. And below each sum was another string of numbers, some preceded by letters.

"But who did this?" Jared asked.

"The guy who was here before you. He was pretty good at hiding stuff. But he couldn't make it completely disappear because they needed a record."

"A record for what?" The answers to his own question swirled in Jared's brain. He knew what that money could be used for.

Jared was a PhD in Economics, and indeed, had pursued that degree because of where he now worked: the Vatican Bank. It had been founded in 1942, but the thing that caught Jared's eye as an undergraduate was its role in the death of Pope John Paul I in 1978.

Pope John Paul I was going to return the Church to the message of the Gospels, and the life of the rabbi from Nazareth at the heart of those holy books. He was going to get it out of the business of being a business. So, he was going to dismantle Vatican Inc., a global criminal conglomerate of Mafia and money laundering that some of the scholars whose books and papers Jared read had said was worth $10 billion.

On September 28, 1978, on just the 33rd day of his pontificate, the new pope did some financial housecleaning. He fired the Vatican Bank's principal, managing director, chief accountant, and administrative secretary.

It was the principal who was at the heart of the story. Archbishop Paul Marcinkus, an American from Chicago served in that role, and Pope John Paul I gave him 24 hours to clear out of his office in the Vatican Bank. A swank office with its leather chairs and chrome and glass tables and bag of golf clubs leaning in the corner with the tag to Rome's most exclusive golf club prominently attached for all to see.

Two other princes of the Vatican, Cardinal Vilot, secretary of state, and Cardinal Poeletti, vicar general of Rome, were to be demoted because of their suspected corruption and their connection to a very dark Masonic lodge called P2, for Propaganda Due, one rife with Mafia. The pope had made a major act in the name of the new Church and was well on his way to doing what he had promised to do: restore the Church to holy honor. People loved him for it. And the next day, John Paul I was dead. A heart attack in his sleep.

After that came the coverups and the conspiracies. The demoted Cardinal Vilot was the camerlengo, in charge of declaring the pope dead and then running things until a new pope could be elected. He quickly had the dead pope embalmed, thus preventing any kind of autopsy that would confirm a sixty-five-year-old man who was in good health, overall, would die of a heart attack so coincidentally to the initiation of his reforms. The official version was that the pope had died from not taking his low blood pressure medication, and from the stress that the papacy had inflicted on this humble peasant from Venice.

The conspiratorial version of the pope's death was that the Mafia, inside and outside the Vatican, had killed the new pope to keep their criminal enterprise intact.

Did Jared believe the pope had been murdered? Not at the time. But his thesis that led to his PhD had followed the money with Marcinkus back in power. To Jared, Marcinkus was the key to everything. He had not been a banker, or an economist, and yet Pope Paul VI had made him the boss of the Vatican bank, with direct access to the pope. Marcinkus had been the pope's bodyguard on foreign trips and had stepped up on some dangerous occasions when knife wielding maniacs came for the pope. Jared figured Paul trusted him and let him inside the Bank.

But just four years after the death of John Paul I, the front pages of newspapers and magazines throughout Europe were screaming in outrage about the collapse of the Banco Ambrosiano. The largest shareholder of that dead bank was the Vatican, which had also managed to acquire debts of up to $1.5 billion. This included debts to the Mafia.

Marcinkus was accused of dealing with the Mafia and the Masons in a manner that saw the Vatican Bank exposed as a money laundering machine. Roberto Calvi, called "God's Banker" because of how tight he was with the Vatican Bank as chairman of Banco Ambrosiano, wrote a letter to the new pope, John Paul II, that said officials within both Ambrosiano and the Vatican were aware of the money crimes happening inside. Nothing happened.

In June 1982, Robert Calvi, who had fled Italy, was found hanging from the scaffolding beneath London's Blackfriars Bridge. Calvi had been a member of that same Masonic lodge as Cardinal Vilot and Cardinal Poeletti, P2. Its members referred to themselves as *frati neri* or "black friars", which was another name for the Dominican order. So, it didn't take much for people to conclude that Calvi, who had fled Italy in fear of his life, had been murdered to send a signal that you don't mess with the Blackfriars. The British government helpfully concluded that Calvi had committed suicide.

In 1984, the Vatican Bank agreed to pay off more than one hundred of the Ambrosiano creditors to the amount of $225 million U.S. in exchange for which, and due to a lack of direct evidence, the Vatican Bank received immunity from criminal prosecution. Archbishop Marcinkus, who had removed himself from the bank a couple of years earlier to avoid the fallout, responded to the settlement by saying, "You can't run the Church on Hail Marys."

The entire sordid story was why Jared had become an economist, and a priest. He had written his PhD thesis at the London School of Economics, his hometown college, as he had grown up in Cricklewood. He knew Blackfriars Bridge, and he knew that it would be very hard to hang yourself from the spot where Calvi's body was found. Subsequent evidence proved him right: Calvi had not died by hanging, but someone had hoisted his body up to the scaffolding from a boat below, on the low tide of the Thames.

So, in his thesis, Jared laid out the various theories about how the Vatican Bank could have been corrupted. Because he also believed the money that the Church had in its possession could be used to help create a kind of global equality, to bring those of the faith up to a standard of living, and not a standard of suffering, he also described a way to fix it.

It was why he decided to become a black friar himself and went into a Dominican seminary. Shortly after his ordination in Rome he was appointed to the Vatican Bank by Pope Francis, to do what he said could be done.

Jared had made progress. The bank once had more than 30,000 account holders, including religious entities and private citizens who held accounts worth millions of Euros. He closed many big accounts, including those of diplomatic missions, and the consulates to Syria, Iran, and Iraq, Muslim countries that had moved millions of Euros around the world through vague cash transactions and which likely fueled conflicts both ancient and recent.

He shut down dubious investments and dodgy real estate deals, but he had discovered it had not been as easy to clean it all up, as to think it could be all cleaned up. That's why he was so concerned now with what his Swiss colleague had found buried in cyberspace.

"How do you think we can break this code?" Jared asked Gianluca.

The Swiss forensics expert grinned at him. "Pretty simply," he said. "It wasn't written by code writers. It was written by a priest. And while he could hide it pretty well, the codes are crap. Yet I think he did them that way on purpose. Just for this day."

He showed Jared how 182 could be, translated to the alphabet, RB. And how 191912123 could be SS LLC. They were the only two codes used in the document. Assuming Gianluca was right that the code writing priest was asking them to take a look.

"I have an idea how we can test your theory," Jared said. "The numbers are big, so let's say they are for real estate," Gianluca said. "The numbers below the codes refer to property deeds, I think."

"Where do you think this real estate is?" Gianluca asked.

Jared looked at one of the numbers, which was preceded by LN. "Let's try the UK. Let's say LN means London."

Gianluca typed in one of the numbers, LN 87921, and then UK Land Titles. Links appeared to the UK government's title search engine, and Gianluca entered the number, paid the fee, and up came the details. A flat in Kensington, London, registered to SS LLC, Cyprus.

Jared smiled at Gianluca, who had been right about the casual code. But in his smile was the fear of what he was now up against. It was a smile that was braver than he felt. "If these codes are here because they were to be discovered, what do you think we would discover?"

Gianluca smiled back. "Only one organization I can think of, and it's criminal."

Jared knew. It was the Mafia.

He remembered what he had promised to Cardinal Matteo, the camerlengo, if he had found anything unsafe. And how the cardinal would keep him safe, if he revealed what he knew.

"I need to get some air," Jared said. "I'll be back in a little while."

Gianluca gave him a salute and swiveled his chair back to his desk.

Jared walked out onto the *Via Sant' Anna* and leaned against the wall of the Bank. His mind was swirling. He did not know what to do. He could go to Cardinal Matteo, and say they had found some numbers that made them suspicious. But that could open a door to a dark world that he did not want to know if Cardinal Matteo was connected to the Mafia.

No, he had to stay silent, and to make sure that Gianluca did as well. He reached into his pocket and pulled out his phone. He punched in Gianluca's number.

"Hello Jared," Gianluca said.

"I have been thinking, Gianluca. We need to keep what we found about the Vatican Bank and the Mafia between us. We do not know who is listening."

"Of course," Gianluca said. "I may be dating a Swiss Guardsman, but he's not interested in bank talk."

Jared smiled. "Good. Until we know what we're dealing with, we don't know anything."

"Understood. See you later."

As he pocketed his phone and began to walk, Jared was so consumed by the discovery that he did not notice the African man with blue eyes standing opposite the Bank. The man had what looked like an iPad out, and was taking pictures, or making a film.

As soon as Jared was out of sight, the man switched off his device, which was not an iPad, but a Kingfisher, a portable device to hack into cell phones. He then opened his own iPhone and pulled up some photos. There was Dan Lanaham, who he had already clocked in the church, and who might be of use to him later. And there was Jared Rossi, who had just been very useful. The last photo was of Gianluca Schmitt and his mother, which he had snagged off some Swiss Catholic site on the internet. He had a feeling that he and Gianluca would soon meet. And that Gianluca would be the most useful of them all.

24

Rome

Pope Leo had spent a terrible night. The pain in his stomach did not disappear no matter what he did. He turned to his left, and to his right, and he lay flat on his face, as if to make the pain drain into his mattress. He prayed to Mary who was his first saint for everything, and then to St. Timothy, the patron saint of stomach disorders. Leo felt that what ailed him was more than what was happening in his stomach, but he had always felt everything in his gut since he was a little boy, so now, why should he not feel death there, too?

It was only the first sip of the orange juice from the glass that Monsignor Van Ardt put on his table that had calmed everything. It was as if, for a moment, the sunshine in the juice of those Sicilian oranges that Cardinal Matteo had sent to him quenched the flames in his stomach.

And then, as if by Providence, Cardinal Matteo was being ushered into the dining room by Monsignor Van Ardt. Chocolate, the pope's handsome Lab, started to bark. An angry bark.

"There there, Choco... he's just saying hello, Eminence." Leo knew that he wasn't. Chocolate was barking because he didn't like the cardinal. And if Chocolate didn't like you, Leo was on guard.

"And I say hello to you both, Holy Father!" Cardinal Matteo said, a warm smile on his face as he bent to kiss the papal ring. Leo raised his hand to accept, despite his own feelings about kissing jewelry. Kissing the ring was an ancient tradition, and he would accomplish nothing but bad press by doing an American thing like abolishing it.

"Monsignor, please set a place for Cardinal Matteo."

"Oh, no," Matteo replied, smiling at the monsignor. "I was up before the sun. I have already eaten, but I will take a coffee, if it is not too much trouble."

"My pleasure, Eminence," the monsignor said, then disappeared to fetch the coffee.

"I am sorry for invading your breakfast, Holy Father," Cardinal Matteo said. "I just came to ask you about a bit of household business that I need your advice on."

Pope Leo smiled. "Of course. But first things first. I want to thank you for this splendid orange juice that you sent to me. *Nasce dalla dolcezza celestiale del sole siciliano.*"

"It comes from the heavenly sweetness of the Sicilian sun. Yes, Holy Father, it does. I am glad that it gives you sustenance."

Monsignor Van Ardt appeared with a cup and small pot of coffee which he put before the cardinal. "I can froth some milk if you would like a latte, Eminence."

"No, this is fine, thank you."

The monsignor nodded, then exited as always, like a ghost.

"So, what do you wish to know, Antonio?" Pope Leo said, taking a bite of buttered toast.

"I had a meeting not so long ago with Renzo Bellocco. You may recall he gave substantially to the Church during the pandemic."

"I do. I do not know much about him."

"He is a very successful businessman. But, as a Sicilian, I must say, he also has that whiff of what we say in Sicily: *Cui nun voli pagari, s'assuggetta ad ogni pattu.* 'Who doesn't intend to pay, signs any contract.'"

Leo took a sip of orange juice and thought about that. What was Antonio Matteo trying to say? This conversational tack was nothing in the usual province of the camerlengo. He had Leo's last will and testament, which he would give to the College of Cardinals when Leo had gone to his heavenly reward, and he would be the one who determined that Leo had departed.

He would take the papal ring, the Ring of the Fisherman, and cut it in half in the presence of the cardinals to end Leo's papacy and prevent any forgeries. Then he would let the Curia and the Dean of the College of Cardinals know that Leo had died, and then prepare for the pope's funeral, and the conclave to elect his successor.

So why did he want to talk to him about Renzo Bellocco?

"I just wanted to let you know, Holy Father, that Bellocco is interested in the papacy."

"Is that a problem? Many people are interested in the papacy. Unless you mean his interest is specific."

Cardinal Matteo looked relieved that the Pope had asked the question.

"It could be. I think we need to consider things at the IOR."

Leo wondered how the conversation had gone from Bellocco to the Vatican Bank.

"How so?"

Cardinal Matteo took a sip of coffee. "I think it might be good to have an Italian at the Bank. You know me, I am of the world, but..." He held out his hands in that Italian gesture of "give me a break".

"Right now, we have Father Rossi, an Englishman, and Gianluca Schmitt, a Swiss. But people like Bellocco are very provincial when it comes to Italy. I think he would feel more inclined to help the Church in the future if a paysan was inside, too, as part of the team."

Leo nodded, as if this was an excellent idea. But now he knew that if Cardinal Matteo was at his breakfast table, suggesting that the Vatican Bank needed an Italian inside to please Renzo Bellocco, that Bellocco was already inside. And that Cardinal Matteo was more than the camerlengo. He was Bellocco's agent.

Leo knew he had two choices. Keep Matteo at a distance, or to bring him closer. To find out what, exactly, was going on.

"We can most certainly address that, Antonio," Leo said with a smile, as if this was the best idea he had heard in a while. "Do you have anyone in mind?"

Cardinal Matteo's eyes flashed in surprise, then he smiled. "I will put together a list of candidates, and you can see who might best."

Leo smiled and raised his glass of orange juice toward Cardinal Matteo. A list would be perfect. Then he could see what the plan was to destroy his legacy after he was gone, and who would do it.

25

Rome

Father Dan had not slept much at all since Khalil's appearance in St. Peter's Square, a function, he knew, of his shock, along with the good amount of whiskey he had downed in the company of Pope Leo. So he was up with the Roman sun, and after showering and saying Mass, he downed 1000 mgs of Vitamin C, and made his way to the *Villino Giovanni* to check in on Khalil. And to tell Sister Marie Therese why he was there.

Jacqueline Brussard was already with Sister Marie Therese when Dan arrived. They were having coffee and toast in the garden of the *Villino*. They were alone. And they looked warily happy to see him.

"Good morning, Sister, Jacqueline," Dan said, and sat down in one of the wicker chairs opposite them. An elderly nun appeared with a pot of coffee, and Dan thanked her as she filled his cup.

"Have you seen our guest, Sister?" Dan asked, taking a sip of the rich black coffee.

Sister Marie Therese shook her head, her brown eyes unblinking as she looked at him. Her youthful face looked a little tired this morning. Dan knew that she had probably been awake all night, wondering.

"What I am going to tell you both about our guest needs to stay here, for the safety of all of us," Dan said, in English. "Understood?"

The two women looked at each other, surprised by this request, but they both agreed.

"It's off the record," Jacqueline said.

"Yes," Dan replied. "For the time being."

And then he told them as much as he could about Khalil without revealing too much of himself. How he had known the boy's family when he taught in Beirut, and how he had helped get Khalil a place at Georgetown Prep.

He had last seen Khalil as a college graduate, Georgetown University, when he had come to Jerusalem to thank Dan for all that he had done. "You have prepared me to change the world," Khalil said.

And then he did. Through targeted violence against western institutions and their military that saw him attack U.S. Navy bases in the Mediterranean with drones. He had attacked Israeli settlements with rockets from Lebanon, and he had shot down British helicopters in Iraq with surface to air missiles. He was everywhere, and yet nowhere. His nom de guerre was Abu Hamza, after the uncle of the Prophet Mohammed, who was known as a lion.

Abu Hamza was careful not to kill civilians, and yet, it was hard to avoid doing so when you fired rockets into villages in Israel. The Israeli intelligence had almost killed him in Paris, but a sympathizer in French intelligence tipped him off, and it was Abu Hamza who ambushed and killed the team of four Israelis sent to dispatch him to wherever he believed he was going.

It wasn't to paradise, as Abu Hamza was no Islamic

militant. He called himself "a sword of justice for the oppressed Arabs," but ever since he killed the Israeli team, he had gone underground, save for that attack on the French train station. He had issued a statement saying they believed they were attacking a military train, when it turned out civilians had died. And once his bombmaker was killed, Abu Hamza went silent.

Until now.

The two women looked at Dan as if he had just spun them a tale of outrageous science fiction. Dan looked up to see three men enter the courtyard and sit at a table within earshot.

"*Buon giorno,*" he greeted the men in Italian. "*Una bella giornata per prendere un caffè al fresco!*" Good day, a beautiful day to take a coffee outside.

The men looked at him blankly, and Sister Marie Therese picked up the point Dan was making. She asked them in German if they were from Germany.

"*Osterreich,*" came the reply. Austria.

"We will continue in Italian," Dan said in English.

"I don't speak Italian," Jacqueline said. "But I get the gist. This guy came to Rome to tell you he didn't do it. The bombing in Jerusalem."

Dan smiled. "That's right."

"And you believe him?"

"Why wouldn't he?" Khalil asked. He had appeared like a ghost. How much had he heard?

He sat down next to Dan and held up a hand when the elderly nun appeared with the coffee pot.

"I see that you have told my story to an audience," he said.

He had heard everything.

Dan ground his teeth together. If Khalil wanted to kill them for this, they were already dead. "I needed to let the people who have been harmed by this bombing, and who want to get to the truth, to know how you can help us. I had to tell them who you were in order to do that."

Khalil thought about this. "You are a nun, I can see that," he said to Sister Marie Therese, "and you are?"

Jacqueline didn't even blink. She handed him the revised business card that Sister Marie Therese had provided for her in case of emergency. This was now that time.

"Dr. Jacqueline Robinson, spiritual advisor, *Donne del Vaticano*," Khalil said.

"Yes," Sister Marie Therese replied. "I am the executive director of the *Donne*, and Dr. Robinson has come here to help us heal, after the attack in Jerusalem."

"Come from where?" Khalil asked.

"Washington, D.C.," Jacqueline said.

Khalil smiled. "Ah, power town. I know it well."

Jacqueline returned the smile. "Have you spent time there?" Dan had just told her that he had gone to school there, and now Dan marveled at how smooth she was in her pretense.

"I was a student at Georgetown Prep, thanks to Father Dan," he said. Then he leaned forward in his chair. "I am not here to cause any trouble, and I will only do so if I feel threatened. In fact, I am here to help you. I did not cause this terrible attack, but I have heard things about who might have done."

He glanced over at the Austrians, who were noisily slurping down porridge and chatting about something.

"They're going to *Castel Gandolfo*," Sister Marie Therese said.

Dan immediately realized he had seen them before. They were the three German-speaking men with Cardinal Friedrich who had been walking in the grottoes of St. Peter's when he had met with Sister Marie Therese and Jacqueline in a grotto chapel. They were going to remodel *Castel Gandolfo*.

"What is this castle?" Khalil asked.

"It's where the pope spends his summers," Dan said. "It's on a hill in a town with the same name about fifteen miles south of here. Mainly a museum today."

Khalil nodded. "All right, are we all in agreement about who I am? Pedro Garcia, a friend of Father Dan's who knew him in Jerusalem."

Everyone nodded.

"Good."

He looked around again, and then up, to see if any drone was hovering. Just to be safe, he took his coffee cup, and put it on the notepad he had pulled from his pocket. Then he scrawled something on the pad and put the cup upside down over it, then passed it to Dan, who looked, replaced the cup, and passed it to the women.

Khalil had written three names on the pad now. Marco Sanseverino, the Papal Nuncio to Israel, along with Renzo Bellocco. But he had added a third name and underlined it. Zug Gruppe.

Dan looked at him, and Khalil smiled. "I think this is your unholy trinity. Find how they connect, and you find the truth."

26

Rome

Gianluca Schmitt was a little drunk. After he knocked off at the Vatican Bank, he needed to blow off a little steam, so he and his boyfriend Jakob had decided to work out at the gym, and then grab a drink afterward. They had run into some of Jakob's colleagues from the Swiss Guards at *Alzati*, a gay bar in Trastevere, their regular haunt. Gianluca had not drunk that much, but he had lifted more weights faster and longer than ever, to try to add some bulk to his slender frame. Jakob laughed and told him he should consider himself lucky that he could eat and drink what he wanted. Jakob was the opposite. If he didn't work out every day, all year, he would become a Swiss suckling pig. And the vegetarian Gianluca would find that unappealing.

Gianluca had never imagined he would meet so many gay Swiss Guards in Rome, but it seemed as if a third of the one hundred thirty-five men who made up the Swiss Guards were gay, or so Jakob said.

Jakob had left the bar because he had pulled the early shift at the Vatican the next morning, but Gianluca decided to stay for one more drink, or maybe two, and think about what he was going to do with what he had discovered. That coded Vatican Bank list had troubled him, because he knew it was evidence of something bad. And he was troubled even more because he knew that it didn't stop there. He had found one smoking gun, but he suspected that there was a flaming arsenal.

What would he do? Tell the Church authorities?

Jared Rossi could be trusted, insofar as Gianluca believed priests were trustworthy. He had not been molested by priests as a kid, or had anything terrible happen to him, but he had seen how their parish priest reacted when his mother left Gianluca's abusive father and took him with her. The priest cut her off from receiving communion and broke his mother's heart.

Part of his work at the Vatican Bank was to get revenge on that priest by finding evidence of a Church crime, and Gianluca had done that.

But in order for his vengeful satisfaction to come true, Gianluca needed to offer proof, and then have that proof accepted, and then have it acted upon. In the words of Pope Leo, "justice must be seen in the daylight."

He took a sip of his cold Azzurro, and decided that for the time being, he would just keep looking in the dark, hoping to find more damning evidence to bring into that daylight.

That's when he realized that there was a guy looking at him. A handsome African guy, about the same age as him, drinking alone on the other side of the bar. Gianluca blinked. There was something unusual about the man. It was his eyes, which were blue, and glistening. When Gianluca realized the guy had those blue eyes fixed on him, the man smiled, and raised his glass.

Gianluca blushed. He was feeling the effects of the

booze, but he hadn't come morally untethered. He knew he wouldn't be in Rome forever, and that his romance with Jakob was not forever either, but it was happening now and Gianluca didn't need to complicate things.

The African guy was now standing in front of him, and smiling, his blue eyes electric. "Do you mind if I join you?" he asked in halting Italian, his voice deep and seasoned with the rhythms of Africa.

Gianluca did not want to be rude, as he knew the daily indignities that Africans in Italy already had to endure, so he smiled and nodded, and said, in English, "Please do."

The man's name was Babatunde, and he was from Nigeria. "I have come to Rome to learn to cook like an Italian," he said, with a broad smile. His face was smooth, and his hair was cut close to his head, which gave him the look of a marble bust that Michelangelo might have sculpted out of black marble, if there had been such a thing.

Gianluca paused when Babatunde asked him what he did. He didn't want to lie, but he also didn't want to tell the truth either. "I work in banking," he said.

Babatunde's face lit up. "Ah, you are rich as well as beautiful!"

Gianluca blushed again. He could not have a hookup, and he knew that that's where this was going, fast. He drained the rest of his beer.

"Ah, I have offended you, I am sorry," Babatunde said. He waved to the bartender and signaled another round.

"I really have to be going," Gianluca said, but Babatunde just smiled. "In my country, it is bad luck to only have one drink with a new friend."

Gianluca took a deep breath. "Ok, I don't want any bad luck! But I do need to use the washroom."

Babatunde grinned, and took the drinks from the bartender, and sat down in the seat next to the one Gianluca had just left.

As Gianluca emptied his bladder he thought maybe he would think of this encounter as making a new friend, who could cook, rather than as a romantic adventure that he didn't want.

He sat down next to Babatunde and raised his glass to the Nigerian. "Here's to good luck!"

They clinked, and Gianluca took a swig of the cold beer.

"Do you have a special friend?" Babatunde asked him. He really was blunt.

"I do," Gianluca said. "He's a Swiss Guard."

"Wow. They have such great uniforms. Do you live with him?"

Gianluca took another sip and shook his head. "No, I live in a flat that my employer provides. It's not really my style, but the price is right."

"Your employer, the bank, pays for this place?" Babatunde said, his eyes wide.

"They do."

"What is the bank? I will have to change my account to them so I can be with such a good place."

Gianluca smiled. "It's a small private bank. They don't have ATMs."

Babatunde thought about this. "A small private bank in Rome. Wow. It's not the pope's bank, is it?"

Gianluca blushed again. And in that blush, he gave away the truth.

"I am right!" Babatunde said and laughed. He clinked his glass against Gianluca's.

"I am just there for a while to help them sort out some things," Gianluca admitted.

"They have very dodgy money dealings, I have heard," Babatunde said.

Gianluca took a long sip of beer to cover any more blushing. "All banks have their issues," he said. "And the Vatican Bank—"

Suddenly, he felt the room start to spin.

"Are you OK?" Babatunde said and put his hand on Gianluca's arm.

"I feel... awful..." Gianluca said. Or that's what he tried to say. The words came out as if they were underwater.

Babatunde waved to the bartender. "How much do we owe?"

The bartender said, "*Dieci* euro." Ten Euros. Babatunde put down a twenty and said, "Keep it."

Then he put an arm around Gianluca and said, "Let me help you get home."

Gianluca tried to say thanks, but he suddenly felt as if he had been buried in cement.

Babatunde flagged down a taxi. "Where do you live?"

Gibberish came back, so Babatunde gently patted Gianluca down and retrieved his wallet.

"*Dieciotto, via Santamaura*," Babatunde said. "It's very close to the Vatican. 00192" His Italian was now much better than it had been in the bar, but Gianluca didn't notice. He felt so weak and tired that all he wanted to do was sleep.

And when Gianluca awoke, the sun streamed into the bedroom of his third-floor apartment, and Babatunde was sitting on a chair opposite his bed. He was no longer smiling.

Gianluca was fully dressed, so this was no date rape night. But it sure felt like he had been drugged.

"This is what is going to happen now," Babatunde said with an edge to his voice. "You are going to tell me what you have learned about secret accounts at the Vatican Bank."

Gianluca shook his head, and tried to rise, but he was still weak.

Babatunde reached into his pocket and for a moment, Gianluca thought he was going to pull a gun. Instead he produced his phone, and on it, a photo of Gianluca's mother. Looking frightened.

"You do as I tell you and your mother will be fine."

Gianluca felt the blood rush to his head. This had all been a setup. And he was probably dead already.

"So, tell me," Babatunde said.

Gianluca could lie, but then, they would find out and kill his mother.

So he told the truth. He told Babatunde about the numbered codes, and how the codes belonged to two entities. He gave him their initials, and his theory about how they were connected to real estate. His voice was calm, though his heart was racing. Babatunde listened to him calmly, and when Gianluca had finished, the Nigerian said, "Are you done?"

Gianluca nodded.

Babatunde took the audio clip of Gianluca speaking that he had recorded on his phone and texted it via Messenger.

Then he said, "Now we're going to do some writing."

What Gianluca wrote was a suicide note. How being gay and Catholic was something he could no longer live with. He hoped one day to wind up in heaven. Then he added a line that he hoped would be a clue: "Father Jared Rossi told me that if I stopped being gay, I would go to heaven."

"Sign it," Babatunde said.

Gianluca signed it, so carefully and clearly that anyone who knew his signature would wonder why he had changed it. Another clue.

Then Babatunde grabbed Gianluca by the neck, hauled him to his feet, and threw him out of the bedroom window. Gianluca didn't even have time to scream.

27

Rome

Pope Leo seemed even thinner and frailer than the last time Dan had seen him, which was a couple of nights ago. Today, his voice trembled as he greeted Chief Inspector Hillel Bennett and Dr. Rachel Ben-Simon in his library, along with Cardinal Alfonso Sanchez, the Vatican Secretary of State, and Vincenzo Pericoli, the head of the Vatican's *Gendarmeria*.

Dr. Ben-Simon's brown eyes were liquid with sadness, as she greeted Pope Leo. "Thank you for your support, Holy Father, after the murder of my friend Mimi Shapiro."

Pope Leo took her hand with both of his and smiled at her like he was her father. "We are all so sorry that it happened, Madame Ambassador. Dottore Pericoli and his team are doing everything to find the criminals and bring them to justice."

"They were two Africans on a motorbike," Rachel said. "Mimi shouted the name of a gun which one of the attackers had, a Beretta something, I heard no gunshots, and then after that, all I remember is that I came out of a coma in the Gemelli Hospital."

"Yes, Madame Ambassador," Pericoli said, "they were Nigerians."

Chief Inspector Bennett had begun to grow a beard since Dan had last seen him, as part of his mourning process for Agent Shapiro, Dan knew, but it gave him the look of a hip rabbi. "Did you have any issue with Nigerians in Jerusalem, Father?" Bennett said, his voice tinged with curiosity.

Dan was surprised by the question. It was as if the Israeli cop was trying to blame the murder on him.

"A couple of seminarians studying at the Institute were from Nigeria, but that's all." And if they were Black Axe, then Dan was the head of the Mafia. Not a chance. He took a breath, then said more sharply than he meant to, "How is your investigation going?"

Chief Inspector Bennett's full mouth tightened, as if troubled by the answer he was about to give. "All we know now is that the IED, the bomb which killed those women, was detonated by military grade C4." He paused and looked at Vincenzo Pericoli. "We think it came from Italy."

Vincenzo Pericoli seemed offended by the suggestion. "Why would you think that?"

"Because we know that someone stole two kilos of C4 from the U.S. military base in Vicenza. And that's what was used."

Pericoli's reaction was dismissive. "The terror groups in your neighborhood don't have that explosive?"

"They don't have U.S. Army C4. We got news of that theft through Interpol. As did you, I imagine."

Dan looked at the pope, and knew he was thinking the same thing. An Italian gun was used to kill Agent Shapiro, and explosives stolen in Italy were used to kill the women in Jerusalem.

"Do you have any suspects, Chief Inspector Bennett?"

Cardinal Sanchez asked.

Bennett shook his head. "We are asking ourselves this one question, though. Who would have access to this stolen C4 from Italy?"

"It is as if," Dan said, "they are sending a message that Italy is somehow behind both attacks."

Chief Inspector Bennett's brown eyes flashed at Dan with gratitude. The Israelis thought the same as he did, but it would have been bad manners to make that accusation in front of the pope.

Leo now began to cough, a hacking which grew in gurgling intensity, and Cardinal Sanchez quickly offered him a handkerchief. The pope waved him off and coughed into his own white handkerchief. When he finished, he glanced at the hankie and as he tucked it into his robe, Dan could see the red stain of blood upon it.

"I think," Cardinal Sanchez said, "we have heard enough for today. We thank God for your recovery, Madame Ambassador, and we thank you for coming to Rome, Chief Inspector Bennett, to inform us of what you have learned."

Rachel Ben-Simon rose and bowed. "Thank you for your concern and support, Holy Father, and to all of you."

"Our investigation will continue," Chief Inspector Bennett said, "and we will keep in close contact with Dottore Pericoli and his team. To see if we can find out more about this Italian angle."

Pope Leo asked Dan to walk him back to his sitting room, dismissing the others with a weak smile and the admission that he would want them to leave no Roman stone unturned to solve these crimes.

As soon as they were in Pope Leo's sitting room, Leo collapsed onto the sofa, his blue eyes hot with pain. Chocolate sidled up and licked his hand.

"Good boy," he said, breathing hard. "Sorry about this, Dan."

"I'm sorry, Patrick," Dan said, using Leo's birth name.

Dan Lanaham and Patrick Malone had been friends for half a century. Now was not the time to stand on ceremony. "Can I get you anything?"

Leo smiled weakly. "Whisky is the only thing that dulls the pain."

Dan grinned. "Thank God we're Irish, Patrick. It won't do us any harm."

Leo shook his head. "It's too early in the day. Imagine the headlines. 'Pope turns to booze to deal with ailing Church.'" He shifted on the sofa and pointed. "There, on the desk. There's a bottle of painkillers."

Dan saw the bottle and retrieved it. He read the label. Oxycontin. The pope's doctor was giving him the narcotic that had caused an epidemic of death and outrage in America. It was so addictive, and so easy to overdose.

He poured a glass of water from the jug on the coffee table and handed Leo the bottle.

"Open it will you, please, Dan? Just one pill. I know how bad this stuff can be."

Dan gave Leo the water and the pill, and Leo showed more strength than he had all day in popping the pill in his mouth and washing it down. "It'll kick in in about half an hour," he said.

Then he gestured to the armchair opposite and said, "Stay awhile, will you?"

Dan sat. "Who am I to disobey the pope?"

Leo chuckled, then coughed again. He pulled out his handkerchief and once again, coughed up blood.

"I don't think we'll have many more days together, Dan," Leo said.

"What are the doctors saying?"

Leo sighed. "That I have some intestinal disorder that is not cancer. It's a load of crap. I'm coughing up blood, I've lost thirty pounds, and my stomach feels like it needs its own exorcist. They just don't want to be straight with me."

Dan considered that. Maybe. Unless, of course, the

doctors were making Pope Leo ill with their treatment, and now giving him the easy out with Oxycontin. Not that his friend would commit suicide, for that was a grave sin. But that someone might give him an extra dose when he was too frail to protest.

"We could get you to different doctors, Patrick. Ones back home."

Leo shook his head. "My time on earth is ending, Dan. I accept that. I just want to be able to go with the knowledge that we changed things for the better. And right now," he took a breath, "I don't believe we have."

Dan wanted to tell him that everything was better, but he knew that wasn't true. Not after the bombing in Jerusalem. Not after what Khalil had told him about the unholy trinity.

"Do you remember when we graduated from Boston College high school and we were looking forward to Boston College ... to joining the Jesuits in action?" Leo took a deep breath. "What enthusiasm we had! The Church was so much a part of our lives, the focal point of so much that we did and what was important to us. And look at us now...."

Dan remembered. Much had happened since then, and he had broken the vows he had made as a priest with Layla in Beirut, but he was as committed as ever to the faith that the rabbi from Nazareth had begun two thousand years ago.

Dan nodded, his eyes a mixture of uncertainty and determination. "Yes, Patrick. I remember. We became so focused on making our beliefs accessible to the modern world that we lost sight of the essence of our traditions. We stripped away those layers without realizing that they were the very foundations holding us up. Can we find a way to blend the timeless wisdom of our faith with the ever-changing tides of society? Pump new life into it with a touch of the old?"

The pope turned his head to look out the window. All he could see from where he sat was the blue Roman sky. Maybe he was gazing at heaven.

"What do you think we should do?" Leo asked. His eyes were soft and searching. He needed Dan's help. "What tradition would you say we need most?"

Dand leaned forward in his chair. "I think that we need to focus on the importance of all the sacraments. Bring them to life in our lives. That can be a healthy source of spiritual renewal. Baptism, Confirmation, Eucharist, Penance and Reconciliation, Anointing of the Sick, Holy Orders, and Matrimony. All of them. From cradle to grave. Make them speak to and for our people and their lives. But in making that connection, we can't abandon the social progress we've made in the last fifty years either. I'm not calling for a return to the veiled woman and the Latin Mass."

Leo smiled. "Easier said than done."

Dan returned the smile. "The sacraments are us, Patrick. We can learn from what we got right, and wrong. Combine the best of our past traditions and know their sacred importance to the Church and her people. And then we wed them to the progress we have made, and we see what child they produce."

Leo closed his eyes, and for a moment, Dan thought he had fallen asleep. Then he opened them and said with clarity, "We cannot let fear govern us. We must admit mistakes made in the hope of progress and maybe at times take a step or two 'backwards' to have a chance of producing a healthy baby, as you put it."

"Amen," Dan said, on a grin.

Leo closed his eyes again for a moment, then opened them and smiled. "Our late Jesuit friend Walter Burghardt wrote something that I returned to the other day," Leo said. "Hand me that notebook, please."

Dan handed him a thin black notebook that was on the

coffee table. Leo opened the notebook to the page he was seeking, and then handed the opened notebook back to Dan.

"Please read it aloud."

So, Dan did.

"Let me make an uncommonly honest confession. In the course of a half century, I have seen more Catholic corruption than you have read of. I have tasted it. I have been reasonably corrupt myself, and yet, I joy in this church—this living, pulsing, sinning people of God, love it with a crucifying passion. Why? For all the Catholic hate, I experience here a community of love. For all the institutional idiocy, I find here a tradition of reason. For all the individual repressions, I breathe here an air of freedom. For all the fear of sex, I discover here the redemption of my body. In an age so inhuman, I touch here tears of compassion. In a world so grim and humorless, I share here rich joy and earthy laughter. In the midst of death, I hear an incomparable stress on life. For all the apparent absence of God, I sense here the real presence of Christ."

Dan felt tears well in his eyes. He heard Walter Burghardt's deep voice in his head as he read, and his words resonated doubly for him. Doubly true.

"Tell me what you think, Dan," Pope Leo said, his voice stronger now, his face more relaxed. The oxycontin had started to kick in. "Not about our theological needs. But about what we're up against."

Dan took a breath and told him, praying that the news would not be the last thing Leo heard on earth. He told his friend about Khalil's visit, and about what he learned. Archbishop Sanseverino, Renzo Bellocco, and the Zug Gruppe. All doing bad things inside the Vatican.

"And you believe this man?" Leo asked. "After all the bad things he has done?"

Dan folded his hands in front of his face, like he was praying. "He did this in the name of justice, and as wrong as they were, as criminal as they were, he thinks there was a noble principle behind them. I believe that the three names he gave me are not doing whatever it is that they're doing for the sake of justice."

"How does he know?" Leo smiled at his own question. "Of course, I imagine his world, like ours, has its own reliable sources."

"It does. He also felt he owed me for getting him into Georgetown Prep. He wouldn't have risked capture to come here to tell me a lie."

Leo put a hand on his chin, thinking. "They could be the Italians sending us a message."

"By murdering people? What is the message? That we're marked for death? Hardly a frightening thought to people in our line of work."

Leo closed his eyes. "No, it's not that kind of message. It's about power. They are saying they have the power to do anything they want. It's what they want, that we need to learn."

Dan thought about this, and Leo looked back out the window. "Soon it will be summer. I wonder if I will be around to make it to Gandolfo."

Dan suddenly remembered the German speaking architects and Cardinal Friedrich. "Patrick, did you give Cardinal Friedrich orders to renovate Castel Gandolfo?"

The pope jerked his head back in surprise, a sure sign of life. "Never. I wouldn't give that German dolt the holy eucharist if I didn't have to."

"You could always excommunicate him," Dan joked, and Leo chuckled.

"It would be war if I did anything to that right wing nutjob. There are too many like him in the Church these days, and we must not confuse tradition with the knee-jerk theology that those guys think is just fine. Why do you ask about Gandolfo?"

Dan told him about the German, or Austrian, architects. "I think in answering our question, we're going to have to take a closer look at Cardinal Friedrich. And who his Italian friends might be."

Leo smiled. "I like the way you think, Dan. Very Jesuitical."

Dan nodded, then chuckled. Leo looked at him with curiosity. "I just heard a story the other day from Father Gerrard, my assistant, who is no fan of Cardinal Friedrich. In it, the cardinal had died. Upon hearing the news, a young priest decided to pay a visit to the cardinal's residence. His old, devoted housekeeper answered the door and asked him what he wanted. He told her he would like to see the cardinal. She told him the cardinal was dead. These visits by the priest to see the cardinal happened again, two more times, and each time the housekeeper became more annoyed with the priest. 'Listen, Father,' she said, 'I already told you three times now, the cardinal is dead. Is there something wrong with you?' 'No,' he replied, 'I just love hearing it'."

Leo's face flushed with life, and he laughed. Dan laughed at the joy his story had brought his friend, who wheezed now, not with illness, but with delight. "Thank you for that, Dan. You have made my day with this story about the cardinal's demise. Just beware, that I believe he is part of the something wicked that closes in on us. You must protect yourself, and the Jesuits from him. I will guard the Church. He hates us, and he will take his revenge however he can."

28

Rome

Father Jared Rossi felt sick to his stomach. It was a way he had not felt since he learned a shocking fact about his birth mother, that she had died giving birth to him, a long time ago. But this time, the news was not about birth, but about death. His colleague at the Vatican Bank, Gianluca Schmitt, had jumped from the bedroom window of his apartment, and Jared was partly to blame.

"I never said anything of the sort to him," Jared said to Inspector Dottore Vincenzo Pericoli, who looked at him like a judge, his brown eyes hard and unblinking. With his shaved head and full handlebar mustache, Jared thought he looked like the kind of Italian cop of a century earlier, who found things out through guile and charm and the occasional round of brutality, but his manner was all twenty-first century: there was only one right answer, and he would find it.

Pericoli had appeared unannounced at Jared's office at the Vatican Bank and told him why his colleague Gianluca would not be coming back. And now, he said Gianluca had died because of something Jared had said about Gianluca going to hell for being gay.

Jared knew the Church's doctrine regarding homosexuality, that it was intrinsically disordered. He also knew that about half the priests he knew were gay, actively, or passively. And he knew with every breath he took, that any God whom he could imagine didn't give a damn about how you loved. The Church should get out of the business of human sexuality. Jesus said God was love, and that should be enough.

Of course, he couldn't say that to the Vatican's chief of the *Gendarmeria*, so he had to be careful. But he knew that he did not have that conversation about damnation for homosexuality with Gianluca because he didn't believe that it was damnable. He just had to make the cop believe him.

"May I see his note, *Dottore*?" Father Jared asked the cop.

Inspector Pericoli looked at Jared as if he might be playing some kind of priestly trick on him, his eyebrows arched, his eyes wide. But he took out his iPhone and opened a document, then placed the phone in front of Jared.

Jared read the note and knew at once that Gianluca had not written it voluntarily. He knew that his Swiss colleague's closest connection to the Church was the revenge he wanted to take for his mother. Gianluca did not believe in heaven. But the proof was in the signature.

Jared knew that the neat, orderly signature at the bottom of this purported suicide note was a fake. He had teased Gianluca about his scrawl of a signature and asked him how he could possibly reproduce the same crazy squiggle each time. Gianluca told him it was his own special talent as a fastidious Swiss, and they had a good laugh at that.

"I never spoke with Gianluca about his sexual orientation, *Dottore*," Jared said, carefully. "It was, frankly, not my concern. We were work colleagues. And if you care to examine any of the many documents Gianluca signed in this office, you will note that the signature on his note is significantly different from the one on the documents, which were his professional responsibility."

The cop looked at Jared with increased suspicion now, as if this was exactly the kind of thing Jared would say if he was somehow involved in Gianluca's death. But if this was a game the priest was playing, then Pericoli would play it, too.

"Show me the documents, please, Father."

Jared walked over to Gianluca's desk, and picked up two documents, innocuous requests for more paper and ink cartridges for the printer, and for some more Vatican Bank stationery and envelopes. Such requests had to be made manually in the IOR.

Pericoli looked at them, then at Jared. "How do I know that he signed these?"

Jared was fuming at the cop's refusal to believe him, but then he remembered the check. It was one that Gianluca had written to his mother, and that he had asked Jared to bless, sort of as a joke but also, Jared knew, out of faith. The check was to pay for a new roof on her house, so it was for five thousand Euros, but Jared didn't want to explain the circumstances.

"Here," he said, handing Pericoli the check. "He sent money home to his mother. He was going to send this today. He got paid today."

Pericoli looked at the check, and Jared said a silent prayer for Gianluca's mother. He prayed that the news of her son's death would not be the death of her. And he prayed that the Vatican's head of the Gendarmeria would not haul him into their offices for further questioning. He already felt as if he had said too much.

"So, Father," Pericoli said, handing the check back to Jared, "if this note was somehow forced, who would want to see Gianluca Schmitt dead?"

Jared had to use the face he had learned when he first heard confession as a new priest. He called it his "Hail, Mary" face, because no matter how outrageous the confession coming at him was, he had to behave as if he had heard it all before, and then he could assign the "Hail Marys" to the sinner who was confessing, and then say one for himself. He could not show Pericoli that he knew anything more than he just said.

"No," Jared said, "he was well-liked and very good at his job."

Pericoli paused and looked out the window at the cloud dappled sky. "Do you think, Father," he said, his eyes gazing on the heavens, before he turned back unblinking on Jared, "that his job had anything to do with his death?"

"Yes," was the answer to that, but Jared did not know where that "yes" would go inside the Vatican once he had given it voice. It could mean that whoever killed Gianluca would come for him next. He needed to tell someone he could trust, someone who had their own cause to be suspicious of the Vatican. So, he shook his head, "No," and flashed his "Hail, Mary" face of total composure. The cop looked at him, the touch of a smile on his lips, as if he would let him get away with ignorance for a while longer. Then he rose.

"Thank you for your time, Father. We will be sending in a team to secure Signor Schmitt's workplace soon. Please do not touch anything."

As soon as Inspector Pericoli was out of the office, Jared was in front of Gianluca's computer. He did not know the password, and hacking passwords wasn't his skill set. But he reckoned the Swiss forensic expert would be extra careful. He had to get into his computer and transfer the file that Gianluca had found with the coded transactions that indicated major money laundering before the Vatican police to get to it. If they had that file, then they could get in the way of what Jared was going to do. He didn't know what that was, yet, but he needed to get into Gianluca's computer fast.

He knew that he had about a couple of hours or so before the police returned, as that was how Vatican time worked. "Urgent" meant in an hour, and "soon" meant in two or three. He could call Gianluca's boyfriend, and ask him if he knew the password, but he instantly rejected that idea. The man was in the army, in a state of grief, and a request by a Vatican Bank colleague to get into Gianluca's computer would have the *Gendarmeria* back to put Jared in handcuffs.

He couldn't ask the Vatican IT people for the same reason.

No, he needed to keep this all quiet, and quick. Who could help him?

Jared walked out onto St. Peter's Square, thinking the fresh air might give him some kind of inspiration. Otherwise he was going to have to explain to the *Gendarmeria* what the curious file that Gianluca had shown him, but not shared with him, meant.

As Jared scanned the square, looking for some miraculous intervention, he saw Father Dan Lanaham, walking with that very attractive Black woman he had seen him with before. She was still here, and presumably, still helping Dan with the investigation into the bombing in Jerusalem. Jared picked up his pace and headed straight for them.

"Father Lanaham," Jared said, extending his hand. "Jared Rossi from the IOR."

"Father Rossi," Dan said, shaking Jared's hand. "The IOR is the Vatican Bank, Dr. Robinson," he added for the benefit of the woman looking with curiosity at Jared. He was dressed in mufti, so unless you knew he was a priest, you couldn't tell from his clothing.

The woman now extended her hand and introduced herself. "I'm Jacqueline Robinson. I'm helping the *Donne del Vaticano* with their healing," she said. Her hand was strong and warm, and Jared felt a connection with her as soon as he touched her.

"I hope that is going as well as it can go," Jared said.

"Yes," Dan replied. "For this place, it is."

Jared smiled. "Yes, the Vatican is its own planet."

Jared had met Dan maybe three or four times, and they had also connected in a strong way, as if they had known each other better than they did. Jared had worked with Dan's predecessor to create a document which outlined the Jesuits' financial health and prospects, and Dan had called Jared to ask about it when he was still in Jerusalem. His question about money had been smart, and thoughtful, and now Jared had an idea. He put on his "Hail, Mary" face, and asked the question that was his own "Hail, Mary".

"Speaking of this place, I need to get into a colleague's computer, who is away today. But there's information he showed me that I need. Do you know anyone who can, for want of a better term, hack passwords?"

Jacqueline shook her head, but something in the casual way that Jared had asked to break into a colleague's computer at the Vatican bank jumped up the electrons of Dan's radar. A priest at the Vatican Bank was asking him for help. To hack a computer. That meant that whatever he needed was secret. Dan saw his opening and took it.

"Could what you want to find on your colleague's computer help us in our investigation?"

Jared was surprised by the question. Could it help Father Dan? It might. And there was only one way to find out. "I don't know," Jared said. Then he took a gamble, trusting that Dan, who was investigating a crime, would not turn him in for one. "But if I get into the computer, I'll show you what I saw."

"Can you just tell us what you saw?" Jaqueline asked.

Jared shook his head. "You need to see it, and I need to explain it."

Jacqueline smiled a little sadly. "I can't hack passwords, I'm afraid."

Dan smiled with a touch of triumph. "I know someone who probably can."

"Here in Rome, who could do it soon?" Jared asked.

"Follow me," Dan said, turning toward the *Villino Giovanni.* He had a feeling that Khalil would know just what to do to get inside the Vatican Bank.

29

Rome

Jared and Jacqueline sat in the courtyard of *Villino Giovanni*, waiting for Dan to return with his password breaking source. Jared smiled at Jacqueline, trying to seem calm, but his heart was pounding. He needed to get back to his office before the *Gendarmeria* sealed off Gianluca's world there, and he had already spent half an hour away from his desk. Jacqueline seemed to read his mind.

"If anyone can help you, Father Dan will find them," she said, and returned his smile. She really was beautiful, Jared thought, with her milk chocolate skin and luscious brown eyes and full, ruby lips that he wanted, he realized, to kiss. He blinked slowly, as if to suppress the thought in his eyes, and gave Jacqueline his serious face.

"I hope that you are right. When I saw you in the Square..."

"You made the right decision," Jacqueline said. "I admit I have a vested interest in the outcome," she added.

"Yes, I am sure. How is the investigation going?"

Jacqueline was about to tell him the truth about who

she was, a journalist from Washington D.C. working on the story, but Dan came around the corner with Khalil, who saw Jared and stopped walking, as if he had seen a ghost. Then he quickly checked his pockets, as if to make sure something was there, and walked over to their table.

"This is my friend Pedro," Dan said. "He can help us."

Jared thought Khalil looked like some kind of scholar, a thin, intense, handsome Mediterranean guy working with Dan in Rome. But then, if that was true, why would he know how to hack a computer?

Khalil did not sit. He just stared at Jared.

"Thank you very much, Pedro," Jared said, rising and offering his hand. Khalil shook it.

"English, are you?" Khalil said.

Jared nodded. "I grew up in London. But I have lived in Rome for a decade now, so I feel a little Italian."

Jacqueline smiled at that idea, in a way that made Jared want to take her for a fine Italian meal. He shook his head. What was he thinking? He was a priest trying to get into a computer before the Vatican police did.

"This computer is in your office?" Khalil asked.

"Yes," Jared said. "We don't have much time."

Khalil's eyes flickered at that. "Yes. Father Dan explained everything. Let's go." Khalil turned to Dan and Jacqueline. "Just Father Jared and me. Don't want to have a parade."

Jared smiled at Dan and Jacqueline. "I will be back with what I promised."

As they walked across St. Peter's Square, Jared told Khalil about Gianluca, and his death.

"You say he found something suspicious in the records of this bank?" Khalil asked.

"Suspicious might be too mild a word," Jared replied. "It was evidence, it seemed, of money laundering."

"By the Vatican Bank."

"Yes."

Khalil thought about that, then looked at Jared again, as if studying him. "Who are your parents, in London?"

Jared thought it was an odd question, but he answered truthfully. "I was adopted. All I know is that my birth mother was from another country, and..." He held out his hands. "So, my adoptive parents are my parents. I was lucky."

"What year was this, when you were adopted?"

"1986. My birth year. Why?"

Khalil frowned, not in puzzlement, but as if he had almost put a puzzle together, and needed a piece, or two, to complete it.

"Do you know what country your birth mother was from?"

Jared was now a little rattled by this interrogation, but he needed Khalil's help. "Yes. She was from Lebanon. But my parents told me to keep that a secret otherwise the British kids would bully me for being an Arab. So I did." Jared stopped walking, before a medieval stone tower. "And here we are. The Vatican Bank"

Khalil looked at the medieval tower that formed the basis of the bank. He smiled. "It looks like a fort."

"It's kind of one," Jared said. "I'm on the top floor."

They walked the stairs to Jared's office and entered. Jared was relieved to see that no one from the *Gendarmeria* had yet entered. He led Khalil to Gianluca's computer and hit the "enter" key. The computer awoke with a photo of the Matterhorn as its screen saver.

"He was Swiss?" Khalil asked.

"Yes."

"And you need a web address he was at, not a document, right?"

"That's right. He had found a buried site, and I need that."

Khalil took what looked like a small motherboard for a computer out of his pocket, one that could fit in his palm, and then a USB cord from his other pocket. He plugged it into Gianluca's computer.

"What's that?" Jared asked.

"It's called Poison Tap. It should take about 30 seconds."

Jared's mind raced. Who was this friend of Dan's who carried hacking equipment called Poison Tap around with him?

"This will get the password?" Jared asked.

"This will get you into all unencrypted web traffic. It will steal any HTTP authentication cookies used to log into private accounts, as well as sessions for the top one million sites from the victim's browser. It will go where your dead colleague went."

Jared was amazed that this little device could so easily get into Gianluca's computer.

"And once you have it, where does it go?" he asked.

"It goes to me," Khalil said. "My server. But you will have what you need."

And you will have it too, Jared thought. "Are you a computer expert?"

Khalil did not reply, he just watched the Poison Tap load up Gianluca's information.

Suddenly, male voices, speaking Italian, could be heard in the distance. Coming up the stairs. Jared felt his heart speed up. "That's the *Gendarmeria*. The Vatican cops. They're on their way up!"

Khalil didn't react, he just kept watching the device work its astonishing magic.

The voices got louder as the cops got closer. Jared could understand what they were saying. "The priest says he was not the type to kill himself. So let's see what we can find."

Jared wanted to reach down and rip the USB out of Gianluca's cable, but Khalil, though not a large man, gave off an air of power that was more of a threat than a defense.

A door down the hall creaked open. Jared knew that creak well. It meant the police were about twenty, maybe fifteen seconds away.

Khalil looked up and motioned for Jared to sit at his desk. Jared sat.

Khalil unplugged the USB and pocketed it and the Poison Tap, then in one swift move sat in the chair opposite Jared and opened the folder on his desk, holding it up before his face as if it was the most interesting thing in the world.

"Ah, Father Rossi," Inspector Pericoli said, leading a short, nerdy guy into the room, with coffee stains on his trousers. "You are still here."

Jared forced a smile. "Well, it is my office. And I wanted to make sure everything was safe."

"Thank you, Father," Pericoli said, then gestured to the guy with him. "This is Dottore Biaggio, head of IT for us. He will take it from here."

Jared nodded to the man, who blinked at him like he was some kind of alien species, then headed straight for Gianluca's computer.

"Shall we go get a coffee, Father?" Khalil asked from behind the folder in perfect Italian. "Let this man do his work."

Jared was impressed by how cool Khalil had been about everything, and now he was offering them a way out.

"Good idea," Jared said, swallowing hard. He realized that he had already broken Vatican and Italian law, and he was already into the coverup.

Khalil rose and was out the door before Pericoli could see his face. Jared noticed that as well. Who was this man who was Father's Dan's friend, staying in a convent guesthouse, breaking into computers, and so coolly dodging the cops?

"Thank you, Inspector," Jared said. "If there's anything else I can do, please let me know."

Pericoli nodded and turned to his IT guy. "Can you get in?"

"It will take some time, Inspector," the technician replied.

By the time Jared was on the stairway down, Khalil was on the street. Jared thought that he had run off with Gianluca's information, but when he exited the building, he saw Khalil standing opposite the bank, smoking a cigarette.

"What now?" Jared asked, wandering over.

"You're going to show me what he showed you," Khalil said.

"I promised Father Dan and Dr. Robinson that I would show them first."

Khalil shrugged. "They can join us."

When Jared and Khalil arrived back at the *Villino*, Father Dan and Jacqueline were sitting with Sister Marie Therese, and they were all looking at her phone, listening to an African woman tell them something that seemed very troubling, judging by the expressions on their faces.

When Dan saw Jared and Khalil had returned, he nudged Jacqueline, who glanced over and then said, "Thank you for this, Chinara. We will resume this conversation later."

Jared knew that they must be speaking with Chinara Bukar, of the Nigerian embassy in Washington. He had met her a couple of times, when she had approached, no, when she had confronted him, with questions about how the Church was helping, on purpose or by accident, the Black Axe. He remembered the calmness in her voice and the fury in her eyes when she told him it was his moral duty to find the funds that were helping these monsters, and to stop them dead from committing their crimes against women and girls. Jared had looked, but had found nothing. He realized that maybe Father Dan and the *Donne del Vaticano* might be looking into the Nigerian crime syndicate, too. And knew more than he did.

"We had quick success, thanks to Pedro," Jared said.

"You were there ahead of the police?" Jacqueline asked. Sister Marie Therese looked surprised by the question.

"They showed up just as we were leaving," Jared said.

Dan looked to Khalil, who nodded once, as if to say, "nothing to worry about."

"And you got the information?" Jacqueline continued.

"We're about to find out," Jared said. "What do we need, Pedro?"

"A laptop will do."

Sister Marie Therese reached into her shoulder bag, sitting next to the table, and produced an HP laptop. "*Voila.*"

Khalil smiled. "*Merci.*"

She powered it up and entered her password. Khalil then sat beside her, and typed in a URL, which was a sequence of numbers and letters, which meant nothing to Jared. But once Khalil hit enter, up came the contents of Gianluca's internet life.

"The device I used moved it all to a special server," Khalil said. "What is the site that you need?"

Jared sat next to them and scrolled through the list. He saw Gianluca's path to the information on the Vatican Bank's internal server, the information that he had shared with Jared, and followed the links down the page until he hit the last one. And there it was.

"This is what he found, and shared with me," Jared said, sitting back so Dan and Jacqueline could see.

There were two documents, one of them in Italian, and the other in code.

"What's this?" Dan asked.

"Gianluca called it the smoking gun," Jared said. He pointed to the coded section. "If you look here, you will see letters and numbers repeat themselves."

Next to each coded entry was a sum of money, not in

code. The entries were for ten and twenty million Euros, adding up to nine hundred and fifty million Euros. Or more than a billion U.S. dollars. And below each sum was another string of numbers, some preceded by letters.

"That's a lot of money," Sister Marie Therese said.

"It is. About an eighth of what the Vatican Bank has in the vault, so to speak," Jared said.

"Do you know what the code means?" Khalil asked.

Jared sighed. "We were just getting started, and then... Gianluca was, he died."

"You think he was killed?" Dan asked.

Jared stared at the computer. "He wasn't suicidal. He was proud of who he was. And he could imagine, and plan for, a future. I don't think he killed himself, no."

"Did you tell Inspector Pericoli that?" Dan asked.

Jared nodded. "Yes." He paused as they all stared at him, to hear the reason. "He was treating me as a suspect. But I did not tell him about what we saw. I didn't know the full meaning of what we saw, and there was no way I was giving that to the cops."

Dan sighed, then smiled at Jared. "Welcome to the team. Now, can you explain what we're looking at, this code?"

Jared showed them how the priest who had been their predecessor at the Bank had created a very crude code. The number 182 could be translated to the alphabet, RB. 18 for R, 2 for B. And how 191912123 could be SS LLC. They were the only two codes used in the document.

"And is there proof of this number letter theory?" Dan asked.

Jared explained that because the numbers were big, he thought they might be for real estate, and that the numbers below the codes referred to property deeds. Jared typed in one of the one of the numbers, LN 87921, and then UK Land Titles. Links appeared to the UK government's title search engine, and because Gianluca had already paid the fee when he and Jared had tested the theory, the details were still there. For a flat in Kensington, London, registered to SS LLC, Cyprus.

"So it seems as if these codes were here to be discovered?" Jacqueline said.

Jared smiled at her, impressed with her intelligence. "Yes, the previous guy at the Bank made them discoverable if anyone was looking. We were looking."

"So who are they for?" Sister Marie Therese asked.

Only one organization I can think of, and it's criminal," Jared replied.

"And there's one person connected to that organization who comes to mind," Dan said, "who has the initials RB. Renzo Bellocco."

"Who's he?" Jacqueline asked.

"He's a very wealthy 'businessman' who wields power and influence in many dark places."

She thought about that, then turned to Jared. "So let's say if that's one of them, who is SS LLC?"

Jared looked at Khalil. "Can you help me find out?"

Khalil, his face suddenly conflicted, looked at Dan. "I think I have overstayed my welcome here."

"But do you know how?" Jared continued, almost begging.

"If you could give us a path, Pedro, then we can take it from there," Dan said.

Khalil looked at Jared and at Dan, and then said very softly. "OK. I will do it for my sister."

"Who is your sister?" Jared asked.

Khalil took a deep breath. "I think she just might be your mother."

30

Rome

Renzo Bellocco was trying to keep calm, but what he was hearing made him want to reach through his laptop screen and strangle the Nigerian with his bare hands.

"You are trying to extort money from me?" Renzo said, smiling like a killer, but his voice was tight with agitation.

"No," said Babatunde, his blue eyes shining like beacons of doom. He certainly knew how to light these WhatsApp video calls, emphasizing his diabolical eyes, and plunging the rest into shadow, like some African Satan. But then, he was the one who called this video meeting, so it was all part of his plan. "I am offering you and Ms. Oberfeldt a business proposition."

"And if we don't accept it?" Alina Oberfeldt said from her London home office, the window that backlit him now dripping with rain, dark clouds scudding behind it. Her face was taught, and her eyes, also blue, seemed dim and defeated in comparison to the Nigerian making this extraordinary offer.

"If you don't see the wisdom of accepting," Babatunde said, smiling, "then we will kill you."

"What if we kill you first?" Renzo blurted.

Babatunde laughed. "That will make your own death much, much worse. I mean, we'll know who killed me. And when we want someone dead, we get our wish. As you know, Signor Bellocco."

Alina Oberfeldt ran her hand over her close-cropped head. Which Renzo knew that she did before he made a counteroffer, though the Italian couldn't see what counter she could make to this naked threat from Nigerian gangsters. "So, you are saying the Black Axe will do proper business with us if we accept this deal? How do I know you just won't take the money and kill us anyway?"

So that was Alina Oberfeldt's counteroffer. A guarantee of life for letting yourself be robbed. Renzo snorted in disgust.

Babatunde, in turn, upped the voltage on his smile. He was enjoying this. "Because we would be killing our partners, who are making us rich."

Renzo felt his heart slamming in his chest and could feel the heat flooding his cheeks. He had not been this angry since he lost $10 million Euros to a Russian con artist, who was now part of the foundation of an apartment building Renzo had built in Knightsbridge. But this Nigerian gangster wanted ten times that amount as a down payment, and twenty percent going forward of all their profits.

"Actually," Babatunde grinned, "we won't kill you. Instead, we'll ruin you. Much better."

He explained that if they didn't accept his proposal, he was going to reveal the money laundering that Alina Oberfeldt and Renzo Bellocco had been doing through the Vatican to Italy's zealous anti-Mafia prosecutors who would take Renzo's empire apart and diminish Oberfeldt's mighty global fund to a kid's piggy bank.

"Why would the cops believe you?" Renzo said, barely hiding his sneer.

Babatunde shook his head, like he was dealing with dimwitted schoolboys. "It won't be coming from me. It will be coming from a very high-ranking Church official. A cardinal, in fact. Who could be the next pope. I hear the current one has not got long to live."

The news hit Renzo like a punch to the face. He immediately knew which cardinal would be doing such a deal with the Black Axe. The German, Friedrichs. To safeguard the deal that Renzo had made with the cardinal. It was insurance for the cardinal, and it was sending Renzo's blood pressure into stroke out territory.

Alina Oberfeldt saw the wisdom in the plan. "I see," she said, nodding wisely. "That would then trigger the investigation in a much more palatable way and get some troublesome Church bodies out of the way at the same time."

Babatunde nodded. "Exactly. Which clears the way forward. You keep doing what you're doing, and we are your silent partners, so to speak. And we will stay silent, unless you make us speak."

Alina Oberfeldt looked toward Renzo at the top right of her screen. She nodded at the Italian, who looked like a Sicilian assassin who had been forbidden to kill anymore.

"All right," Renzo said. "We will go along with it."

Babatunde laughed, one more suited to the punchline of a delicious joke, breaking slowly, and then heaving into guffaws that the two people on the other end of the call had to endure. Then just as abruptly, it stopped. "That is what I call the right answer," the Nigerian said, his blue eyes sparkling in triumph. "You will be hearing from us."

And with that, he logged off the call.

Renzo stared at Alina Oberfeldt, his anger cresting into a plan.

"I see you thinking, Renzo," Alina said. "Do you know

how to get to this Nigerian?"

Renzo nodded. "Yes, but as he said, if we harm him, they will just kill us with more of their vigor. No, I am not thinking of him. I am thinking of the cardinal."

"You know who it is?" Alina leaned forward, a smile playing on her full lips.

"I can find out," Renzo said. He had to be careful here. The deal he had made with the German Friedrichs was not one whose particulars he had shared with Alina Oberfeldt. He had just said they had a man in Rome who would do their bidding, and that he had a way forward.

"Where is this Nigerian based?" Alina asked.

"Why do you care?" Renzo replied. "He can get to us anywhere. But he is here, in Rome."

Oberfeldt nodded. "It would seem to be the place to be." She picked up a plexiglass box from her desk, with a vase inside it, and she looked as if she was going to inhale the fragrance as if it were a miracle, except for the fact the vase was encased in that glass box. "This is my favorite assistant, Renzo," Oberfeldt said, cradling the plexiglass box like a baby. Inside the vase were white flowers that looked like old fashioned nun's wimples, hanging from thick green stems.

"Nice," Renzo replied, wondering if Oberfeldt had early dementia. How could he be talking about flowers at a time like this?

"It's a very special flower," Oberfeldt continued. "If you put this vase in your room, it will eventually kill you."

Now she had Renzo's attention. "It's a killer flower?"

"Angel's Trumpet, it's called. "All parts of the plant are toxic. If you touch it, you will feel intense thirst, difficulty with speech and swallowing, then you will have vomiting and diarrhea, followed by fever, confusion, hallucinations, delirium, dilated pupils, seizures and coma. All these wonderful things. Then death. The perfume from this heavenly beauty can cause respiratory irritation, headaches, nausea, light-headedness... Eye contact with the sap may cause dilated pupils and temporary blindness. Any way you look at it, the Angel's Trumpet sounds the death knell of whoever has it in hand."

"Who needs a Beretta?" Renzo said. "I am impressed that you know all this, Alina."

Oberfeldt smiled. "My father was a doctor of chemistry, after all."

Yes, Renzo thought, who committed gruesome experiments on Jewish inmates at Mauthausen. Doctor Monster they had called him.

"How long will the death take?"

"About a day, depending on the ventilation. If you touch it, then much faster."

"And you are sending Angel's Trumpet to someone, Alina?"

She nodded. "I am having it delivered tonight, as a matter of fact."

"To whom?"

On that, the doorbell to Renzo's villa sounded. Three loud gongs. Renzo knew that one of his guards would get the door, but when he turned back to Oberfeldt, she was gone from the screen.

"Signor Bellocco, it is for you," his guard's voice said on his office intercom.

He rose, and walked down the marble staircase of his villa, surprised to see the young woman he had last flirted with at Oberfeldt's London mansion, now standing in his.

Looking even more luscious than he remembered. Her hair seemed blonder and her eyes greener, and her mouth, so rich and red and so very needed to be kissed. And he saw, in her arms, that she had a metal tube. One that his guard indicated was not a weapon by pointing at it and giving Renzo a thumbs up.

"*Signorina*," he said, taking her hand and brushing it with a kiss.

"I told you I would see you in Rome," she said, with a sly smile.

"You did. And you said you would tell me your name."

She handed Renzo the tube. "Angel's Trumpet is sealed inside this tube. Frau Oberfeldt said to have it delivered at once. To whomever you wish."

Renzo felt a chill run up his spine. Oberfeldt had given him a way to do what the doctors had failed to do. A way to kill Pope Leo, quickly.

But now, he needed a little more time. He needed to get the German cardinal back onside.

"I see," Renzo said. "And will you be staying here until I do?"

"Am I to take that as an invitation?" she asked, still smiling.

"You haven't told me your name. Once you do, I will invite you."

Her smile disappeared. "That's too bad," she said. "I prefer to remain anonymous. *Bonne notte, Signor*," she said, and was out the door before he could reach for her glorious ass and pull her back in.

He stared at the metal tube she had left. Oberfeldt had planned this before he even knew of the call. What if the Angel's Trumpet could kill him, in the tube? He couldn't take that chance.

"Take this thing and get rid of it," he said to his guard, handing him the tube. "But whatever you do, don't open it, or it will kill you."

The guard gave Renzo a stoic look. "How much time before it explodes?"

Renzo shook his head. "It's not that kind of bomb. It's a very poisonous flower. You can bury it in the sand along the Tiber. We just don't want it floating around and being discovered by some curious school kids who die because of it."

Renzo wasn't concerned about the schoolkids. He was

concerned about the investigative trail that would lead back to him if such an incident occurred.

The guard nodded, and carefully cradled the tube as he exited the room. As Renzo watched him go, he was reminded of what he had always known. A killer must always expect to die. Before his own death happened, though, he would make sure a few people went ahead of him. And if Alina Oberfeldt thought this was the best way to send the master of messaging a message, then she would be high on Renzo's list of those to die first.

31

Rome

Khalil could not tell who was more surprised. Father Dan, or his son, Father Jared. They were in Dan's office, with the door shut. Father Martin Gerrard was happy to see the handsome Mediterranean man back in his vicinity, but when he read the look on Dan's face, he knew that this meeting was not an ordinary one. He silently brought them bottles of water, to help cool the heat he saw burning in Dan's eyes.

"But how?" Jared asked, looking from one to the other, his blue eyes lit with astonishment.

"I fell in love with Layla in Beirut," Dan said.

"My sister," Khalil added.

"But you're Spanish," Jared said.

Khalil shook his head. "No, Lebanese."

Jared stared at him, unblinking. "But how do you know she's my mother?"

"Because... it all fits together," Dan said.

"You knew?" Jared asked. "She was pregnant?"

Dan shook his head, no. "I didn't know. I had our story buried deep within me. When Khalil pointed out your resemblance, you might say there was a resurrection."

Jared put his head in his hands, as if to hold in all the emotion running through him. Dan was his father, and Pedro was his uncle. If it was all true.

So, Dan told him the story of him and Layla, but that he did not know she was pregnant. Neither did her family, Khalil added, until she arrived in England. When Jared was born, she had no choice but to give him up for adoption, because the pregnancy had almost killed her.

"I thought it did kill her," Jared said.

Dan looked to Khalil, who nodded. "You were adopted by a good English-Italian family, and here you are now. With a father, and an uncle you didn't know you had."

Jared rose and steadied himself by putting his hands on Dan's desk. "I need some air."

He exited Dan's office, the pain on his face when he looked back at them both suggesting he would not return any time soon.

Dan sat back in his office chair, his face a mixture of wariness, sorrow, and protective joy, of the very kind on the face of Mary in the *Madonna della Strada*, the painting he so loved that hung in the *Gesù*. He had a son, and that son was a priest in Rome. He had to smile at the divine irony of it all, and then a tear rolled down his cheek at the thought of Layla, dying because of him. That was not irony. That was tragedy.

Khalil watched the emotions crossing Dan's face, and then stood. "I have to go, Father Dan. I have already stayed here too long. And the police saw me, or at least part of me, today."

Indeed, Khalil had risked much by coming to Rome. But then, if justice caught up with him because of his crimes, would Dan feel regret?

For now, he only felt gratitude and shame. He stood and

had to steady himself by placing his hands on his desk, just as his son had done. The fact he was a father and Jared was his son and Layla was dead was a force field around his body, squeezing him with both joy and pain. "Thank you for everything, Khalil," he said, his voice breaking.

They stood awkwardly, now united by blood, and death. Khalil was the one who broke the moment by stepping forward and embracing Dan. "I will be in touch about the banking stuff," he said. "I know someone who can help. And as for Jared, I hope you and he will find a way forward."

He turned to leave the room, then stopped at the door, and turned back.

"I know you have heard much today, and it will take time. But I cannot leave without telling you one more thing. Layla did not die in childbirth. She wanted Jared to go to a Catholic family, because of you."

Dan sat down with a thump, looking as if he had just survived the ten count, barely, but would not make it back into the ring. "She's alive?" Dan asked, his voice sounding like sandpaper.

Khalil nodded. "I have not seen her in some time, for obvious reasons. But yes, she lives in England. Oxford, actually, where she teaches religion at St. John's College."

Dan felt the room begin to spin. The woman he had loved but would not leave the priesthood for that love in order to save her brother, had now come back to him by that brother he had saved.

"Jared doesn't know..." Dan said to himself.

Khalil nodded. "He will only know if you tell him. It is your choice, now."

Khalil said no more. He just gave Dan a quick bow of his head, and then he was gone, too.

Dan clicked on his computer, and Googled St. John's College, Oxford. He found the faculty page and there she was, his Layla, known now as Professor Layla Penner. She looked as he remembered her, wearing her beauty as an afterthought, her fierce intelligence shining through those stunning blue eyes.

He wondered about her surname and Googled her to see if she came up on Wikipedia. She did not, but a bio of her on the International Congress of Religious Scholars site revealed that she had been married. Her husband, Duncan Penner, had been a law professor at Oxford, who had died of stomach cancer.

Dan felt as if his veins had been injected with ice. The boy he had helped go to Georgetown Prep to save him from a life of violence in Beirut had become a man who killed, and a man who brought the dead back to life, the woman Dan had loved. The mother of their son. He wanted to see Layla again, he wanted to confess his sorrow to her, but he realized that any attempt to see Layla must come from Jared.

And he knew Jared would be flailing to stay afloat and breathing in the surging tidal wave of murder and corruption and unexpected family that had come his way in the last twenty-four hours. Dan was now Jared's father, something he had not been when he awoke this morning. He was responsible for his son's wellbeing, now, even if he was the reason for the shock.

The whirling images in his head were interrupted by a knock on his door. Father Martin Gerrard poked his head in, and read Dan's face, and returned the look with a broad Irish smile.

"There's someone here to see you, Father," Gerrard said. "Sister Marie Therese."

Dan felt a jolting pull of the other reality hanging around his neck, the death of Sister Maureen and all those women in Jerusalem. And then he felt a touch of relief. He would return with full commitment to the investigation, if only to help in his own redemption.

"Send her in, Father," Dan said, and stood to welcome

the nun into his office.

No sooner had he issued the invitation than she was standing in front of him, her eyes lit up with the fire of an idea.

"Sister Marie Therese, please," Dan said, gesturing to the chair opposite his desk.

She shook her head. "We haven't time, Father. I have been thinking about what Chinara Bukar told us about the Black Axe and their connection to someone in the Vatican."

"Do you know who it is?" Dan asked.

"Not yet," she replied, her voice strong with courage. "But I have an idea of how we can find out."

"You do?"

"Yes. I need to meet with the Black Axe."

"But they had a part in killing Sister Maureen."

Sister Marie Therese smiled, almost daring Dan to stop her. "Yes. But they won't kill me. Not when I tell them what I know."

"And what is that?"

She puffed up, seeming to grow three inches taller with her plan. "The truth. I am going to tell them the truth. And it will make them afraid."

Dan thought about this truth. He thought the Black Axe were so welded to their own truth that they would never hear what Sister Marie Therese was going to tell them. But he admired her bravery, and her spirit of vengeance. She burned to get justice for Sister Maureen. "How will you get to them?"

Sister Marie Therese smiled, like she had all the aces. "Chinara gave me a contact. He's here in Rome. She said I can't miss him. An African with blue eyes."

32

Rome

When Jared emerged into the bright Roman sunlight, he didn't see her at first. But she had been waiting for him to exit Dan's office, so that meant that she had followed them here, after she had heard Khalil's astonishing revelation that Dan was Jared's father. And now, Jacqueline Brussard walked up to Jared and asked, "Are you OK?"

He blinked in the sunlight at this stunning African American woman who was inquiring about his well-being. Just looking at her made him smile. He also realized that she had been waiting for him. What did that mean? What did he want that to mean?

"I don't know," he said.

She looked at him, her brown eyes liquid with compassion and concern. "I can't even imagine..." she said.

"Neither can I, really," Jared replied, and then he laughed, and so did she. In the vast scheme of things, he had just learned he had a father and a mother whom he didn't expect. That was all, and yet, that was everything.

"If you're free," Jared said, the impulse of the idea firing his boldness, "I'm going for a drive to one of my favorite spots. It would be lovely if you could join me."

Jacqueline smiled. "It would be my pleasure."

Jared had a red Fiat 500 hatchback, which was perfect for the narrow Roman streets, with its compact body and nimble handling. And it could get up a good head of steam now, as he and Jacqueline sped along the SP 217 to Nemi, about thirty miles southeast of Vatican City. It was a place Jared liked to go to clear his head when things got to be a little cloudy in Rome, and right now, they were beyond cloudy. He felt as if everything he understood had just been plunged into darkness, and now he had to find a way to see himself and his life through a lens that could see through the darkness, a lens that he had to find.

The first part of the trip was silent, as Jared navigated them out of Rome. Jacqueline knew that talk would come, so she looked out the window as he drove them out of the city into the countryside and to a place where he said she would want to return. So, she was a little surprised when he began to speak by asking her about her own family. There was a long story, and a short one. So, she opted for the short.

"Just me and my Mom, mostly. And my grandma. Who's 92. My mom looks after her."

"Did you grow up in Washington?" Jared asked.

Jacqueline nodded. "I did. In the southeast part of the city, across the Anacostia River."

She looked out the window again, knowing that she was at her own crossroads of truth if Jared pushed her story further. He thought she was a Catholic women's advocate. How could she tell him she was a journalist for the *Washington Post*?

"So, it was just the women in your household?" Jared

asked.

His voice was calm, but she could feel the intensity in his questioning. He wanted to know if she had a happy family, as if to calibrate the state of his own.

"My father left when I was little," she said.

"I'm sorry," he replied.

"I wasn't," Jacqueline said, surprising herself with the words that just came out of her mouth. But now that they had, she needed to provide context. "He drank too much, and when he was drunk, he was nasty."

"Oh, I am sorry," Jared said, glancing at her, his blue eyes lit with compassion. "Did he hurt you?"

She smiled. "He hurt my mother pretty often, but he stopped at hitting me. Maybe he saw himself in my face. I don't know. But my mother left him, and that was the end of it."

Which was not the entire truth. Her mother divorced her father, and the divorce court decreed he was never to come back. But the divorce had been a problem for her mother with the Catholic Church, and she didn't want any opinion on it now, from Jared.

"So," she continued, "we lived with my grandmother, my mother's mom, and we were fine."

Jared smiled. "Did you go to college in Washington?"

"Yes, I went to Georgetown." She didn't add that she went on a basketball scholarship, and then to journalism school at Columbia.

"Close to home, then."

"Yes, close to home."

They drove along in silence for the next ten minutes, and then Jared grinned at what he saw ahead.

"There it is! *Lago di Nemi!*"

As they crested a hill, Jacqueline could see a turquoise lake ahead. "*Bella,*" she said.

Jared smiled. "Wait 'til you see the rest of the place." He seemed, for the first time since she had seen him today, to be, if not happy, then more at peace.

The town was the smallest of the *Castelli Romani* villages, and as Jared pulled the Fiat into the center of town, Jacqueline could feel the history oozing from the pores of the town's cobbled streets.

"You can smell the ancients in this place," Jacqueline said, but she also knew that you could smell them in Rome as well. What was it about *Nemi* that brought Jared here in this state of mind? The lake was beautiful, and the town was yet another charming Italian community, but that wasn't the reason.

"This used to be the domain of the goddess Diana," Jared said, sweeping his hand over Lake Nemi. "Two thousand years ago this Sanctuary of Diana was filled with ancient religious pilgrims. Locals used that grove next to the lake as a sacred place of worship. It became an important religious center – with a temple, baths and even a theater – and was visited by people from the surrounding cities until the 2nd century CE. Until people stopped believing in her. And now...."

His voice trailed off, as if he was disappointed that Diana was no more.

"She was my favorite goddess when I was a kid," Jacqueline said, as they sat on a stone bench, the warm sun flooding the town square around them. "Goddess of the hunt."

"I liked her, too," Jared said. "Also, the goddess of childbirth."

Jacqueline let that remark sit, as they gazed out on the people doing their daily business in the markets and cafes.

"So did you like the hunter Diana because you like to track things down?"

Jacqueline felt her heart thud. If there was a time to tell him the truth, it was now. Unless he already knew. Either way, she did not want to lie to him.

"Yes. It became my profession," she said, watching his

reaction. He looked puzzled, so he did not yet know who she really was.

"You mean advising progressive Catholic women?"

Jacqueline took a breath. "Only if they read what I write."

He looked even more puzzled.

"I am not an advisor to progressive Catholic women, Jared. I am a journalist. I cover politics, mostly, for the *Washington Post.*"

His look of puzzlement shifted into a brief cloud of alarm, and then he smiled. "That's wonderful," he said. "Of course, that's why you're here. To get the story of what happened."

Jacqueline smiled in relief. "Yes. I knew Father Dan from his time in D.C., and I had to have cover to help him tell his story because we didn't know who was doing what."

"As I know all too well," Jared said. He was looking deep into her now, his blue eyes like laser beams, searching for something. "And what have you found?"

Jacqueline shook her head. "Nothing good." She looked around, to see if anyone was listening to them, but the villagers were still going about their afternoon business without giving them a second glance. Unusual, a priest in a collar, sitting with an African American woman in the middle of an Italian town, but maybe, to them, it looked like a moment of pastoral care with some unhappy refugee.

"Can you say anything more?" Jared asked.

She sighed. "I pretty much know what you know. That bad actors are using the Vatican Bank to launder money, but maybe to buy influence. And that the Black Axe might have had something to do with the attack in Jerusalem."

"Is that what the Israelis are saying?"

Jacqueline shook her head, no, then looked around. She saw a man watching them from a table at an outdoor café. He took a drag from his cigarette and blew it in their direction, as if he didn't like what he saw.

Jared rose. "I know somewhere better to speak," he said.

They walked in silence up the *Piazza Roma*, which swung around to reveal the white stone façade of a church. It had a covered portico, and a small belfry rising to the right of the entrance. Jacqueline realized that Jared was taking her to church.

"The Sanctuary of the Crucifix is what it's called," Jared said. "Come in and you'll see why..."

They entered the small sanctuary and inhaled the perfume of incense. They were the only people inside the cool and tranquil church. Jacqueleine immediately saw the reason for its name as they walked toward the altar. A wooden crucifix hung above it, the face of Jesus almost blissful in the torment of his awful death.

"It was founded in the mid-17th century for the Franciscans," Jared said. "That crucifix is considered miraculous, as it was discovered fully made. Presto. Another miracle..." He stopped and then turned to her. "I'm sorry, I assumed you were a Catholic, helping the *Donne*. But if you are not, I am not trying to convert you! Just talking history."

Jacqueline smiled. "I am Catholic, though not a very good one."

Jared nodded, but remained silent, encouraging her to say more.

"When my mother left my father, they got divorced," Jacqueline said. "Her parish priest excommunicated her."

"Ouch," Jared said, then blushed. "Sorry, not a time for shorthand. That must have been awful for your mother, and you."

Jacqueline felt his compassion and liked the fact that he had caught his own tendency to respond before thinking. He was also so very handsome, as the afternoon light slanted through the upper windows and created a world of soft shadow, in which Jared stood.

"It changed my view of how I saw the Church," Jacqueline said. "My own view of God was that he or she didn't care about marriage or sex. Just about love. And what that priest did was not about love, but about power."

Jared looked at her as if seeing her anew. "I could not agree with you more," he said.

Jacqueline wanted to ask what he was agreeing with, exactly, but she tamped her instinct as both a journalist and a Catholic woman down, and remained silent, as she felt he wanted to continue. Instead, he stepped forward and knelt at the altar. Jacqueline followed him.

He had his eyes closed, and his head bowed in prayer. Jacqueline looked at the crucifix, which seemed, in so many ways, a strange symbol to hang above an altar, as if Christianity was some kind of death cult.

She turned her gaze to a nearby statue of the Madonna, who looked wise and at peace with her role as the goddess of this Church that thought itself so masculine.

Jared opened his eyes and smiled at her. "I put in a word for your mother. And for us," he said.

Jacqueline put her hand on his out of gratitude for the gesture, and he squeezed it. Then he released her hand and stood.

"You were going to tell me something about the Black Axe," he said, his voice soft, and uncertain.

Jacqueline nodded. "Sister Marie Therese has a plan to connect with them. And to reveal that we know that they killed Sister Maureen and those women in Jerusalem."

Jared blushed. "Do we know that?"

"She thinks we'll know from their reaction. There's a Black Axe operative in Rome."

Jared nodded. "She's very brave."

"So are you," Jacqueline said.

"I am?"

She smiled. "I think after what you learned today, the fact that you're still standing, is pretty brave."

Now he looked as if he was going to reveal a great secret. "I feel like a coward," he said. "I came here to clear my head, but it has only become more foggy."

"Why is that?" Jacqueleine asked.

Jared smiled at her like a shy schoolboy, then stepped forward and kissed her on the lips. More than a peck, but the kind of test kiss you would give to someone you hoped loved you, because you loved them.

"That's why," he said.

Jacqueline smiled back at him, then said, "Here's to clearing those clouds."

And she kissed him back, as if kissing the first of a million kisses.

They had crossed beyond the dark cloud into a world where the only light would be them. With many, Jared knew, trying to snuff it out. There was only one thing to do. He kissed her again, and their new journey began.

33

Rome

Cardinal Wolfram Friedrich drained the last of his Monchschof and raised his tankard to summon more of the ice cold and sparkling beer. He was in mufti tonight, at the request of his host, Renzo Bellocco, who sipped his glass of Riesling like an abstemious nun, but other than that, there were no disapproving eyes aimed at this rotund German man enjoying his schnitzel and his spaetzle and his beer.

Fredrich had suggested they dine at *Taverna Otto*, a popular German beer hall near the Vatican, decorated with red and yellow and black bunting, the colors of Germany, along with beer barrel tables, and buxom blonde waitresses in low cut white blouses and swirling red skirts giving the whole place the feel of a perpetual Oktoberfest. Friedrich knew it would be full of witnesses should Renzo try anything dastardly.

He was certainly not going to meet Renzo at his villa with his security guards hanging around like twitchy black shirted goons, or anywhere that Renzo might have muscle with the management. No, Friedrich was friendly with Otto, the owner of the Taverna, as a good Catholic man from the same hometown as him, Holzkirchen, just south of Munich. "The town of wooden churches." Friedrich knew that wood was a poor choice for a Church, vulnerable to fire and rot and time. No, a Church built to last would be made of marble. Just like what he was doing to the chapel at *Castel Gandolfo.*

"I think you should put a pause on that little reno down south, Wolfram," Renzo said, slicing a bit of bratwurst as if it was a dangerous science experiment, then taking a careful bite.

"And why is that, *Maestro?*" the cardinal asked. He always called Renzo the Maestro as a kind of flattering gesture, but in reality, it was a diminishing tactic. He knew the power Renzo had due to his wealth and his unflinching use of crime to get that wealth, but he also knew that keeping him disarmed as the Maestro also kept him at arm's length. The last thing he wanted was Renzo Bellocco telling him what to do, as he was doing right now.

"Because you are not the pope. And behaving as if you are is something that will ensure that you are not going to be, when that time comes."

Cardinal Friedrich grinned. "So, you plan to vote in the conclave, *Maestro?*"

Renzo Bellocco snapped his fingers at a passing waitress "Bring me a glass of Italian wine. Montepulciano, *per favore, signorina.*" The waitress nodded and went off to fetch the proper drink for an Italian suffering in a German tavern.

Renzo could see that the cardinal was much more confident in his manner, tossing off the *Maestros* with more of a challenge in his voice, as if asking Renzo to show him his power. If that's what he wanted, that is what Renzo would give him.

"Tell me, Eminence," Renzo said, using the formal term of address to remind Friedrich that he was still just a cardinal. "What do you see as the most important thing facing the Church today?"

Friedrich shoveled a mouthful of spaetzle in and then washed it down with the fresh tankard of Monchschof the waitress had delivered, along with a modestly poured glass of red wine for Renzo. "I think, *Maestro*, the most important thing for the Church is to stop turning the other cheek."

"You mean go against the teaching of Jesus?" Renzo asked, feigning disbelief. He knew exactly where Friedrich was going with this.

"Not at all, *Maestro*. Far from it. I mean taking the teaching of Jesus to heart and taking his message out there to the pagans. Not flinching, not afraid, but telling them that here is the one true faith, and if they don't get onboard with our two thousand years of majesty, well, then we shall make sure they regret it."

Renzo took a sip of the Italian wine and grimaced. "Sounds as if you think the Vatican has an army."

"Oh, we do, *Maestro,* we have a small and mighty army that wants the Church to be a beacon for the righteous, and not a dingy cafeteria for the riff raff."

Renzo nodded. "I see. Well, I will tell you what I think the Church needs. A pope who listens to his closest advisors and does what they advise. The Church is not a democracy."

Friedrich chortled at that idea. "I never said it was, *Maestro*. But I do know the pope must be strong, and lead, and not be led by the sheep."

"So, you think you can be that kind of pope, Wolfram?"

Cardinal Friedrich squirmed at the question. "He who goes into the conclave a pope, comes out a cardinal."

Renzo smiled; the way Friedrich imagined that he might smile before he slit your throat.

"Well, just remember that I am an advisor to many cardinals, and I have told them about your virtues. I can keep telling them..." He shrugged and took another bite of bratwurst.

"I have friends too, *Maestro*," Friedrich replied.

Renzo nodded. "I know you do, and I hope that they don't desert you when they discover you're working with, how do you say it in German, *die Schwarzen*?"

Now Friedrich looked like a man who had just lost his appetite. "I don't know what you mean, Renzo," he said. He took a swig of beer and put his knife and fork down beside his plate.

Renzo Bellocco leaned forward and said in almost a whisper. "If you do the bidding of die *Schwarzen*, then I promise you that you will never be pope."

Friedrich, however, had not lost his appetite. He was waiting to strike back, smiling now, as if he was enjoying what was coming. "Ah, I see, Renzo. So, you do have a vote in the conclave. Well, let me put it this way, the Blacks, as you call them in your not so good German, have made me an offer that I can very much refuse. They don't scare me because they need me to be alive, one way or another. If I help them, I will ruin you. But you might ask why I would want to ruin you. I do not. I have made a wager with the devil, *Maestro*. It is a bit like that wager the Frenchman made."

"Which Frenchman do you mean?"

"Pascal. He said he believed in God because if he won, then he won eternal life. If he lost, then he lost nothing."

Renzo felt his blood pressure spike, as he now saw what was coming.

"And as for me, *Maestro*, if I win, then I win the papacy, and if I lose, then you lose."

Friedrich stared at Renzo in a way the Italian recognized. With the blazing eyes of a killer. He knew that Friedrich was right. Now all he had to figure out was how he could stop the Black Axe before Friedrich became pope. And shift the power back to himself. He smiled at the cardinal and raised his glass of wine.

"To your health, Eminence," he said, in a way that Friedrich knew meant that his health could change in an instant.

But he raised his tankard in turn and replied "And to yours, *Maestro*. I think it can only get better, if we stick to God's plan."

They clinked glasses, with each of them thinking that they knew what God's plan was.

34

Rome

It was cloudy and threatening rain outside the pope's study, as Father Dan, Pope Leo, along with Secretary of State Alfonso Sanchez, listened as Inspector Domenico Pericoli laid out what he and his *Gendarmeria* team had found in Gianluca's computer.

"Just banking information, Your Holiness," the Inspector said. "Nothing suspicious."

Dan didn't know if Pericoli was telling the truth or not, but he felt relief, nonetheless, that the cop had not said more here. There was only a small group who knew what Gianluca had found, and he had kept it all online. The *Gendarmeria* didn't track it, or if they had, they weren't going to tell the pope.

Dan looked to Leo, who had wasted so far into his bones that his white robe hung off him like a king-sized bed sheet. He coughed, as well, pretty much constantly now, and into a handkerchief that was stained with red. Dan knew that the Pope could die at any time. And he didn't want to speed his journey to heaven with bad news about the Vatican Bank. And yet, he knew that Leo needed to know, and that knowledge might even fuel the life force in him.

"Do you have any further information on Gianluca Schmitt's death?" Dan asked, changing the focus of the conversation.

"So sad, the death of that young man," Leo said, and coughed up some blood.

"Well, not much," Pericoli replied. "We found he went to a bar the night before he jumped, or fell, from his bedroom window."

"And that is unusual?" Cardinal Sanchez asked, his hands resting on the scarlet fascia encircling his plump belly.

Pericoli pursed his lips, solemnly, as if what he was going to say might offend the pope.

"It is a bar called *Alzati*," Pericoli said.

They looked at the cop, not knowing this bar, or how it mattered.

"It is a bar for the intrinsically disordered," Pericoli said.

"You mean it's a gay bar?" Dan asked. He was surprised by Pericoli's reticence to declare a simple fact.

"Yes."

"And what is the significance of this bar, other than it being for the 'intrinsically disordered'?" the pope asked, his voice scratchy, but his eyes alert.

"We know that Gianluca left the bar with someone. Another man. An African, with blue eyes."

Dan felt heat run up his spine. An African with blue eyes was the guy he had seen in the Gesù. It was the man who Chinara Bukar said was the Black Axe operative in Rome. How many blue-eyed Africans were there in Rome? It must have been him. And if it was him, Gianluca was already in grave danger.

"You are thinking something, Father?" Pericoli asked, reading Dan's eyes, which were heavy with a realization. The African was after what Gianluca had discovered about the Vatican Bank. But how would he have known about that discovery? Had the Black Axe hacked into the Vatican Bank? And what did Gianluca tell him, before he was thrown out of his own bedroom window?

"No, Inspector," Dan said. "Just thinking of poor Gianluca. Why, do you think this African is significant?"

Pericoli pursed his lips again. "You will recall the Israeli agent was killed by an African."

Dan remembered all too well. And he knew that Rachel Ben-Simon who survived the attack could not remember much, except that he was an African.

"Where are the Israelis in the investigation of Sister Maureen?" the pope asked, his voice more sure, now, as if he had found some energy in what he had just heard.

"They say that it was not the usual suspects. They have, despite the failures that led to their last war, good intelligence. It was not Hezbollah or the Iranians."

"Then who was it?" the Pope asked. His question was met by silence, and the Secretary of State stood up.

"Thank you for this briefing, *Dottore*," he said to Pericoli, who also stood.

"We will let you know what else we find."

"Thank you," Pope Leo replied, then he raised a hand to dismiss the cop.

Once Pericoli had gone, the pope turned to Dan and Cardinal Sanchez. "What did you make of that?"

Before Sanchez could answer, Dan said, "I think you need some rest, Holy Father. It was a lot of information."

Leo immediately understood what Dan was doing. "Yes, you are right, Father Lanaham. Will you help me to my chamber?"

"Of course, Your Holiness," Dan replied. Then he turned with a sympathetic smile to Cardinal Sanchez.

"Let's hope we get good news soon, Eminence."

Sanchez nodded, then he bowed to Leo, and bid them both good day.

Dan held Leo's bony arm as they walked slowly along the hallway leading from the study to Leo's bed chamber. He slept in a simple single bed, and Dan helped him to sit down on its edge. Chocolate, the dog, was already snoozing on the end of the bed.

"Do you want help getting into bed?" Dan asked.

Leo shook his head. "I want to know what you know."

So, Dan sat down in the armchair next to Leo's bookstand. He took a breath, and then he told the pope what he knew. And what he did not. When he had finished, Leo looked as if he had indeed been revived by the news. The fire in Leo's eyes that Dan had seen as a young priest in Boston was back. Not as bright, but still as hot.

"So, you are telling me that you think Renzo Bellocco and some other entity have been laundering money, lots of money, through the Vatican bank?"

"Father Jared and Gianluca Schmitt thought that."

Leo nodded slowly. "And Gianluca was so upset by this knowledge that he jumped out of his bedroom window."

Dan smiled at his friend, who still had the life of sarcasm in him. "Yes, agreed. He was pushed. By someone who got what they needed. And that someone, I think, is the blue-eyed African."

"Why do you think that?"

"Because we have a Nigerian contact who told us that the Black Axe has an operation in Rome. And their leader is a blue-eyed African. I have, in fact, seen him."

"You have?"

Dan nodded. "He was in the Gesù when I came back for the election. I thought nothing of it, but for his blue eyes."

"Do you think he was following you?" Leo asked. Dan had not thought that until now.

"I think he was making his plan. Seeing where I would

go. So he was not in church, I think, by coincidence."

Leo smiled. "No, not."

"I think the Black Axe has something to do with the murder of Sister Maureen as well. She was deep into her investigation about their kidnapping and trafficking of young girls."

Leo closed his eyes, and Dan could see the pain in his face. He felt a wave of sadness flow over him, as he could see his friend was willing himself to live until this mystery was solved. But Dan didn't know if it ever would be.

"Why would they kill so many if they were just after Sister Maureen?" Leo asked, his eyes still closed. Dan looked at the bottle of Oxycontin on Leo's table. It looked almost empty.

"Do you want a pill, Patrick?" Dan asked softly, using his friend's birth name.

The pope opened his eyes, and shook his head, no. "I have learned to live with the pain, Dan. It is my reality, and I am at peace with my mortality. Before I go, I just want you to find out who did this, and why?"

"I think they were sending a message, Patrick. A message that the Mother Church was not safe. A message to me, by attacking Sister Maureen and those women in my building. And a message to the pope who will follow you. They wanted attention, and that was a way to get it."

Leo closed his eyes again. "But who are they?"

Dan grimaced. He had some idea, but not enough proof. "I am finding out, Patrick. I just need to chase a couple of things."

Leo smiled, his eyes still closed. "Don't make the chase a long one, my friend."

Dan rose. "I won't, Patrick. Do you need any help—"

The pope waved him off and stood up. "I am going to my chapel to pray, Dan, For us all."

As Dan walked across St. Peter's Square, he felt the pain he had seen in the pope's face now swirling in his own heart. He knew they were in the end days with Leo, and he knew he had to find an answer so that Leo could die in peace. Then he smiled. Leo was at peace. It was Dan who was not. His thought was a very Jesuitical way of restoring his emotional order.

Then his cell phone vibrated. He had it switched to vibrate mode while he was meeting with the pope. He fished it out of his jacket pocket and looked at the number. It was "Unknown". Dan was about to hit the stop button, thinking it might be spam, but then the word "Unknown" resonated in a way he didn't expect. He was in the unknown and trying to find the truth. So, he said "Hello."

"It's me, Dan," the man on the other end said. "Don't use my name."

It was Khalil.

"OK," Dan replied.

"I have what you need," he said.

"Great." Dan knew that Khalil had cracked the code SS LLC on the Vatican money laundering discovery.

"But not on the phone."

"OK."

Then the call went dead. Dan stared at the phone to see if the call had dropped, or if it had ended. The "Unknown" had vanished from the screen. Khalil was sending him a message. He had what Jared and Gianluca had been seeking. But how was he going to deliver it?

As Dan walked across the Square, he considered Khalil's options. He could send it via some encrypted server. But he didn't ask Dan if he had one, so that was out. He could send it by old fashioned mail, hand-written, and unhackable. No, Khalil wouldn't risk someone other than Dan opening his mail.

That meant Khalil was coming back to Rome. Dan looked around, to see if he could spot Khalil watching him register the thought. But the Square was filled with tourist groups flying their national flags—the Netherlands,

Poland, the Philippines – and Dan could not see Khalil among any of them. And Khali would not be so foolish as to call Dan when he could see him.

He would wait. Khalil would know when it was best to make his move. As he always did. This time, though, Dan very much hoped that it would be in the service of a different kind of justice, where no one who encountered it would wind up dead.

35

Rome

Sister Marie Therese did not feel at all nervous as she walked into the Church of Saint Agnes, in Piazza Navona. Chinara Bukar had given her the contact details for the Nigerian, and she had texted him. When he texted back and suggested she meet him in some park in the northern suburbs where stabbing a knife into her back would be easy, Sister Marie Therese had calmly responded that she would meet him in church. Especially in this one, dedicated to the saint killed during the persecution of Christians under Diocletian. It was a fitting place to remember Sister Maureen. And besides, if the Nigerian killed her in a church, then she was confident that her trip to the afterlife would be swift and sweet.

Not that she wanted to leave this life, and not for quite a long time. There was work to do, and she was going to make sure that what Sister Maureen had begun would not be left unfinished.

As she stepped from the *piazza* into the church, its interior shaped like a Greek cross, with pink and white marble and colorful frescoes, her eye was immediately drawn up to the cupola, which made the small church look much bigger by directing the eye to the infinite.

Sister Marie Therese marveled at the eight ribbed and gilded Corinthian pilasters of the cupola that were placed between large windows, the sunlight bouncing in and lighting the fresco depicting St. Agnes rising up to heaven, surrounded by the four cardinal virtues of Prudence, Justice, Fortitude, and Temperance which were painted on the curving vaults.

It was Justice that Sister Marie Therese had come for, and she closed her eyes and said a quick prayer that it would be lit by the lantern containing the dove of the Holy Spirit. The face looking back at her was Sister Maureen, her face angry in its eyes, and yet full of hope from the smile on its mouth.

Sister Marie Therese opened her eyes and blinked. Of course, Sister Maureen had seemed to be standing before her, but that was her mind's eye doing the seeing. She now directed her gaze outward and took in the church. There was a group of Spanish tourists standing before the green marble-columned high altar, while a tour guide told them the story of how the high altar was intended to feature a sculpture of the Miracle of Saint Agnes, but the artist died shortly after receiving the commission. Instead, in 1688, another artist created a white marble relief showing the Holy Family, which now adorns the altar.

There were a few other people at various stages in the church, one kneeling in prayer, a couple looking at the side altar of Saint Cecilia, patron saint of music and musicians, and a group of Dutch school children apparently taking a test, scribbling answers in a notebook as a teacher asked them questions.

Sister Marie Therese turned and saw a man standing in

the small chapel that occupied the right arm of the Greek cross, its altar made of red cottanello marble and above it, a statue of St. Agnes Among the Flames. It was the man she had come to meet.

"*Buon giorno, signor,*" Sister Marie Therese said.

The man turned to her, and Sister Marie almost gasped at the intensity of his blue eyes against his Black African skin. He didn't say anything. He just smiled and gestured to one of the pews.

They sat, and he stared forward at the altar for a moment, as if considering how he would kill the Holy Family depicted above it. Then he said, "I am listening, Sister." His Nigerian lilted English was both a statement, and a challenge.

Sister Marie Therese took a breath and said, her voice firm and low, "Why did you kill Sister Mauren and all those women in Jerusalem?"

Now he turned to her, his blue eyes flickering with curiosity. "What are you saying?"

Sister Marie Therese said it again. This time adding, "What did you think killing them would accomplish?"

Now his eyes shifted from curious, to angry. "We did not kill those women."

Sister Marie Therese was surprised to hear this. She had expected the usual terrorist rhetoric, but he sounded offended by her question.

"But you had threatened Sister Maureen to stop her work investigating your trafficking of young girls."

He looked at her, his eyes not blinking. "Yes, we asked her to stop. Did we think that she would, no? But what could she do? She was just a woman, sticking her nose into our business. In fact, we told her if she would stop, we would make a donation to her organization. The ladies of the Vatican. And we did."

Now Sister Marie Therese was offended. This thug from the Black Axe was telling her Sister Maureen had stopped her work in exchange for money? Or maybe, she had taken the money and she had not stopped.

He seemed to read her mind. "You are thinking, why would she do this? Well, she did not stop after taking our money."

Sister Marie Therese glared at him. "That sounds like a reason to kill her."

He shook his head. "It was too, shall we say, expensive for us to kill her, to tell you what is the truth. It would bring down the wrong kind of attention to our business. We let her keep the money, too."

Now Sister Marie Therese blushed in confusion. This man was telling her that they had not killed her friend and those women, that they actually admired her work, and they let her keep their donation after she bailed on their agreement? It didn't make sense.

"How can I know that what you say is true?"

Now he looked at her as if she was a naïve schoolgirl whom he might kidnap and export to some hellhole of abuse. "Because she was no threat to us. She was saving a few, but we have many. Letting her proceed was a smart move on our part. As for this sister, she was doing work that was a threat to other people though."

Sister Marie Therese didn't know what type of work that could be, but Babatunde read her face like a children's book and told her anyway.

"She was looking into bad money things here, in the Vatican. She was looking into the Mafia. She was looking into a guy named Renzo Bellocco."

Sister Marie Therese felt ice cold race up the back of her neck. She had heard this name with Father Jared and that man from the Middle East. She knew he was a businessman, but why would he kill Sister Maureen and all those women?

"So, you are saying he was behind the murder of Sister Maureen and the others in Jerusalem?"

He smiled at her. "It wasn't us, and it wasn't our jihadist friends, despite what the Israelis are trying to prove. It was him."

"How would he do that?"

He now laughed, a soft ripple of amusement at how disconnected she was from the world. "He can buy anything. And everything is for sale. Even death."

Sister Marie Therese felt tears well in her eyes, and she quickly wiped them away. "But if Sister Maureen was no threat to you, how was she a threat to them?"

"Because she had access to the pope. That's why."

"And so, killing her was to send a message to him?"

"No, it was to deliver a message to the next one," Babatunde said.

"What do you mean?"

"To any cardinals who thought they might be the next pope, he sent a message to say this is what happens if you poke into my business."

Sister Marie Therese felt like she had been hit hard in the stomach. This man was telling her the Mafia killed Sister Maureen and those women to send a message to the next pope?

He nodded. "We would never do something like that. It was what you call an overreaction. Bad for business."

Now Sister Marie Therese was angry. "No, you just kidnap girls and sell them. You rape, and cheat, and extort, and torture, and kill all in the name of what? Talk to me about overreaction."

Babatunde leaned back in the pews and looked again at the altar. "Why did you come to speak to me today?" he asked.

"Because I wanted to know the truth."

He looked at her, his eyes suspicious. "I think you planned to have me arrested outside the Church, after I confessed."

She had thought about that plan but had rejected it as

too dangerous. The police might start shooting and more innocent people would die.

"You are right about the confession," she said.

"I have told you the truth."

"Why have you done that?" Sister Marie Therese's voice was soft now. She believed what he was saying was true.

He leaned forward now and pointed at the altar. "Because if you believe that, then you need to know what I said is true. Because there are people trying to destroy it for their own purposes. And I would think you do not want that to happen." Then he gave her the kind of smile she imagined that those he had killed had seen, one in which he enjoyed his knowledge of what was to come. "It is bad for your business. So, take what I have told you, and decide. Do you want to live? Or do you want to die?"

Then he rose as swiftly as an assassin and was gone. Sister Marie Therese looked up at the cupola, at the lantern of the dove representing the Holy Spirit. She had prayed for Justice and her prayer had been answered. But justice had not been done yet. And now, getting it for Sister Maureen was up to her.

36

Rome

Jared and Jacqueline were stopped in the hallway leading to Father Dan's office by his secretary, Father Martin Gerrard, who looked as if he was carrying a heavy secret of state, his open Irish face now creased with worry.

"I would be asking you to hold on out here for a bit," Gerrad said, his voice high and tense, his face flushed with apology. "Father Dan has a visitor who asked for privacy."

Jared looked to Jacqueline, who smiled at the Irish priest as if he was the luckiest man on earth, next to Jared, of course.

"Can you just please tell Father Dan that we are here, Father Gerrard?" The implication being that it was for Father Dan to decide if they could enter, not the gatekeeper.

Father Gerrard grinned at that suggestion in gratitude. "Of course, I will be back in a jiff."

He dashed off down the hallway and into his office. Jared took Jacqueline's hand and squeezed it. "That was smooth."

Jacqueline replied with a kiss to his mouth, then they quickly broke away. "I know, I know, we're not saying anything until we have solved this case," she said.

Jared smiled at her with what he felt in his heart. Love. "But we can still steal a kiss."

Before they could steal another one, Dan's secretary poked his head into the hallway.

"Father Dan will see you both," Father Gerrard said, his tone now light and relaxed. As if relieved not to have to keep a secret any longer.

Jared and Jacqueline walked through the Irish priest's office and into Dan's, surprised to see that Sister Marie Therese and Khalil were already there. They knew which visitor required the privacy.

Khalil rose and embraced Jared, as an uncle might, while Dan stood back, still not in any way knowing what to do as Jared's father, except to raise his hand in a gesture of awkward welcome, half salute, and half a call to the waiter for another round.

"We are glad you're here," Dan said. "Pedro, sorry, Khalil has news. As does Sister Marie Therese."

"We have news, too," Jared said, and Jacqueline flashed him a panicked look as if he was going to give up their budding romance on the spot. He smiled at her, and continued, "I know that Jacqueline is really a journalist. She told me."

"I had to," Jacqueline said. "To truly be a help to you."

Dan smiled at them both, as if the truth had suddenly become so contagious in his office that no one could dodge it. "Good, well, we have a way forward it seems. Khalil?"

There was a touch of something that sounded like hope in Dan's voice. Khalil looked uneasy, as if having a journalist nearby while he did what he had come to do was not the safest way forward for him. But he was here, and he had made that choice, so he nodded and took a piece of paper from his jacket pocket and unfolded it on Dan's desk.

On the paper was a series of numbers, linking cash transactions to SS LLC. And beneath the name of the LLC was the name of the principal owner. Alina Oberfeldt. Head of Zug Gruppe.

"Wow," Jared said. "How did you..?"

Khalil shook his head. "Best if you don't know. But you know who this woman is?"

Jared looked grim. "I do. She runs Zug Gruppe, which is a global investment fund. She had some trouble with the SEC due to sketchy trades with Iran during sanctions, but she got off with a fine. She comes across as a female Bond villain without charm. Gianluca Schmitt had a special hate-on for her. She is also Swiss, like Gianluca is. Was."

There was a short pause, then Sister Marie Therese said, "Her father was German. Oberfeldt was not her father's birth name. It was her mother's name."

Everyone looked at her, in surprise, and curiosity.

"I know this because my grandfather was imprisoned by Oberfeldt's father. My grandfather served in the Belgian army in World War II and was captured in 1940. He was sent to Mauthausen and served as slave labor."

She shuddered in memory of the things he had told her when she was old enough to hear them. "For a few weeks, there was a doctor, Heim, known as Doctor Death, who did medical experiments on the prisoners. He would inject toxic fluids into their hearts, and then record how they died. My grandfather had to serve as his butler. This man, Heim, was Oberfeldt's father. That's probably why she called her LLC "SS". Her father was a member of the SS and committed war crimes in their name."

She stopped and closed her eyes in prayer. "I wish I did not know this," she added, "but I do."

Silence followed her words. Dan reached out and put a

hand on her shoulder, and she smiled. "I know all about Alina Oberfeldt," Dan said. "I was part of an investigation into her when she wanted to start a business in Israel. The Israelis asked me to look into her, and I did. I stopped her business, because of her very bad father. And now she is doing very bad things inside the Vatican."

"Along with RB," Khalil added.

"Renzo Bellocco," Jared said. "He's Mafia. Big Time gangster, untouched by the law."

"And Sister Marie Therese met with a Black Axe representative who added to that," Dan added, which caused everyone to look at her with astonishment, at her bravery, and at the fact she was still alive.

"I did," she said. "A blue-eyed Nigerian named Babatunde. He said that they had nothing to do with the murder of Sister Maureen and those women in Jerusalem."

"And you believed him?" Jacqueline asked.

"I did. I mean, he had no reason to lie to me. I would be the person to whom he boasted about it, if they had been involved. He said it would have attracted the wrong kind of attention to them."

Khalil smiled grimly. "Yes, it would."

Jared looked at his uncle with curiosity. Who was he, really, to find out all this information that was now so dangerous to know?

Dan caught the look and stepped in with a plan. "We need to keep this all to ourselves for the time being."

"You're not going to tell the cops?" Jacqueline asked.

Dan shook his head. "Right now, we have money laundering in the Vatican by a Mafia boss, and the daughter of a Nazi war criminal. Along with a murdered Israeli agent, a murdered Vatican bank official, and murdered Sister Maureen along with the women who were killed with her."

"So how do we get what we need to put these people in jail?" Jared asked.

Dan turned to Sister Marie Therese. "The Black Axe rep, he said something very interesting to Sister."

"He said that there were people trying to destroy the Church for their own purposes."

"Or destroy the parts of it they don't like," Dan said.

"So, these people are RB and SS LLC," Jacqueline said.

Dan put his hands together, in a steeple, as if praying. "Yes. We just need to connect them to the crime."

Dan knew that he could not do this from Rome. He had to go back to Israel, to Jerusalem where it all began, to tell the Israelis what he knew, and find out what they thought.

"We need to go back," Dan said. "To the scene of the crime."

Khalil gave him a grin. "I think I will give that one a miss."

Jared and Jacqueline exchanged glances. There was no mirth in Khalil's voice that merited a grin. He was hiding something.

"First," Dan said, catching their look and wanting to redirect their attention, "we need to check in with a cardinal. Just to make sure that what Sister Marie Therese was told passes the smell test of someone who knows the Black Axe all too well."

"Cardinal Omahu?" Jared asked.

Dan nodded. "I think it is best if just Sister Marie Therese and I go to see him. You and Jacqueline can go over the documents Khalil has produced. See what your trained eyes can unearth. We'll meet back at the *Villino Giovanni* this evening.

Khalil's brown eyes darkened with concern. "I really do have to be on my way. This was just a short visit."

"Can you hang on until later today?" Dan asked. "Just so we can all be on the same page?"

Khalil looked at Dan as if this was a very dangerous request, but then he caught Jared's eye, which was filled with hope. They needed his help. He knew that. But he also knew that coming to Rome twice in the time period he had done so was totally against his protocol. He had risked it out of gratitude to Dan, and love for his sister. He still felt both, so he nodded. He would stay. He just hoped that their reason was better than his instinct. At least for a few hours.

As Dan and Sister Marie Therese exited his office, Dan knew that he did not need to go to Israel. Chief Inspector Hillel Bennett was walking into Father Gerrard's outer office. He had lost weight, though his dark features looked heavy with concern.

"Chief Inspector Bennett, what a surprise," Dan said, offering his hand. The Israeli cop shook it, then nodded to Sister Marie Therese.

"Might we have a moment, Father?" Chief Inspector Bennett asked.

"Sister and I have an urgent appointment, Chief Inspector," Dan replied, glancing at Father Gerrard in a way that made the Irish priest add, "And you're going to be late."

"I can walk with you then," Bennett replied.

Dan was relieved to have removed the Israeli cop from such a close call to Khalil, and it was Khalil that Hillel Bennett wanted to talk about as they crossed St. Peter's Square.

"We understand that Abu Hamza has been in Rome. The international terrorist."

"Do you think he was behind the murder of Sister Maureen?" Dan asked, trying to deflect.

"No," Chief Inspector Bennett replied. "We think it was an inside job. And Abu Hamza is not on the inside. Or is he?"

Dan stopped walking, and turned to Chief Inspector Bennett, looking at him with anger in his eyes. "What are you saying?"

Chief Inspector Bennett held up both hands in a gesture

of peace. "I am not saying anything. We know you knew him when he was a kid in Beirut. And helped him to get to the U.S. We think he may try to contact you."

Dan cocked his head to one side, thinking about that. "And you came all the way from Israel to tell me this?"

Bennett shook his head on a weary smile. "No, I came all this way because I think Abu Hamza is here. And if he is, I want to do a deal with you."

Dan smiled in return. "A deal with me for someone I knew when he was a child?"

Bennett looked stern, the cop once again. "No, for someone I believe that you know now. Give him to us. And we will tell you who killed Sister Maureen."

37

Castel Gandolfo, Italy

It was early evening and the sun had just begun to set behind the papal palace at *Castel Gandolfo* and turn the turquoise waters of the volcanic Lake Albano which the palace overlooked into a shade of purple, maybe the color of purple worn by a bishop.

"Or an archbishop," Renzo Bellocco said, raising his glass of Montepulciano in the direction of Archbishop Marco Sanseverino, who stood with his back to the window in the pink wallpapered Clock Parlor in the Papal Palace. "Until, of course, he is made a cardinal by the next pope."

Bellocco then raised his glass to Cardinal Wolfram Friederich, who glanced at Sanseverino, the sleek Papal Nuncio to Israel, and then looked back to Renzo, who stood next to the Papal Camerlengo, the portly Cardinal Antonio Matteo, who remembered that Renzo would one day want a favor and feared that today was that day. He took a healthy sip of wine and vowed to stay as silent as he could. What if someone were listening in? Someone who could do him harm?

"I would think, *Maestro*, that the next pope will have a lot of candidates for cardinal," Cardinal Friedrich said, and took a swig from his glass of beer, which was Italian, and not really to his taste.

Renzo Bellocco smiled at Archbishop Sanseverino and said, "By all means, Marco. Proceed."

The archbishop reached into his cassock and produced a tan manilla folder. He walked across the red carpet covering the marble floor, to the mirror on the wall behind the table clock, where the cardinal was sitting. He handed him the folder.

"What is this, *Maestro*, mail from the Jews?" Friedrich said.

"After a fashion," the archbishop replied.

Friedrich rested the envelope on his ample belly and peeled it open, then extracted a sheet of paper.

"What is this?" he asked.

"It's the record in World War II of the father of one of your greatest supporters."

Friedrich blinked and looked at the document. "This says he was an SS war criminal who murdered thousands of Jews."

Cardinal Matteo looked at Renzo, who betrayed nothing. The archbishop ran his hand through his slicked back black hair and smiled at the German. "No, that's who we're going to say you took money from to make renovations to the Papal Palace."

Cardinal Matteo looked around the room. The Vatican acquired the Castel Gandolfo castle in 1596 as a payment for a debt owed by the Savelli family. The palace was then built in the 17th century for Pope Urban VIII and was designed by the noted architect Carlo Maderno. Since then, the palace had been used by many popes as a summer residence until Pope Francis turned it into a museum. Pope Leo had stopped the artifaction of the palace but had left it in a state of limbo. Leo had been here maybe twice in his papacy, and never for long.

It was Cardinal Friedrich who had the initiative to restore the palace to a place fit for a pope, and Cardinal Matteo could see that the pink wallpaper in the room where they stood was new. He must have done every room and there were a lot of them, so the whole venture must have cost a lot of money. Cardinal Matteo knew he could not unhear what he was hearing, so he tried to make himself small.

"Alina Oberfeldt, and you, *Maestro*, gave me this money," Friedrich replied. "For the good of the church. To make this place a proper papal palace."

Renzo Bellocco now walked over the cardinal and stood next to the archbishop, like a pair of gangsters looking at their prey.

"No, Wolfram. I told you to stop. It was not your place. But that doesn't matter because now you have two choices."

The customary flush in Cardinal Friederich's face had faded, and there was fear in his blue eyes as he stared at the two Italians before him, knowing that the choices they were going to offer would not be about the type of schnitzel he wanted.

"What are those choices, *Maestro*?" he asked, his voice too hearty, revealing his fear.

Renzo Bellocco smiled and walked over to a side table where a bottle of Montepulciano stood, and topped up his wine, then topped up Cardinal Matteo's glass. He enjoyed making the fat German puppet wait for his command, and he just hoped that he was smart enough to obey it. He swirled the wine in his glass, took a sip, gargled a little, and then swallowed.

"Please, Marco, enlighten our German friend."

Archbishop Sanseverino extracted another envelope, this one white, from his cassock, and handed it to Cardinal

Friedrich.

The cardinal opened it up and raised the paper within it to catch the light reflecting from the mirror behind him. He read the sheet of paper, and then put it face down in his lap and looked at them as if they were some kind of magicians.

"This is on my official letterhead as the prefect of the Congregation for the Doctrine of Faith."

Archbishop Sanseverino nodded. "Of course. It's an official statement."

Cardinal Friedrich turned over the sheet of paper and looked at it again.

"You want me to abandon Alina Oberfeldt because her father was a Nazi?"

Renzo shook his head. The cardinal really could be thick. "No, we want you to condemn her for using the Vatican Bank to launder money, and when the American nun got too close to discovering this, Alina had her killed. That's what you're condemning. The fact her father was an evil Nazi is just icing on the cake."

"But she did not do this," Friedrich said plaintively.

"You know this for a fact, Wolfram?" Bellocco asked.

The cardinal shook his head, no, and looked to Cardinal Matteo, who looked at the ground, toward hell.

"Well, Archbishop Sanseverino knows. Because the Israelis told him."

Now Friedrich looked offended. "And you believe the Jews over Alina Oberfeldt?"

"You believe in Jesus, Eminence?" the Archbishop asked.

"Of course!"

"Well, he was a Jew."

Friedrich's face now reddened. "He was a different kind of Jew."

Bellocco took a sip of wine. "I really think we're going to have to get you some lessons on how to speak to the media, Wolfram. Because attacking the Jews after this terrible attack on them by Hamas, and then on us by the Nazi Oberfeldt, will not look good."

The cardinal stood up and put down his glass of beer. "I want to see the evidence before I sign."

Renzo Bellocco opened his hands in a gesture of "be reasonable." Then he said, "Come in, *Dottore*."

On that invitation, the head of the *Gendarmeria*, Inspector Vincenzo Pericoli entered the room, looking, in his back suit with his shaved head and fat mustache and unblinking brown eyes like the messenger of death.

"I have seen the evidence, Eminence, and I believe it."

"Do you understand now, Wolfram?" Renzo asked.

The cardinal sat back down. He looked pained. He understood.

"Wolfram, we're offering you a chance to get out in front of it, as they say in the world of politics," Renzo said, as cheerfully as he could. "It will make you look good."

Cardinal Friedrich looked at the Italian billionaire, and the Vatican cop, and frowned.

"And if I do this, what will happen?"

Renzo Bellocco raised his glass to the cardinal and grinned. "Well, I think Archbishop Sanseverino will enjoy being a cardinal. Because you will be the next pope."

Cardinal Friedrich thought about that, then turned the paper over. "Do you have a pen?" he asked.

Inspector Pericoli reached into his inside breast pocket, retrieved a pen, and handed it to Cardinal Friedrich. As the cardinal signed the statement, Renzo took out his phone and snapped a picture of the signed statement. Then he attached it to a text he sent on Signal.

Do it at midnight.

38

London

A thousand miles away in London, Alina Oberfeldt switched off her computer, and yawned. She had spent a most profitable day moving money around the world and making more of it. A lot more of it. In fact, she had taken ten million Euros out of the Vatican Bank and turned it into thirty million on a land deal in Dubai.

She rose, and switched off her desk lamp, though she left her computer on, its glow casting her features in a sinister light. In the reflection of the screen, Alina Oberfeldt saw a pair of eyes staring at her, blue eyes, on a black face. A face she had last seen trying to extort money from her. An extortion to which she had agreed. If this man was in her office, undetected, that could only mean trouble.

She could press the panic button beneath her desk to silently summon his guards, but if this guy had managed to get past them, maybe they were dead already. And if the intruder wanted Alina Oberfeldt dead, then she would be slumped over her desk with a bullet in the back of her head and not in a position to do what she did next. Which was to turn to the man and smile.

"I didn't expect to see you here in London," Alina Oberfeldt said, her hands in front of her so the man could see she had no weapon.

"I like London," the man said. "Much friendlier to Africans than Italy."

Alina Oberfeldt nodded, then said, "And you have come all this way to see me because?"

Babatunde stood and let Oberfeldt see the Glock pistol in his hand, and the suppressor screwed on to the end of it. "Actually, I came here to help you commit suicide."

Oberfeldt's legs wobbled, and she steadied herself by placing a hand on the top of her desk chair. "Why would I want to commit suicide?"

Babatunde reached in his pocket, and Alina Oberfeldt flinched, but the Nigerian was not producing a poisoned syringe. He pulled out his phone, and unlocked it, then handed it to her. "Because you have done some very bad things."

Alina Oberfeldt took the phone and read the statement she saw on the screen. She handed the phone back to the Nigerian, then said "Let me show you something. On my computer."

The Nigerian seemed puzzled by Alina Oberfeldt's response to the statement that Renzo Bellocco had sent him, but he walked over to her computer, and saw the trading screen come to life when she woke the computer up.

"You see this, Babatunde?" Alina Oberfeldt said, pointing to a line that revealed the journey of SS LLC cash from the Vatican to the Caymans, to Cyprus, to Ukraine, to Bulgaria, and then to Dubai. "You can see it started out this morning at ten million Euros. And now I have turned it into thirty million. A third of which is yours. Why would

I want to commit suicide if I am so good at making money for us?"

Babatunde looked at the screen, then stepped back. He put the gun back in his pocket and scratched his head.

"Just because Renzo Bellocco wants me dead, I do not have to die," Alina Oberfeldt said. "In fact, my father was dead for years, and living in Argentina the whole time. I learned some things."

She had the Nigerian's attention. "You are saying you have a place to hide? A safe place?"

Alina Oberfeldt looked at him, unblinking. "Did Renzo ask you to bring him my head on a platter?"

Babatunde shook his head, no. "They were just supposed to find you dead in your bed, from an overdose, in reaction to the publication of the statement. Tomorrow."

Oberfeldt cocked her head to one side, as if envisioning this situation, and then grimaced, finding it not to her taste.

"Do you want to kill the one member of our partnership who can actually make you real money?" she asked.

The Nigerian shook his head. He did not. "But what will you do to escape?"

Alina Oberfeldt smiled. "Better if you do not know that. You can just tell Renzo that there was no one home. After you killed my guards, which I take it you did."

Babatunde nodded, as if acknowledging killing them was nothing more than agreeing that it was raining.

"So that is good," Oberfeldt said. "Renzo Bellocco will have to sleep with one eye open if he knows that I am out there."

"What about the statement, saying you killed that nun and those women?"

Alina Oberfeldt shrugged. "Renzo was the one who killed them. I tried to stop him, but he said it was necessary to send a message to the next pope. The one he plans to install. So that we can keep our business open. The thing is, would you trust a partner who tried to have your other partner killed? He'll be coming for you next time."

Babatunde's eyes flashed with fury. "Not unless I kill him first."

Alina shook her head. "I wouldn't do that. I would let him see that I know how to turn off his spigot. You and I are partners now."

Alina Oberfeldt held out her hand to the Nigerian, who extended his and they shook.

"My one piece of advice to you, Babatunde, is do not go back to Rome. Rome means death. Besides, I will need you to be alive when we kill Renzo Bellocco. And kill him we shall."

39

Rome

Dan sat at his desk, staring at the statement that Jared had put before him, the one published in the *L'Osservatore Romano*, the Vatican's daily newspaper, and which had now been picked up by everyone else, including the *Washington Post*, *The Guardian*, and *CNN*, who all had requested interviews with Dan and with Jared.

"I don't suppose this would be the time to tell them we're related," Jared said, and Dan flashed a smile. He liked his son's dark sense of humor, as it was certainly needed now.

"No," Dan said. "But we need to relate. I need to learn how to become your father. Your other father."

Jared thought about that. "I need to learn how to become your son."

Dan smiled. "So we will learn together."

Jared returned the smile, then took a breath. "I'm your son in more ways than I imagined," he said. Dan remained silent, looking into his son's electric blue eyes.

"I, too, have fallen in love with a woman." Jared knew he had agreed with Jacqueline not to say anything until the investigation was over and the truth had been found, but they were close, and something inside him made him want to tell Dan something he would understand. He needed to tell his father this. Dan looked relieved to hear the news.

"I know you have. I could see it in the way you and Jacqueline are together. As in, you are together." He paused, and then asked the essential question. "Are you going to stay together"?"

Dan knew that I Jared said "Yes," that he would be leaving the priesthood. Instead he said, "I am praying over it, Dan."

"Then may your prayers be answered," Dan replied. "She's a wonderful woman and a great journalist. Her articles about the Black Axe in Rome since we learned the truth have put pressure on them, I am sure."

Jared smiled proudly, just as Dan's secretary, Father Gerrard, popped his smiling Irish face through the door and announced, "Sister Marie Therese and Dr. Robinson are here."

The words were half out of his mouth when the young nun burst into the room, fury in her eyes, followed by Jacqueline, who looked frustrated. "I cannot believe that this woman killed Sister Maureen," she said.

"And we can't ask her, as she has disappeared," Jacqueline said. "*The Guardian* just said the Metropolitan police went to her home this morning and found three bodyguards dead, and Alina Oberfeldt gone."

"Do you think she was kidnapped by whoever killed the guards?" Dan asked.

Jared shook his head. "No, I think she was allowed to go by whoever killed the guards."

"And who would that be?" Jacqueline asked.

"The Black Axe," Sister Marie Therese replied, her face taught with anger. "That is something they would do, especially if they were working with her."

"But why would they kill her guards and not her?" Jacqueline asked. "Unless the killer changed their mind. She might have said something to convince them otherwise."

"Yes," Dan said. "Maybe whoever sent the Black Axe to kill Alina Oberfeldt learned something that was more important than killing her."

Everyone thought about that, then Sister Marie Therese asked softly, "Who would send the Black Axe?"

Jared took a breath, and looked at Dan. They were thinking the same thing. "Renzo Bellocco," Jared said. "They were partners. Maybe Khalil knows something."

Dan put a finger to his lips. "He's gone. And he was never here. In fact, the only one who has ever seen him is me, and that was when he was a kid, OK?"

The force with which Dan spoke made them all pull back a little. Clearly, Khalil, or Pedro Garcia as he had first been, was trouble.

Dan turned back to the statement and shook his head. "Cardinal Friedrich is the Prefect for the Congregation of the Doctrine of Faith. How would he know this stuff? And he's a known anti-Semite himself, so why would he turn in a fellow German?"

"Someone made him." The voice belonged to Chief Inspector Hillel Bennett, standing in the doorway, with Father Gerrard looking like he had done someone a favor by not announcing them.

"Chief Inspector Bennett," Dan said. "Please come in."

Hillel Bennett entered and pulled a chair from the side of the room to the middle, opposite Dan, and sat.

"And please, continue," Jared said.

Chief Inspector Bennett smiled at him, the way you might smile at an unruly child who didn't grasp the rules of the game. "I am here to make a trade."

Dan shook his head. "I told you, Chief Inspector, he is

not here."

Chief Inspector Bennett held his smile and extracted a laptop from his briefcase. He opened it and it powered up, and then he placed it facing Dan.

"You'll want to see this, then."

Everyone crowded behind Dan, and Chief Inspector Bennett hit play.

Onscreen, Khalil was entering the *Villino Giovanni*. And then exiting it. And then entering it. And then exiting it.

"You can see the last time code was late afternoon, yesterday. So, Abu Hamza was in Rome, staying in your house Sister Marie Therese, and visiting his old friend Father Dan."

"Abu Hamza?" Jared asked, disbelief in his voice.

"That's his *nom de guerre*. You might have heard it connected to various acts of terrorism around the world, many of them aimed at us in Israel. His birth name is Khalil Khoury. Which is how Father Dan knew him in Beirut."

Dan looked to Jared and smiled reassuringly. He knew that it was useless to deny that Khalil had been in Rome, since Bennett had obtained footage from the security cameras at *Villino Giovanni*. Surely Khalil knew they were there. Or maybe, Dan thought, he was sending a message, knowing they would be found.

"Yes, Chief Inspector, Khalil Khoury was in Rome. To see me." Dan wondered what payment the Israeli cop was going to demand.

Hillel Bennett was still smiling. He was enjoying his moment. "But I cannot trade him for anything, as he is no longer here."

Dan felt relief at hearing that Khalil was gone. Unless, of course, Hillel Bennett meant "no longer here" to mean dead.

Bennett turned off his smile and looked serious. "He has not left Italy by train or plane, and we have looked at the autoroute footage and did not see him in any car. Unless, of course, he was in the trunk, and had someone friendly to drive him."

He looked at each person in the room, and they all shook their heads.

"Yes, you are right," Bennett said, as if to a class of gifted children. "He did not leave by car. He left by boat."

He hit play and another video was a zoomed satellite photo of a man resembling Khalil getting into a Zodiac. "There he is in Ostia," Bennett said.

And then Khalil zooms off south, and into the dusk, and the satellite loses him.

"Satellites see as well at night as in the daytime," Bennett said. "However, temperatures tend to invert between day and night, so at dawn and dusk, details of what the satellite sees can be washed out as the temperatures change. He knew what he was doing, leaving at dusk."

Chief Inspector Bennett then turned to the gathered. "So where is he now?"

Dan stood up. "I have no idea. He came to Rome to help me find out who killed Sister Maureen and the women in my house, in Jerusalem."

Chief Inspector Bennett nodded. "And did he help you? After all, you once helped him."

Dan did not know how deeply Chief Inspector Bennett knew of his relationship with Khalil and his sister and their family. But he wanted to get off this track as cleanly as possible.

"I did help him get to the United States, where he developed his political sensibility to hate us all. And he did some terrible things. But as a priest, I am obliged to forgive sinners."

"Did he ask for your forgiveness?" Bennett's eyes shone with interest.

"Not directly, but by coming to Rome to help, it was a

form of atonement."

Chief Inspector Bennett thought about that. Then he turned to Jared. "So, what do you think? Did Abu Hamza help?"

Jared looked to Jacqueline who gave him a smile of love, and so he said, "Yes, he did. He helped us find out who was laundering money through the Vatican, and why."

"Why?"

"To make money, of course, but also to put their stamp on the Church, to allow them to make more money."

"They knew Sister Maureen was getting close to exposing them," Sister Marie Therese said.

Chief Inspector Bennett nodded. "Yes, that's what we found out as well."

Another silence hung over the room, then Dan said, "I'm sure you saw the statement from Cardinal Friedrich about one of the players we discovered."

Bennett nodded. "I did. Very odd that he would do this, I thought."

"As did we," Dan replied.

"So, I came here to make a trade, but it seems like your trading piece has left the country. Or not."

Silence hung over the room for a moment, of the kind that could turn lives upside down when it ended.

"However, I appreciate your honesty in the face of such powerful evidence he was here, and so I will tell you who was behind the killing of Sister Maureen."

They all looked at him, hoping he would confirm their suspicions.

"It was not Hamas, or Hezbollah, or Islamic Jihad, or even Abu Hamza. It was Archbishop Sanseverino who provided the intel, and a team from Italy who carried it out."

"The Papal Nuncio?"

Bennett nodded. "In the last few days we decided to listen in to a few of his conversations. We tapped into his phone, so we heard everything. Including the conversation that he had last night with Cardinal Fredrich. And Renzo Bellocco."

Dan knew immediately what had happened. The archbishop and the gangster had made the cardinal sign the statement.

Chief Inspector Bennett read Dan's mind. "Yes, they made Cardinal Friedrich sign it. And why did they want him to sign? To get rid of a rival. And why did he sign? To—"

The door to Dan's office burst open, and Father Martin Gerrard staggered in, sobbing. Dan knew what he was going to say before he opened his mouth, and his heart ached already.

"Pope Leo," Gerrard said, his voice heaving, "will not last the day. You have to go now. He wants to see you."

40

Rome

Monsignor Van Ardt was his usual calm self at seeing not just Father Dan, but Father Jared and Sister Marie Therese at the papal apartment doorway.

"Please," he said, his eyes heavy with sorrow, "he is resting in his chamber."

They walked behind the monsignor as he led them down the hallway to Pope Leo's bedroom. Leo was propped up on three pillows, and his eyes flashed with a soft blast of light when Dan entered the room, along with Jared and Sister Marie Therese. Chocolate was lying on the floor, his brown eyes wide, watching everything, as if he knew.

"Hello, Patrick," Dan said, and put his hand on Leo's shoulder.

"Hello, Dan," Leo said, his voice weak. "Thank you."

Dan knew that Leo was thanking him for being here. And now, Dan had to thank his old friend with the truth.

"Patrick, I don't want to cause you any more pain, but I have news."

Pope Leo smiled, and tried to wave Dan on, but his hand only rose an inch off the bed. So he conveyed with his eyes, soft and blue, that he was ready.

"I will let Sister Marie Therese tell you what we have learned."

Sister Marie Therese looked as if she was more stricken by seeing the pope so close to death than by what she was about to say. But she smiled, and pulled a chair next to Leo's bed, and sat, resting her hand on his.

"Holy Father, we know who killed Sister Maureen. We have learned that Archbishop Sanseverino and Renzo Bellocco had Sister Maureen and the other women from the *Donne del Vaticano* murdered."

The pope's eyes went wide, and he looked at Dan, who nodded, that it was true.

"They did it to send a message to a cardinal who they intend to make the next Pope," Dan said.

"Renzo Bellocco," Jared added, "is laundering money through the Vatican Bank. We discovered that, and my colleague was killed because of it. But it is Renzo who wants to control the papacy."

Leo closed his eyes and for a moment, Dan thought he had breathed his last, but then he opened them, and he looked angry.

"Get a pen and paper," he said, almost in a whisper. "And the monsignor."

Monsignor Van Ardt appeared with a notebook and a pen. "Your Holiness?" he said.

"Write this down," Leo said, his voice a rasp. "I hereby elevate Father Dan Lanaham to the College of Cardinals. Effective immediately."

Dan felt blood rush to his head. Just weeks ago, he had become superior general to the Jesuits, and now the pope had made him a cardinal.

"You need to be at the conclave, Dan," Leo said. "So, you need to be a cardinal."

Leo had made Dan a cardinal so he would be present at the election of the pope who would follow Leo. It was his way of ensuring Dan continued to know and serve the truth.

Dan smiled and grabbed Leo's hand. "I will do my best, Your Holiness," he said.

Leo smiled. "Now please Father Jared, add that Dan will serve on the Council of the Economy as cardinal, and then sign my papal order as a witness. Just in case they think I am not of sound mind."

Leo slumped back on the pillow, exhausted, but still smiling.

Jared looked to Dan, and so Dan now pulled up a chair next to Leo's bedside. And he sat, resting his hand on Leo's arm.

"I have one more bit of news, Patrick," he said quietly. "When I was in Beirut all those years ago, I fell in love with a woman there. She loved me. Together, we made Jared. I just found out recently that Jared is my son."

Leo shut his eyes again, and Dan was sure this news had killed him. But then he opened them and smiled. He looked at the paper, and then at Sister Marie Therese. "You make the addition and then sign it, please sister. Forgive me, I should have asked you first. I am not quite up to speed." Then he looked at Dan and Jared, that heavenly smile still on his lips.

"Glory be to the Father, and to the Son, and to the Holy Spirit," Leo said. "As it was in the beginning is now and ever shall be, world without end. Amen."

"Amen," they all replied. It was his blessing of the news he had just heard.

Then Leo closed his eyes again, and softly said, "Hail Mary, full of grace, the Lord is with thee, blessed are thou amongst women, and blessed is the fruit of thy womb Jesus. Holy Mary, Mother of God, pray for us sinners, now and at the hour of our death..."

"Amen," Dan said, but Leo's eyes remained shut, that little smile still curled on his mouth, as if he could see the Mary to whom he prayed, watching over him as he left the earth. On his journey to heaven, where he would, Dan knew, as the tears rolled down his cheeks, keep them, and guide them, and watch over them all.

41

Vatican City

Jared stood with Jacqueline and Sister Marie Therese in Saint Peter's Square, the night air warm around them. The conclave to elect a new pope had begun three days earlier, and the cardinals who had gathered in the Sistine Chapel had yet to give a majority to any candidate, as the four votes they had taken saw the black smoke of a failed ballot belch out of the chimney attached to the roof of the Sistine Chapel. Only when the smoke was white would there be a new occupant on the Throne of St. Peter.

Cardinal Dan Lanaham sat in the Sistine Chapel with the other papal electors on this hot August night, and thought back to the funeral of his friend, inside the very Basilica. It had been a gorgeous late summer day, the kind that Leo, when he was Patrick, used to love to spend outside, meeting his people, hearing about their lives.

And now his was done. Dan felt the emotion of that funeral, just a week earlier, rise within him. It had been more than a funeral for a pope. It had been a funeral for his friend.

The changes that Leo had made, the progress that the Church had seen, could be undone in the next ballot, depending on who the cardinals chose.

And Dan could see, in his conversations with those cardinals whom Leo liked, that they were going to have a pope very different from the one who had just died. "The Holy Spirit has the deciding vote," a cardinal from Quebec reminded Dan, but Dan knew that it was a Mafioso from Rome who had that deciding vote, and the vote was rigged. There was nothing Dan could do to stop it. He just, as Leo had intended, had to see it happen. And then find a way forward.

Outside the Basilica, Rachel Ben-Simon squeezed in behind Jared and Jacqueline and Sister Marie Therese who were pressed against the front barricade.

"How do they make the smoke white?" Rachel Ben-Simon asked.

"Ambassador, how nice to see you!" Sister Marie Therese said, shaking her hand.

"I don't know how much longer I will be the ambassador," she said, gazing at the chimney as she shook the nun's hand. "So, I wanted to find you all tonight."

"Well, I would imagine the same holds true for several of us, if they pick the wrong pope," Sister Marie Therse replied.

Rachel Ben-Simon smiled. "Ah, but does not the Holy Spirit have the final vote?"

"Yes," Jared replied. "And maybe that's why it is taking them so long."

She laughed, and then turned back to Sister Marie Therese. "Do you have a favorite, Sister? I am sure that 'favorite' is not the proper term, but what I mean is there a person you think would make a good pope?"

Sister Marie Therese looked wistful. "I do. Sister Maureen would have been brilliant..."

Rachel Ben-Simon squeezed the nun's hand. "Yes, she would have."

She left the "but" unsaid, but they all heard it drifting in the night air.

"Pope Leo was making real inroads in raising the role of women in the Church," Jared said. "Who knows, maybe the next guy will see the wisdom in following suit. After all, it was women who put the rabbi from Nazareth on the map."

Rachel looked to Jacqueline and Jared, and Jared nodded. "Yep, 'These women were Mary, also called Magdalene, from whom seven demons had gone out; Joanna, whose husband Chusa was Herod's administrator; Susanna; and many other women. They provided financial support for Jesus and his disciples.' So says the Gospel of Luke. Just like Pope Leo reminded us at Sister Maureen's funeral."

Rachel looked proud. "So Jewish women paid for Jesus and his disciples."

Jared nodded. "Women were critical in the development of the early church. St. Paul, formerly Saul of Tarsus, wrote about them and to them in his letters. It was only about the 4th century after Jesus where men started to control the show."

Jacqueline gave Jared a little squeeze on the arm for that. Rachel Ben-Simon noticed.

"But it is changing," Sister Marie Therese said. "Because of the work we do here. And if the next pope tries to stop us, we will do it elsewhere."

Rachel smiled at the nun. "Well, you would be most welcome to do it where it started, in my country."

"Thank you, invitation accepted, should we need it." Sister Marie Therese looked luminous tonight, as if no matter what happened, she would find a way forward.

"Dr. Robinson," Rachel said turning to Jaqueline, "as a scholar of these things, what do you think?"

Jacqueline looked down, then shyly up at the ambassador. "I am not a doctor, in the way you are. I am not a doctor at all. I am a journalist for the *Washington Post*. I was here to help my friend Father Dan find out who killed Sister Maureen and those women, and the doctor was just a cover."

Rachel Ben-Simon nodded. "I understand completely. You can't be too protected in this world." Then she softly said, "And I hear that you discovered the perpetrator."

Sister Marie Therese opened her mouth, to say that it was a topic best left unsaid here, but her words were drowned out by the roar of the crowd.

Above the Sistine Chapel, white smoke unfurled from the chimney into the night air, softly and thinly, as if reluctant to do what it had to do.

"In answer to your question, Ambassador," Jared hollered "They make the smoke black by using potassium perchlorate, anthracene, and sulfur. They make it white by using potassium chlorate, lactose, and rosin."

"Thank you, Father Rossi," Rachel shouted back on a smile. "Another mystery solved."

About twenty minutes later, the camerlengo, Cardinal Antonio Matteo appeared on the central balcony of St. Peter's Basilica, and the crowd cheered.

"They picked an Italian?" Rachel Ben-Simon exclaimed as if this was the worst choice possible.

Jared put his hand on her shoulder. "No, Madam Ambassador, he is the senior cardinal deacon at the conclave. He gets to tell us who they picked."

Cardinal Matteo stepped forward to the microphone, and said, as if being forced to speak, *"Annuntio vobis gaudium magnum; habemus Papam..."*

"I announce to you a great joy, we have a pope," Jared translated.

"Eminentissimum ac Reverendissimum Dominum..."

"The most eminent and reverent Lord..."

"Dominum Wolfram..."

Jared said nothing, he was too stunned to speak.

"Sanctae Romanae Ecclesiae Cardinalem Friedrich qui sibi nomen imposuit Urban."

"Cardinal of the Holy Roman Church Wolfram Friedrich, who has taken the papal name Urban."

Jared finished the translation, his voice seeping with bitterness.

"They elected as pope the German cardinal who made the statement against Alina Oberfeldt?" Jacqueline was aghast.

"Yes, and now we have confirmation of who killed Sister Maureen," Sister Marie Therese said. "The man who put Cardinal Friedrich on the Throne of St. Peter. Renzo Bellocco."

Rome

SIX MONTHS LATER

Renzo Bellocco was so angry that he was calm, like the assassin he was. He knew that emotion made mistakes, and so he had strapped emotion to the floor of his psyche as he told Cardinal Marco Sanseverino what he was thinking.

"The time has come, Marco. The time has come."

Cardinal Sanseverino, who had been elevated to his princely status about two weeks after Wolfram Friedrich became pope, just smiled at the gangster. He knew what time had come.

Cardinal Antonio Matteo sat at the side of the room in Bellocco's study, looking pale and thin. He had lost about fifty pounds since Cardinal Friedrich became pope about six months earlier, just from knowing how it happened. And now, Bellocco enjoyed the fact that Matteo was going to know what would happen next, as he was still the camerlengo, and he had access to Pope Urban's inner sanctum.

"Since Alina Oberfeldt disappeared, I have lost seventy million Euros from my Vatican Bank account. I have a team looking for her, but like her Nazi father, she is good at hiding. The only way I can get control back is to make another statement, one that Alina Oberfeldt will understand."

"What do you have in mind, Renzo?" Cardinal Sanseverino asked.

Bellocco smiled at Cardinal Matteo. "This is where our friend the camerlengo comes in."

"I do?" Cardinal Matteo asked, his voice thin and trembling.

"You do." Bellocco reached into his pocket and extracted a small dark bottle containing a liquid. He handed it to Matteo.

"It's thallium. Put five milligrams in his beer tonight, and ten tomorrow night, and he'll be dead by this time next week."

Matteo looked at the bottle as if it was Satan himself.

Bellocco held it in front of his eyes. "Remember the orange juice supplement that you gave Pope Leo? The sunshine from Sicily? It was all laced with polonium. Took a few months to kill him, but you did it. This is much faster."

Cardinal Matteo looked like he would rather swallow the thallium himself than do what had been commanded by this evil man. Bellocco caught the thought and squashed it. "Oh, and if you die suddenly, Antonio, then so does your sister and her husband and their three lovely children, Gianni, Luca, and Emilia. Understood?"

Cardinal Matteo's face became even paler, and he nodded, then took the bottle from Bellocco. He rose and nodded at both men. "I shall be on my way."

"And so shall Pope Urban," Bellocco said, with a smile.

Once Cardinal Matteo was gone, Bellocco turned to Cardinal Sanseverino. "Do you have the votes? I mean, you've only been a cardinal for a few months."

Cardinal Sanseverino smiled. "I will get the votes if Pope Urban leaves a will saying he hopes that I replace him. It will be seen as a sign of divine continuance. And I will work the room with it."

"What about that Cardinal Lanaham? He's a trouble-some Jesuit. He's Leo's spy."

"Leo is dead, Renzo. It matters not. The College of Cardinals want Italian blood to steady the rocky ship. They will see me as a virtue."

Bellocco nodded. "And we will help them to see that. The dead pope's wishes for you to continue his work will be in his will, Marco." He smiled at the Cardinal and raised his hand in salute. "Just think of what name you want to take as pope."

Across the city, Cardinal Dan sat in his office in the Apostolic Palace, with the late Pope's dog, Chocolate, lying at his feet. Leo had left the dog in Dan's care, and Chocolate thought that Dan was only his temporary guardian. His alert brown eyes told Dan that he expected Leo to return. Dan loved the dog, and knew that in time, Chocolate would accept him for who he was. They would miss Leo together.

Dan was now a cardinal sitting on the Council for the Economy, which supervised the economic management and financial activities of the Departments of the Roman Curia, institutions connected with the Holy See and the Vatican State. It supervised the Vatican Bank. Leo had put him there so he could have access to what crimes were being committed inside the Bank, and that he could do something to stop them.

Dan knew, from his experience as a cardinal so far, that he would need help. Jared would be there, and so would the new woman they had hired from England. A former

Oxford professor in finance at the Said Business School. Dan had not yet asked her if she knew Layla. That was on Jared's time, once Dan had met the right moment to tell him.

Father Martin Gerrard had accompanied Dan on his elevation to the College of Cardinals, and now he knocked on Dan's door, then popped his head in. "Father Jared is here to see you."

Dan stood, and said, "Please, show him in."

Father Jared entered Dan's office, dressed in civilian clothes, carrying a heavy backpack. Dan felt his blood rush to his cheeks. He knew what was coming.

"Hello, father," Jared said. The way he said "father" was soft, and intimate. Dan heard it and knew how he had to answer.

"Hello my son. You look like you're going on a trip."

Jared smiled. "I am. I am going to Washington, to see the woman I love, Jacqueline Brussard."

Dan took a breath. "And so, you are leaving us?"

Jared nodded. "I am leaving the priesthood, yes. But not the Church. And I am not leaving because I fell in love. I am leaving because I fell out of love with the place I was in, and what I was doing. I feel that I can do more good for us all on the outside of these walls."

Dan stepped forward and embraced his son. "I know that you will. I will pray for the success of your journey."

"You're not going to try to talk me out of it?" Jared asked.

Dan shook his head. "It is your decision, not mine. All I can do is support you. And I will still need your help."

Jared had tears in his eyes, and Dan now did too, knowing how hard this decision had been.

"I have taken a leave from the Vatican Bank," Jared said. "The new guy who the pope put in place is an idiot."

"You can help me from the outside, then."

Jared smiled, and looked suddenly shy, as if what he

was going to say next was somehow forbidden. But he asked softly: "Did you ever think of leaving the priesthood, father?"

Dan wiped his eyes and nodded. "Yes, I did think of it. I thought of leaving for your mother. But I knew that if I was no longer a priest, I could not be true to myself. I did not know she was pregnant with you, and that she would leave for England."

"If you had known?"

Dan's eyes traveled back in time, and he smiled. "Then I would have gone with her. But..."

"But what?"

"There's still time to tell her how much we love her."

Jared looked at Dan as if he had been punched in the face. "What do you mean?"

"I mean that your mother, Layla, is alive. She's a professor at Oxford."

Jared sat down and put his head in his hands, sobbing now. Dan sat next to him and put an arm around his son. "It's OK, Jared. Now you have two families. Consider that a blessing."

Jared's sobs turned to laughter, and he hugged his father. "OK. OK. You're right."

He wiped his face and then looked serious. "My uncle told you, didn't he?"

"Yes. And he told me to tell you when I knew the time was right. That time is now."

Jared smiled. "Are you going to contact her?"

Dan felt his own heart flinch. "Yes. But not without you. We will go together."

Jared hugged his father again. Then he asked, "Do you know where my uncle is?"

Dan shook his head. "No. But he did a good thing for us."

"Helping us find out that Renzo and his mob killed all those holy women to put that awful man in as pope?"

Dan smiled grimly. "Yes, but your uncle showed us the truth. Pope Leo told me many times that something wicked was heading our way."

"And now it's here."

"It's here, Jared. And it's just beginning..."

—END—

John F. Myslinski

John F. Myslinski was born in Salem, Massachusetts and was raised in the Boston area, where he attended Catholic schools and university. Jack graduated from **Bishop Fenwick High School** in 1965. He received his BA from **Boston College** and then joined and remained a member of the **Jesuits** (New England Province) for eight years. Jack served as a *Federal Officer* with the **United States Capitol Police** in Washington, D.C. and graduated No.1 in his class at the **Federal Law Enforcement Center** in Georgia.

He entered the seminary at **Mt. St. Mary's,** where he received his **Master's Degree in Divinity.** He was ordained to the priesthood for the **Archdiocese of Washington** in 1980. As the "TV Priest" for the **District of Columbia,** he was the host of the tv program *"Real to Reel"* for six years and celebrated the television Mass for the Washington Metropolitan area for eight years.

He also served in the **Air Force Reserves** as a Captain. He was the pastor of **Holy Face Parish** in St Mary's County and **St. Mary's Parish** in Rockville, Maryland, for over a decade. Msgr Myslinski was elected and appointed Dean of St Mary's County and also of Montgomery County. He spent many years working with and for the homeless community in the D.C. area.

He has the double honor of being named "Washingtonian of the Year" by *Washingtonian Magazine* for his work with the homeless, and being named a **Monsignor** by **Pope John Paul II** in 2005.

In a letter of commendation to Msgr on the occasion of his honor by the magazine, **President George H. W. Bush** wrote, *"I commend you for your selfless commitment to those in need, and I thank you for helping to make our Nation's Capital a better place to live."*

He recently co-authored a novel STRANGE GODS and in the last couple of years attended book signings through out the country.

He lives and continues his ministry as a Catholic priest in the Berkshires in Western Massachusetts.

Michael McKinley

He is a journalist, author, screenwriter, and filmmaker educated at the University of Oxford.

He co-wrote A QUIET LIFE, a cybercrime thriller, *Skyhorse Publishing*, 2024; FACETIME: A PSYCHOLOGICAL THRILLER; THE PENALTY KILLING: A MARTIN CARTER MYSTERY, nominated for an **Arthur Ellis Award** as best first crime novel, *McClelland & Stewart*; ICE CAPADES: A MEMOIR OF FAST LIVING AND TOUGH HOCKEY, with Sean Avery, *Dutton & Viking*; THE CODEBREAKERS: THE SECRET INTELLIGENCE UNIT THAT CHANGED THE COURSE OF THE FIRST WORLD WAR, with James Wyllie, *Ebury*; FINDING JESUS: FAITH. FACT. FORGERY, his companion book to the highly popular CNN series, with D. Gibson, *St. Martin's Press*; DIAMOND DUST, a memoir with Utah's most successful Mormon counterfeiter, Russ Swain, *Pierian Springs Press*, 2024

As a journalist, he has written for *The Guardian*, *The Daily Mail*, *Los Angeles Times*, *Sports Illustrated*, *Vancouver Sun*, *National Post*, *Saturday Night Magazine*, *Chicago Sun-Times*, *Food & Wine*, *New York Observer*, *New York Daily News*, *Politics Daily*, *Washington Post*, and has won national news and magazine writing awards.

His TV and Film credits include co-creator and co-executive producer of EPSTEIN'S SHADOW: GHISLAINE MAXWELL, the three-part series for *NBC Peacock*. He wrote, directed and produced OUR LADY OF STATEN ISLAND, a feature documentary; and LINCOLN'S LAW, a TV drama series; and DEAD RIGHT, a TV drama series. He created, co-wrote and produced THE TWO MARYS for *CNN*, winner of the **Gracie Award for Best Hour-long Documentary** aired in the U.S.